The House on Hatemonger Hill

By

Eileen Haavik McIntire

*A*manita Books
Columbia, MD 21045

Library of Congress Control Number: 2021904644
ISBN: 978-1-7368214-0-4
Cover design by Earthly Charms, earthlycharms.com

Published by Amanita Books, an imprint of
Summit Crossroads Press, Columbia, MD USA.
Email: sumcross@aol.com

The author welcomes your comments. E-mail her at eileenmcintire@aol.com. Also visit her website and subscribe to her newsletter at www.SecretPanels.net

If you enjoy this book,
we would greatly appreciate your
writing a review on Amazon.com.

Books by Eileen Haavik McIntire

The Shadow Series of
Historical Mysteries
Shadow of the Rock
In Rembrandt's Shadow

The 90s Club Series of Cozy Mysteries Featuring
the 90s Club at Whisperwood Retirement Village
The 90s Club & the Hidden Staircase
The 90s Club & the Whispering Statue
The 90s Club & the Secret of the Old Clock
The 90s Club & the Mystery at Lilac Inn
And coming in 2022
The 90s Club & the Clue in the Old Album

Psychological Suspense
The Two-Sided Set-up

Historical Suspense
The House on Hatemonger Hill

Reviewer Comments

The Two-Sided Set-Up — "...a fast-paced and multilayered thriller with well-developed characters and colorful settings...An engaging tale for aficionados of psychological suspense." *(Kirkus Reviews)*

The 90s Club & the Hidden Staircase (No. 1) — "With plenty of humor and its own original tale...a 'must' for readers of cozy mysteries." *(Midwest Book Review)*

The 90s Club & the Whispering Statue (No. 2) — "A fun read...nostalgia and...social commentary wrapped up in an engaging mystery novel." *(Foreword Reviews)*

The 90s Club & the Secret of the Old Clock (No. 3) — "An impressively well-crafted and thoroughly entertaining mystery that plays fair with the reader..." *(Midwest Book Review)*

Shadow of the Rock — "A riveting tale of time and humanity, highly recommended." *(Midwest Book Review).* "A bold adventure...Chapters move quickly in a mixture of danger, excitement, and pure enjoyment..." *(Foreword Reviews)*

Table of Contents

Chapter 1

January 9, 1964

I'd heard of George Lincoln Rockwell, founder and head of the American Nazi Party, but I never expected to meet him, certainly would not support him—he's a Nazi. Robbing him was an absurd idea. But I couldn't predict the future, and my path took an abrupt detour on the fateful day Aunt Kay unexpectedly asked me to lunch. We met at venerable Woody's Department Store in downtown Washington, D.C.

Lee Harvey Oswald had assassinated President Kennedy less than two months before. We all remember where we were that day. Disbelief, horror, fear, and immense sadness succeeded each other as we adjusted to a new reality. It still feels like a nightmare as I write about it. Lyndon Johnson became our president. Change was in the air, and George Lincoln Rockwell was planning his campaign to run for president in 1972.

I didn't know Aunt Kay well, since we saw each other only at family events, but she was a hat, white gloves, and pearls kind of person. I wore jeans, sweatshirts, and sneakers most of the time, stopped wearing hat and gloves in grade school, and only put on a dress when forced to. Why did she want to talk to me?

This meeting for lunch was strange, and it worried me. I admired her and craved her approval, but she intimidated me. She was sophisticated and bold, and her job sent her traveling all over the world. She could speak French, Spanish, Italian, German, and a little Russian. Next to her I felt like an ignorant kid from the country, even though I was twenty and a junior at the University of Maryland.

What did she want with me?

Woody's was a familiar place. Every Christmas, my family came into D.C. to stand outside the store and admire the holiday scenes in the windows. The displays now featured a Valentine theme, and when I walked into the store, I heard a soft medley of instrumental Broadway tunes. Salespeople hovered. The spicy fragrance of perfume hung in the air as I passed the cosmetics counter.

The store's open and airy ambiance reassured me. Since classes began last fall, attacks of claustrophobia and panic have plagued me in closed spaces, but in Woody's I could exit at any time, so I felt comfortable. Under these circumstances, a panic attack shouldn't occur, so I left my flask at home. No one needed to know about my problem, and a swig of vodka kept it at bay.

That's the only time I drink alcohol. I don't want anyone to think I'm an alcoholic. Anyway, pills for whatever my problem was required a doctor's prescription, and I wasn't ready for that yet or for hours on a psychiatrist's couch. I wasn't crazy. Besides, a couple of swigs of vodka helped get me through the attacks. No need for tranquilizers. This was a weakness I preferred to keep secret.

I saw Aunt Kay standing at the escalator.

"Sue!" she called, stepping toward me. "Good to see you, my dear." She enveloped me in a rose-scented hug, gave me the once-over, and smiled at me with bright red lips and heavy eyelashes dripping mascara. Her wavy brunette hair was teased and varnished into place, and her navy blue suit emphasized the curves on her slim body. "We'll go upstairs to the restaurant. It's quite good here."

"I know," I said, feeling gauche and out-of-place in jeans, although my sweater and coat were acceptable. Woody's was where genteel ladies lunched. My brown hair, cut short in a pixie style, didn't know what curls were. I had dabbed on lipstick but stayed away from the heavy black eyeliner so many other students used.

As we boarded the escalator, I noticed two colored women admiring a selection of rings in the jewelry showcase. Good for them, I thought. The sales clerk watched them, suspicion written on her hard little face. Were they welcomed in Woody's? I wasn't sure, but they were inside.

Aunt Kay noticed them, too. "About time," she muttered.

I agreed, but I would never have said anything if a security guard had forced them out of the store. Aunt Kay would fight for the women's right to be there. I would slink away. I never stuck my neck out. My Mom said I should get some gumption, but how do you do that? In fact, I'm a coward. I don't like to make waves. In the fight for justice and freedom, I am mostly irrelevant.

But then I had no idea what Aunt Kay had in store for me and civil rights foe George Lincoln Rockwell.

Aunt Kay read my thoughts. "What bothers you most, I think, is you don't speak up to help the underdog."

"No gumption," I agreed. She was right, but what would I say? Would anything I say make a difference? I may be a moral coward, but I did write letters to Congressmen urging them to support the landmark Civil Rights Bill. There was no question where Aunt Kay stood on the issue.

Why did she want to see me, anyway? Something was up. I wished I'd brought my flask. My stomach was full of butterflies.

"Is everyone okay?" I asked. "Mom? Dad?"

She glanced at me, amused. "Everything's fine with them."

If it wasn't something to do with the family, what was it?

We found a table in the restaurant despite the lunchtime crowd, took seats, quickly scanned the menus, and gave our orders. I glanced at the other diners as I waited for Aunt Kay to tell me what she wanted. She said it was important.

Now she regarded me with such speculation I felt even more uncomfortable. She tapped her long fingernails on the tabletop and looked like she itched for a cigarette. "Tell me again what you're studying, Sue."

I recognized a delaying tactic. Still trying to size me up, I thought. Not sure she wants to go ahead with whatever she has in store for me. Not sure I can do whatever it is. Not sure I'll take the assignment. My self-assessment of cowardice made me think she was probably right.

"My major is English literature," I said cautiously. "I'm taking art as a minor and adding some journalism courses." So maybe I can get a decent job, I added to myself. The word was still circulating that if women wanted a job, they'd better know how to type. That meant no matter how well-educated and competent, women were relegated to a clerical career. I glanced at Aunt Kay, my role model. She had a good job buying for an import company and a secretary who did the typing. Furthermore, she had experience in the business world, and she never asked if I could type. Unlike me, she had gumption.

"Excellent. You're including a trade with liberal arts." Aunt Kay spoke absently. "And how are your grades?"

Why did she want to know that? It was none of her business. "They're all right," I hedged, deciding to cut the pain short. "Why did you want to see me?"

She leaned forward, ready for business, but waited as our sandwiches and drinks arrived. I became even more nervous. Something was clearly afoot.

Kay bit into her sandwich and then put it aside. "I need to go on a buying trip for my clients," she said, all career woman now. "To Europe—you know, Germany, Switzerland, Turkey..." She paused as she studied my reaction. I kept it bland. "And other places. I'll be gone several months—probably till June."

"I'd be glad to go for you," I said to lighten things up, "or with you." The semester hadn't started yet. I could take off for a few months.

Kay laughed. "You don't have the know-how," she said bluntly, "but I do need someone to stay at my house and watch over things while I'm gone. You can commute to school, and I have a vehicle you can use.

I breathed a sigh of relief. I was worried about all kinds of dire pronouncements, but what she wanted was for me to house-sit. I almost laughed.

Kay misinterpreted my sigh. She quickly added, "You'd stay at my house free, and I'd give you a stipend." Then she rushed forward as if to stall any objections. "You wouldn't have to pay the fees for a dormitory room, and I own a whole house. You won't be lonely, either, because I have five roomers—all interesting people you'll like. Everyone takes care of themselves." She sat back and grinned at me. "Staying there should save you a ton of money."

I nodded. She'd thought of everything. I'd get free room and board in a house away from the chaos and noise of the dormitory and my obnoxious roommate, plus I'd broken up with my boyfriend. I wanted to get away from that whole scene. It was driving me nuts. "What will I have to do there? Clean up the place after the roomers? Chaperone them?" That's a laugh.

Kay grinned at me with confidence now. I hadn't shaken my head so far. "Nothing like that. They're all decent people with good jobs, or they're going to school. I want you to stay at the house to represent me, to make sure they don't trash the place, you know. Not that they would. They have access to the kitchen, living room, the house, in fact." She laughed again, this time uneasily. "But you'd be doing me a huge favor, and it will help you with your college expenses. Put the money you save toward grad school in a couple of years."

"What about meals? Will they expect me to cook?" That was an appalling thought.

She shook her head. "A cook comes in weekday evenings and makes dinner, and a cleaning woman also comes in once a week, so you don't have to worry about those details. I'll set up a bank account for you to deposit rent checks and pay the help. Will that work for you?"

"I'd stay there, go to school, and keep an eye on things, that's it?" It sounded too good to be true. I liked the idea of a cook. Good food for a change.

"That's right. You'll enjoy living there. The boarders are a lot of fun, but they are out much of the time. The place is close to the bus stop. You can go to the museums, galleries, shows."

"Stop," I said. "I'm sold. When should I bring my stuff over and move in?"

"I'm leaving next Wednesday. You can take me to the airport

and move in then. I'm sorry it's such short notice, but the woman who usually house-sits for me had a family emergency."

The university was on break. I could take care of any hassles about giving up the dorm room between now and next Wednesday and be ready to move in when Aunt Kay left.

There had to be a catch somewhere, but it was such an unexpected reprieve. I hated living in the dorm, although the people staying at Aunt Kay's house might be worse. "Tell me about the boarders," I asked.

Kay laughed again. She was trying too hard to act carefree as she rummaged in her purse. This time, she pulled out a pack of cigarettes and withdrew one with a questioning look at me. I shook my head, and she lit up. She blew out a long stream of smoke. "There are three young guys, twenties. One is Sean Wolfe, an artist and filmmaker who works for some government agency's film division. Then there is Clark Wolfe, his brother, who thinks he's a writer." Kay frowned in distaste. "He's a neurotic social ignoramus trying to find a job here in D.C." She grinned and added, "Not that I have an opinion." She winked. "Anyway, Sean is paying for him until he can earn his own way. He's okay but tedious. Ignore him and let him do his thing."

She took another long drag on the cigarette and blew out the smoke. "Mike is a student who fled Hungary with his sister."

My ears pricked up. "He fled Hungary?" Hungary was a communist country under Soviet control. He must have an exciting story to tell. My neophyte journalism instincts kicked in.

Aunt Kay grinned. "Ask him about it. He works as a lunchtime waiter downtown while he takes night courses. Drinking lunches among the bureaucrats are quite lucrative in D.C. Mike also likes to bake, so encourage him if you want some excellent pastries."

"Sounds like a good person to have around," I said, joking while I wrapped my mind around living in a real house on my own except for the five roomers who would all be out most of the time. So far, the lot seemed harmless. Maybe the others, like Mike, would have exciting stories to share, too.

"He's quite nice," said Kay. She waved her hand, and ash

from her cigarette sprinkled the tablecloth. She didn't notice.

"The others are women?" I asked. "You said five roomers."

"Of course," said Aunt Kay. "There's Ellen, who has a job with some nonprofit downtown. She's quite pleasant—imaginative, you know? And there's Gail Bernstein, who lives in the basement which has its own bathroom and a small refrigerator. She's a graduate student. Quiet. She only comes upstairs for dinner and to leave and return. You'll hardly ever see her."

"Where will I stay?" It had to be better than a shared dorm room.

She smiled. "You'll have your own room next to the kitchen. It's quite small, but then you can use the entire house as well."

I sat back and considered the situation. I'd be living with three working people, one student, and one unemployed person seeking a job. They all seemed like people I could handle and maybe even enjoy—unlike the fruitcakes in my dormitory. That Clark guy is probably away searching for a job most of the time. Gail kept to herself, so she wouldn't be a problem. The Hungarian waiter-student might be interesting, but he and the rest had jobs and would be out of the house a lot of the time. Yep. It seemed like a good deal, and what I needed to keep from going completely nuts at the university.

"Is there anything else I should know?" I asked, keeping my eyes on her face. What was she not telling me?

She didn't quite meet my eyes. "Nothing you can't handle," she said. "I'm so relieved you'll do it." Kay clapped her hands. Her grin appeared again. "You'll have a great time there, and I'll be back by mid-June, so you can line up a job for your summer break."

Six months. I can get through six months even if Aunt Kay is holding back some detestable detail, and it's a hellhole. It has to be better than the dormitory.

"One more thing," Kay added slowly as her eyes watched me. Here it comes, I thought. Here's the catch.

She stubbed out the cigarette and pulled another from the pack without taking her eyes off me. It was as if she were measuring me. "Last summer I was away for several months. You remember the March on Washington?"

"Of course," I said. "I was there." Martin Luther King's speech, "I Have a Dream," still rang in my ears.

"All the boarders were there, too, and inspired by it. Since then they seem more driven, and they're all working on projects that ..." She paused and studied me before she added, "...that I think you'll find interesting."

"What kind of projects?" I asked.

"You'll have to ask them," she answered, "after they get to know you."

Aunt Kay finished her sandwich, staring off into space. She didn't say anything as we took the escalator down to the street floor, but at the door she stopped and turned to me. "These are turbulent times," she said, "you have a chance to make a difference. The next six months will let you see what you're made of." She held up her hand to hail a taxi before adding, "I think you'll be surprised."

As she climbed into the cab, she added, "It will be a test."

Chapter 2

January 15, 1964
On Wednesday morning, I drove Aunt Kay to National Airport as we'd agreed, then I stopped by the dorm to pack all my stuff into her red and white Volkswagen bus. The bus was such a surprising vehicle for her to own. I'd never seen it before. It didn't fit my image of Aunt Kay at all. She seemed more like a Porsche or Jaguar person. I shrugged. She may need it to haul items for her clients in the import business. She used cabs to get around town most of the time. I didn't know much about Aunt Kay at all.

The VW bus was big enough to move my boxes, phonograph, and clothes out of the dorm hellhole. Then I had to stop by the university's finance office to take care of the paperwork. By early afternoon, I had trundled my stuff over to Kay's row house on Kilbourne Place in the Mount Pleasant area of Washington and settled in. I'd always thought of Kay as a rather remote penthouse type. I had no idea she owned a row house in the middle of Washington and took in roomers.

What was her major in college? How did she get a job where she made enough money to buy a house and go on travels worldwide? That kind of job was my dream.

Most people would call her row house conveniently located. It was near the Sixteenth Street bus lines, the National Zoo, and Columbia Road with its shops and restaurants. I could take the city bus to the University of Maryland, but Kay's VW bus would be faster and more fun. The commute was about thirty minutes, not a bad price to pay for saving my sanity. The liquor store was on the corner, and anyone over eighteen could buy alcohol in D.C. Made my life easier.

Thank goodness none of the roomers was around when I moved my stuff in. I needed to calm the jitters and get used to the place before I met the other residents. What if we didn't get along? I was stuck here until Kay came back in June.

Her row house stood in the middle of a block of similar houses, each with a front porch and steps to the sidewalk. The architect arranged rooms like a train. I entered from the covered porch into the living room. Then I walked through it to the dining room, down a narrow hall past the bathroom to the kitchen. Across from the kitchen was my bedroom. It was tiny, but bigger than half of the dorm room I shared with my awful roommate at the university.

The place was surprisingly wide for a row house. Judging from the handsome staircase in the living room, it must have belonged to a wealthy family in its early days. I surmised that my bedroom was at one time the housekeeper or cook's room. Except for the kitchen, which smelled of Comet Cleanser, the house had a faint scent of furniture polish mixed with tobacco smoke. Not surprising, since glass ash trays lay on every table.

A Persian-style carpet, thick and beautifully designed with leaves and flowers against a beige background, covered the living room floor. Aunt Kay probably bought it in some Middle Eastern bazaar on a trip for her import house. The wood floor was stained a shiny dark walnut, visible around the rug's edges. A similar carpet covered the dining room floor except, again, for the walnut-stained floor around the edges. She'd arranged comfortable easy chairs and a couch for conversation in the living room and set up a long table in the dining room. A folding metal table stood against one wall with two stacks of paper flanking a typewriter on top. I had imagined a more formal set-up for my Aunt Kay.

The living and dining rooms were dark. Every flat surface

carried a lamp. Natural light filtered in through windows at the front and a small window in the dining room where the house became slightly narrower. The kitchen was cheery and faced south, so the sun poured in through the back windows most of the day. That meant the sun would brighten my bedroom, too. A high chain-link fence surrounded the petite concrete backyard where Aunt Key kept the garbage and trash cans. I watched a squirrel poke down the alley until I realized its tail was bare. Not a squirrel, then. I grew up in rural Maryland where squirrels, possums, raccoons, deer, and foxes roamed. I'd never seen a wild rat before.

I quickly explored the second floor—all bedrooms and a bath. I peeked into each room, and they seemed quite small, as if someone divided two larger rooms into four small ones. One bathroom served them all. Then I climbed a plain wooden staircase to an attic bedroom. It was obviously Aunt Kay's. The rose scent she wore was everywhere up here. Light gray walls along with a pale blue and gray rug made the room seem restful. She'd placed a double bed with a blue-flowered spread against one wall opposite a white dresser and bureau. The room even had its own bath. Double glass doors led out to a balcony at the back. At last, something that did fit my image of Aunt Kay.

Being in that room calmed the jitters I felt at the move I'd made. I briefly considered taking over this room but decided against it. Aunt Kay had her reasons for assigning me the cook's room next to the kitchen. I should stay there, so I reluctantly descended the stairs back to the living room.

I picked up a textbook and sat on the couch trying to read but couldn't concentrate. What kind of people were going to come through the door?

I didn't have to wait long for the first of the roomers to arrive. Light footsteps tripped up the porch steps, the key and doorknob rattled, and in walked a short young woman with bushy black hair and wearing a plain blue overcoat. She glanced at me. "You're Kay's niece?"

I nodded. "Sue Millard. Are you Gail?"

"Yeah, I'm in a hurry and can't chat now, but I'm really glad to meet you." She came forward to shake my hand. "I stopped by to drop off my books, and then I have to run out to a meeting."

"Kay tells me you all take care of yourselves except for dinners during the week. Is that right?"

"Sure. Don't worry about us." She waved and headed to the basement door in the dining room. "See you later."

She didn't stop to talk, thank goodness. She wouldn't be a problem, but what about the others? I didn't want to deal with them any more than I had to. Aunt Kay said they were working on projects and once they got to know me, they'd invite me to join them. Like I'd be pleased at the honor. Sorry. I was here to house-sit. Nothing more.

The next person to arrive wore heavy shoes that clomped up the steps outside. He pushed himself backwards through the door and didn't see me at first. He seemed twisted up inside his scarf and coat and took a minute to unwind himself. Then he noticed me. "Ah, the concierge." He grinned as if he'd been clever.

"What? I'm not a concierge," I said. This wasn't a French hotel. "I'm Kay's niece, Sue Millard."

"Maybe chaperone then." He studied me as if I were some rare specimen, stroking his beard. I guess he was trying to appear sophisticated, but his beard had dark bits stuck in it, and his dirty, reddish hair was matted with grease or hair oil. "Glad to meet you." He paused at the stairs. "I'm Clark Wolfe. I'll be right down after I get this heavy coat off." He stomped up the stairs. The bottom hem on his pants leg had come undone and dragged on the steps. Was he the unemployed brother? If so, no wonder. I hoped he wouldn't be underfoot during the day.

A while later, a dark-haired, tall, athletic-looking man entered, spotted me, and held out his hand. "You must be Miss Millard," he said formally with a slight bow. His eyes were a soft, warm brown against his olive skin. He looked to be about my age. At first glance, he was appealing and attractive. I'd like to know more about him. I had to wrench my eyes away but recovered quickly enough to offer a smile. Take it easy, Sue, I told myself. You don't even know the guy.

He spoke with an accent and carried a bundle of books and papers, setting them on a chair as he struggled out of his coat.

Something about him immediately touched my heart. He must have endured great hardships before he came to America. Aunt Kay said he worked as a waiter while going to school. His black slacks and white long-sleeved shirt were probably his work uniform.

He picked up the books and papers as he spoke to me. "I am Miklos, but everyone here they call me Mike. Welcome. I hope you enjoy your time here, and we will try much not to annoy you."

I noticed a small green star on his shirt collar. "What is the green star about?" I asked.

He glanced down at the star and grinned at me. "The green star, *la verda stelo*, it identify me as *samideano*, a same thinker, you know, a speaker of Esperanto and believer in the ideals. Peace... brotherhood."

I'd never heard of it. "What is Esperanto?" It sounded like some kind of weird religion.

"Esperanto is the international language, *la internacia lingvo*," he said. "Esperantists are all over the world."

"Really." He was an idealist, but he seemed quite sweet and likable. Even his accent was adorable. Wait. Did I use the word "adorable?" So not me.

"It's easy to learn so everybody can study it and be able to speak to anyone," he added, "especially if they travel."

"Does Aunt Kay speak it?" I asked.

"Yes, she is excellent student and knows many words. She use it, too, in her business." He paused and scratched his chin. "Because she travel much."

"Okay," I said tentatively, not wanting to get into a lecture and hoping he wouldn't turn out to be a bore.

"But yes. Your aunt, Miss Kay, she allow me to hold Esperanto meetings here once a month. We have class at library close by. Meeting here is okay, yes?"

I shrugged. Of course it was okay. Maybe I'd learn a few words, too. "If I can take part," I said, jokingly. It would be a good way to get to know him better. And I would like to know him better.

He laughed. "But you are American flibbertigibbet—that is

okay word? Not serious student."

My mouth dropped open. He thought I was a flibbertigib-bet? "Who told you that?" I asked, suddenly angry and upset and a bit disappointed. Where did he learn such an old-fashioned word? Is that what Aunt Kay thought? Is that how she described me to the roomers here? I rubbed my arms. She didn't know me at all.

He backed away, hands warding me off. "Sorry, sorry. That is wrong word? I apologize."

"I am not a flibbertigibbet," I said forcefully and turned my back on him as I answered a knock at the door. A tall, heavy, col-ored woman stood outside with a huge purse hanging from one arm and the other wrapped around a paper grocery bag. "Hello, Missy. I'm Hannah Owens, the cook for all you. You must be Miss Kay's niece."

I heard Mike head up the stairs. Good riddance, I thought, as I greeted Hannah. "My name is Sue. Aunt Kay told me you had your own key."

"That's right, Missy, but seein' as how it's your first day here, I thought I'd better give you fair warnin', so to speak."

That was thoughtful of her. "Thank you. I'm just now meet-ing everyone. Come on in." A faint smile appeared, and she had a twinkle in her eye. She might be fun with her friends.

Hannah walked in, handed me the grocery bag, and dropped her purse on the floor to shrug off her coat. "I'll hang it on the hall tree and get it when I'm done here. I'll have dinner ready in an hour." She took the groceries and disappeared into the kitchen.

Hannah diverted me briefly, but I couldn't curb my disap-pointment in Mike. Did Kay tell him I was a flibbertigibbet? How else would he know that word? I respected Aunt Kay and wanted her to like me. Now I felt hurt and upset at Mike, Aunt Kay, and myself. I was not a flibbertigibbet.

Ellen was the next one in, a victim of the fad for cat's eye glasses. Her car coat was bright red. She threw it off and hung it on the hall tree behind the front door. She was taller than I and wore a gray wool skirt and plain white blouse, dressed up with a blue and green scarf and a wide blue belt. On her feet she wore low-heeled, black pumps. She had one foot on the stairs when she saw me. "Oh! You're our keeper," she said, grinning at me. "Welcome. I'm Ellen Olson." She held up an attaché case. "I work downtown."

"I'm Sue Millard. Glad to meet you." She seemed like someone I'd like. "What do you do?" I asked.

"I'm assistant director for the Association of Partnerships." She grinned. "Don't ask. Too complicated to explain what it's about."

She was several years older than me, and she seemed to have a responsible, professional job. How much typing did she do?

Only one person left to meet. Sean Wolfe, the filmmaker. He didn't arrive until after six. By then, Clark had returned and opened a gallon jug of Gallo wine. He brought glasses from the kitchen to share the wine with the rest of us in the living room. I refused the wine. Whatever Hannah was cooking in the kitchen smelled delicious, and I was hungry.

Unlike his brother, Sean was clean-shaven and neatly dressed in a suit and tie, although the wind had tousled his red hair. He nodded at us as he ran up the stairs, whipping off his tie. He came back a few minutes later wearing jeans and a flannel shirt. He grinned at me and said, "So you're our keeper, are you?"

"That's what Ellen called me." I shook my head. "I'm Aunt Kay's niece, and my name is Sue Millard. I don't plan to keep any of you."

He pretended to pout. "We're not all bad." He spotted the Gallo and glanced at me with a question. I shook my head. He filled glasses for the others, and I chatted pleasantly with Ellen and Clark in the living room. Mike was there, too, but I ignored him. We moved to the dining room table when Hannah announced dinner.

So far, I felt comfortable with the boarders, Hannah, the house. Everyone seemed likable, except maybe Clark. And Mike. How dare he think I was a flibbertigibbet? How did he even know the word? Which one of them used it in the first place? That word didn't come out of nowhere.

How did Aunt Kay happen to meet such a collection of

characters? No one ever told me she ran a boarding house. Were these people somehow in her social world or did she advertise?

And what was she worried about? I wasn't feeling tested, but my aunt had good sense, and she put me in this position to protect her house. Did I have something to fear from this group of mostly pleasant strangers? I hadn't noticed any undercurrents— at least not yet.

Chapter 3

After dinner, I brought out my sketch pad and drawing pencils, preferring a relaxing pastime rather than tackling the stack of books I needed to read for the next semester.

Mike had retreated to his room. "To study," he said, and I remembered Aunt Kay told me he was taking night classes. He also baked. Pastries and pies, I hoped, which might be something redeemable about him I could appreciate.

Sean sat at the dining room table, pulling film from a reel out of one box and laying it flat on a board in front of him. As he finished working on a stretch of film, he let it drop into a box on the other side of his chair.

"What are you doing?" I asked. It seemed odd to me.

He glanced up. "Experimenting."

He was a filmmaker, Kay said, but was this any way to make a movie?

He glanced at me and saw my puzzlement. "I'm drawing an animated cartoon directly onto the film," he explained, adding a red dot. "Got the idea from an animated feature put out by the Canadian Film Board." He sat back in his chair and grinned at me. "I guess it seems weird to you."

"Never heard of it," I said with a lifted eyebrow. "Looks like a lot of tedious work."

He shrugged. "I'll see how it goes."

Clark sat at the small table holding a typewriter in the dining room. He sipped a glass of wine and contemplated a blank
sheet of paper. A white Meerschaum pipe hung from his lips and
gurgled with each breath. Noxious fumes from the pipe hung in
a cloud around Clark's head. He'd set the scene for his role as
famous author.

Apparently, the creative muse was missing tonight. He
ripped out the paper, crumpled it, and threw it into a wastebasket
in the living room. Ellen sat on the couch studying what looked
like a topographical map. She'd set a pile of books beside her.

"What are you working on?" I asked Clark. Probably his
novel.

"My novel," he said. "Science fiction." He spun another
sheet of paper onto the typewriter roller and stared at it.

Sean and Clark in the dining room, Ellen and I in the living
room, all of us quietly pursuing our own interests together. I liked
the companionable feeling. I guess Aunt Kay did, too.

Clark put aside the pipe. "I'm out of inspiration." He left
the typewriter to sit next to Ellen. She spread the map out wider,
and they both peered at it.

Idly, I walked over and glanced at the titles of the books
piled up next to Ellen. Civil War history. Virginia campaigns. Virginia history. Then I noticed the map was of Virginia. "Planning
a trip?" I asked, out of curiosity.

Clark looked up at me with narrowed eyes. "Why do you
want to know?" He folded the map as if he didn't want me to
see it. Ellen didn't protest. "We're not doing anything," he said.
"Nothing. Seeing if there's any place we want to visit, that's all."

He sounded suspicious of me, which made me even more
curious.

"Sorry," I said. I suppose Clark and Ellen were an item, and
I was an interloper. "It's all right, Clark." Ellen picked up one of
the books as she looked at me. "It's a project we're working on."

Was this the project Aunt Kay mentioned? The test? If it
was, why were Clark and Ellen reluctant to tell me about it? I
returned to sketching. Sean bent over the film. After an hour of

this, Sean stood up, stretched, and glanced at my sketchpad.

"Not bad," he said, making me feel self-conscious. I was only messing around with a pencil. "Do you suppose," he added tentatively, "your aunt would mind if I bought a piano?"

"A piano?" What an odd request. Would Aunt Kay object? I didn't know. He should have asked her. Had he deliberately waited until she was gone?

"Where would you put it?" I asked.

"It'll fit in the living room." He gestured to a likely spot against a wall. There was plenty of room for an upright piano. "A friend is selling one. It's small and won't take up much room."

I ruminated over the question but didn't see any objection. "I guess that would be okay." If Aunt Kay didn't like it, let her tell Sean to get rid of it. "Sure. Go ahead," I told him.

The piano arrived the following Saturday. Sean spent the afternoon wrapping aluminum foil around the keys. "Why?" I asked.

"Wait and see," he said.

That evening, after dinner, he sat down at the piano and banged out a Beatles tune, "I Want to Hold Your Hand," which was a current hit. The foil-wrapped keys gave it the sound of a honky-tonk piano, or even a bit like a harpsichord. It was his thing, not mine, and I wondered if Aunt Kay would appreciate it.

A couple of weeks passed quietly. My classes at the university began, and I was out of the house much of the time. I was also monitoring the Civil Rights Bill and wishing his colleagues would force Rep. Harold Smith, a Southern segregationist, to move the bill out of committee. I got my wish. A bipartisan group of Representatives told him they'd take over the committee if he didn't conclude hearings on the bill that week. That ended the foot-dragging. He closed the hearings on January thirtieth, and the House debate opened the next day. The prospect for passage looked good.

I had my fingers crossed. I got mad every time I thought of how badly some white people treated African Americans. Last year I'd read *To Kill a Mockingbird*, a powerful book. About the same time, I was walking down Pennsylvania Avenue near the

White House and saw a bunch of white boys hurl racial slurs and stones at a Negro woman who desperately tried to protect her young son from them. As usual, I did nothing to help her, and the sight of her tear-stained, bloody face haunts me.

Did Negroes like being called "colored"? That's the term most of us used in polite company, but was that an okay term or a derogatory one? I didn't know. Theoretically, every one of us was "colored," whether it was pink, orange, beige, or brown.

The following Monday, after dinner, Gail came bursting into the house, carrying a manila envelope stuffed with papers. "Sorry I missed dinner," she said. "I had an important meeting." She bounced down on the couch. "Did you hear the Northern Democrats defeated an amendment today that would rip the guts out of the Civil Rights Bill?" She grinned at me. "Hooray for our side."

I looked up from my modern art textbook and smiled at her. The fight in Congress was in full swing, but I agreed. Hooray for our side.

Mike had come down to sit in the living room, reading a book. I ignored him. Nobody calls me a flibbertigibbet and gets away with it. He glanced up at Gail, and she stopped to chat with him as she glanced through the papers she was holding. "How's it going?" she asked.

"Good. Tomorrow I take off work and do some exploring, I think." He closed the book he was reading with a snap. "Good to see place. The situation there, you know?"

Gail looked at him thoughtfully. "That is dangerous. You're not going alone?"

Mike shook his head. "Stuart. He comes along."

"Even more dangerous for him," Gail said, frowning.

He nodded. "But we need to know house and ground, what they do." He picked up the book again and thumbed through it.

"Let me know when I can help." She disappeared through the basement door for her apartment without another word. What were she and Mike involved in? I saw the meaningful look they exchanged.

What kind of exploring was Mike going to do? And who

was Stuart? "Mike, where are you going?" I asked, out of innocent curiosity.

Mike laughed. "Nothing you would find interesting."

He was an overbearing and patronizing jerk. "I see," I said, controlling my irritation, "because I'm a flibbertigibbet."

"I am sorry I use that word," he said. "Funny word, but you say it is not a good one."

"No, it's not. Where did you hear it?" Not from Kay, I hoped. I watched for prevarication.

"Professor say it in my class. He call all girls flibbertigibbets. I think it okay if professor use."

I felt sick. "Your professor is a very bad man. Don't ever use that word again." I meant what I said. Women everywhere have to endure that kind of abuse, part of everyday life. We had to erase that attitude. I changed the subject. "So what are you going to explore? I'm interested."

Mike searched my face. "You would like to know, but this I cannot tell you. It is secret. Big secret. I am sorry."

Ellen and Clark had a secret project. Mike and Gail had one, too, it seemed, but nobody was going to clue me in. I didn't know anyone named Stuart. I supposed I had to earn my spurs first. Prove myself worthy. Was Aunt Kay involved in either of these projects? What did I know about Aunt Kay? Apparently, my assumptions were completely off-base, but I thought she would support a cause she believed in and the people involved. But would she take an active part? Would she risk losing her job? Or this house?

Mike again threw the book down and got up. "I make cookies," he said and headed for the kitchen, adding "I will leave some for you."

Cookies might make up a little for calling me a flibbertigibbet. Maybe.

I heard a knock on the door and got up to peer through the peephole. A young colored man and woman stood outside. I hooked the chain and opened the door cautiously, wondering if I should. This was downtown Washington, and I was white. The situation was tense between the races. I felt ashamed of myself.

"I hope it's not too late," the woman said. "I'm Tanya from next door." She laid an arm on the young man. "This is my brother, Stuart. Gail was at a meeting in our house and left her notes." She held up a blue spiral-bound notebook.

"Come in," I said, unhooking the chain. "I'm Kay's niece, Sue Millard. Have a seat. I'll get Gail."

Tanya smiled. "Thank you. Kay told us you were house-sitting. She's very proud of you."

Her eyes traveled from my face to my clothes. I'd changed into jeans when I came home from class. I had no idea what she expected to see, but she wore a simple and elegant skirt, blouse, and navy blue jacket. She'd pulled her hair back into a bun, but her face captivated me. It had good bones, the kind found on well-paid models. She was quite an attractive young woman. Her brother Stuart was probably around twenty, slim and athletic. He wore a Baltimore Orioles sweatshirt.

"She's my favorite aunt," I said. My only one, I might have added, but didn't. Aunt Kay told the roomers all about me. I wondered what she said. They were friendly and accepting of me, but guarded. Clark and Ellen refused to tell me about their project, whatever it was. Gail went to meetings next door. What were those meetings about? She wouldn't say. Mike and Stuart were going exploring. What did they hope to discover? They wouldn't tell me, but so what? None of it mattered, because whatever Aunt Kay thought about her boarders' activities, my job was to house-sit and that's all.

Tanya stood uncomfortably in the living room, while I called Gail. Stuart took a chair as Mike came out of the kitchen with flour on his hands and a touch of it on his nose. "We look around tomorrow," Mike said. "You will be ready?"

"Ready for what?" I asked. Both of them stared blankly at me.

"Nothing," said Mike. Stuart shifted his eyes to the floor.

The film project engrossed Sean, but he turned around, and I saw his face brighten. He almost knocked over a box in his haste to get up and talk with Tanya.

"Have a seat," he said. "Would you like anything to drink?"

His eyes spotted the Gallo bottle. "A glass of wine?"

"No, no. I'll only stay a minute." She was still standing, but she was smiling at Sean.

Gail bounded up the stairs and stopped as she saw Tanya. She glanced at Sean and then winked at me. Gail had noticed, too. Tanya handed her the notebook and turned to leave.

"Come over anytime," Gail said to Tanya. She looked at me. "That's okay, isn't it?"

I nodded. "Anytime."

Gail smiled at my response and nodded to herself. Was this some kind of test? The test Kay talked about? Of course Tanya was welcome to come over, especially since Sean has a thing for her. How interesting. But she is colored, and he is white. Can anything come of their romance? Aren't mixed race relationships against the law in some states? In Virginia, a biracial couple was waging a legal battle for the right to marry. It was 1964, and we still had a long way to go in racial relations.

Last fall, a display at the Maryland State Fair purported to show the result of integration. A sixty-ish, gray-haired woman in a housedress stood next to a large poster depicting silhouettes of a black person and a white person with a plus sign between them. "Segregation is essential to racial purity," she said. "When you start mixing the races, they'll intermarry. Then...,'" She pointed to a gray silhouette of a child. "You've got hybrid kids. Mongrels."

Okay. I guess she was saying if a black person marries a white person, the result is a bunch of gray children.

"We've got to prevent this," she asserted.

Her ideas were too bizarre for me.

Stuart got up to follow Tanya. "What time?" he asked Mike.

"We leave at five a.m. so we get to the place early before anyone is around."

"That sounds good. By the way..." Stuart paused and eyed Mike. "I've asked my friend Darrell to come along."

Mike frowned. "Is that good? He is smart mouth. He will see the trees and plants and forget what we look for. Not much help, I think."

"I know, but three is better than two," Stuart said, "In case there's trouble."

"Okay," Mike said, doubt in his voice. "We make sure he not start trouble."

Stuart nodded and ambled out the door behind Tanya.

"I haven't met Darrell, have I?" I asked Mike.

"Doesn't come around here much," said Mike without interest. "He is grad student. Howard University."

"Good person to have along if you're going exploring," I observed. "Where would you go at five a.m.?" I asked, being nosy. "Nothing's open, not even the parks."

Mike shook his head. "Checking out a place in Virginia, that is all. No big deal." He headed back to the kitchen. "I finish cookies and then go to bed since I am up early."

They were off to explore someplace at 5 a.m., but they wouldn't tell me anything about it. I didn't like the secrecy. It seemed odd, and now I was curious. Was Aunt Kay in on their secrets? Did she approve? Was she the law-abiding person I thought she was?

Were they?

Chapter 4

February 4, 1964.

I heard Mike foraging in the kitchen before he left the next morning. My clock said four forty-five, so he was serious about leaving at five a.m. I heard him open and softly close the front door. What were he and Stuart and Stuart's friend Darrell up to? If they were simply looking for a new place to live, they wouldn't need to leave at five a.m.

I wanted to spend time in the university library before classes, so I was dressed by seven and finishing a bowl of cereal and cup of tea by seven-thirty. The others stumbled around me for coffee and whatever they fixed for breakfast. Even Clark surprised me, already dressed and getting ready to go out. I retreated to my room to fill the flask from the secret stash of vodka I hid in a drawer. Nobody else needed to know about that. That flask was a lifesaver.

I left the house for the university, feeling the joy of knowing I was free. Free of the dormitory and free of the campus whenever I wanted to leave. I still faced a day of classes. The worst one was in linguistics that placed the professor in front of the only exit. I'd disrupt the class if I had to leave. I was stuck, trapped.

That class was a nightmare. I don't know how I sat through it with my stomach clenched, my hands sweating and cold, every ounce of me struggling to control the mounting urge to flee. But

I needed a good grade in the class, so before I entered the room, I hid in a restroom stall and drank a couple of sips of alcohol. It was enough to feel a calming glow to get me through the class without a panicky run to the door, but not enough to hamper note-taking and listening. I didn't participate in any discussions. By the time class was over, the effects of the alcohol had dissipated, and I was free of the classroom and free of the claustrophobia.

Why was I a victim of these attacks? They appeared suddenly last fall when I got trapped in an elevator, but they continue to occur whenever I feel trapped. I wish they'd go away.

The house was empty when I returned in the late afternoon. Clark was gone, too, I was relieved to find. He was underfoot most of the time. When did he ever look for a job? Such a pleasant surprise for me to find no one was home. I opened the back door and let fresh air in. The stench from Clark's pipe smoke hung over his typewriter.

The house seemed eerily silent. Even the neighborhood outside was quiet. I was reading when Gail popped in later that afternoon. "Mike and Stuart back yet?" she asked.

I glanced up at her serious face. "Haven't seen them," I said. "Where were they going so early in the morning?"

She hesitated and finally said, "I'm not sure. You can ask them."

Oh, yeah. She was lying. The three of them were in some kind of secret project. Were Ellen and Clark in it, too? They didn't want to talk about their project either, but it seemed to involve a map and the Civil War and had nothing to do with Mike and Stuart's project. Somebody's hidden treasure? Sure.

Sean walked in the door, shrugged off his coat and hung it on the coat tree. "Where is everybody?" he asked.

I looked up from my book. "Don't know." I glanced at my watch. Almost six. I saw Hannah climbing the steps. She walked in and headed straight back to the kitchen, head held high. "I'm putting dinner on the table by six-thirty. I don't wait around for nobody."

Clark hustled in at a little after six, nodding at me as he

passed and climbed the stairs. Ellen came in a little later. Mike still hadn't shown up. Should I be worried?

We ate dinner without him. Nobody said anything, but the empty chair was the elephant in the room. As we finished and sat chatting around the table, I heard a knock on the door. Tanya stood outside.

"Have you seen Stuart or Mike?" she asked, sounding upset. She wore no jacket, only a sweater, and pulled it around to hug her body.

I shook my head. "We haven't seen either of them. They left together."

Tanya bit her lip. "Now I am really worried."

I poked my head out the front door to look up and down the street but didn't see them. "I am, too." I noticed how cold she was. "Come inside."

Sean came to the door behind me and took her by the hand. "You can wait with us." He led her to the couch, and they sat down together self-consciously, and then moved slightly apart. They were smitten with each other. What would Tanya's parents think? Or Sean's, too. Where would it end?

"They should be home by now," Tanya said, rubbing her arms compulsively. "They were looking over the place. I told them not to, but they had to do it, anyway. I hope they were careful and nothing happened, but where are they?"

"Damn fool thing to do. We're not ready yet," said Sean, glancing at his watch. "It's after eight."

"Stuart's friend Darrell was with them," I said.

"That's not good," said Tanya. "Now I really am worried. If there's trouble, Darrell will find it."

"But he's a grad student," I said, "and must be older than Stuart. Shouldn't he show some sense?"

Tanya shook her head. "You don't know Darrell."

I sat on a chair facing them. "Can I help? Would you like tea or coffee while we wait?" I asked, needing something to do. Neither Sean nor Tanya wanted to talk, and my efforts went nowhere.

After half an hour with no word from Mike, Tanya left her

chair and walked to the door. "Mom and Dad must be worried sick by now. I better stay with them in case Stuart calls." She opened the door and peered down the street. "Let me know if Mike shows up." She threw another sharp glance at Sean. Her eyes slid from Sean to me, and she bit her lip. "I've got to go." She left. I locked the door behind her.

What kind of expedition had Mike and Stuart gone on? They hadn't returned, which upset Tanya and Sean. They knew what was going on. They talked all around the fact that it was dangerous. The look Tanya gave Sean contained some hidden message, and whatever it was worried Gail, too. I stood at the door uncertainly. What should I do to help? Start calling hospitals? The police? I glanced at Sean, but he sat at the table, pulling film out of the box. The clock indicated eight-thirty. It was still early yet. Mike and Stuart might be stuck in traffic.

Sean plugged away at his animated film project, Clark stared at his typewriter, and I sat with a textbook in the living room. Ellen had gone out shopping. I tried to read but didn't see the words on the page. They were drinking from a new gallon bottle of Gallo wine.

"Is Mike out late often?" I asked.

"He has night classes," Clark said, "and he works as a waiter. Anyway, he's a foreigner. I heard they eat dinner at midnight sometimes." Clark walked to the door and out onto the porch steps, staring up the street. "Here she comes," he said.

I heard the relief in his voice, as I listened to Ellen's steps on the porch, and then Clark ushered her into the living room.

"Have you seen Mike?" I asked.

Ellen shook her head as she glanced at her watch. "He hasn't come home yet?" She looked at Sean's anxious face.

"He usually tells us if he'll be late for dinner," said Sean. "He's a thoughtful guy, and he doesn't like to inconvenience Hannah. He might have gone on to his night class."

Then where were Stuart and Darrell?

At nine, the phone rang. I answered, but I barely understood what they said. The voice spoke with an accent. It sounded like Mike. He was slurring his words. Was he drunk? But some of the words sounded foreign, like maybe Hungarian? I asked him to repeat what he said and listened carefully. It was Mike, and something was terribly wrong. "Where are you?" I asked, but instead of relief I felt fear.

"Emergency Room," he mumbled. "Arlington Hospital in Virginia. Can you pick us up?" He spoke slowly as if it hurt to talk.

I gripped the phone. "Are you all right? Where's Stuart? What happened?"

"Stuart and me, we are okay." His teeth were chattering. "We lost Darrell. We need ride home. I tell you about it when I see you."

Where was Arlington Hospital? Never mind. Kay had a map of Virginia in the VW bus. "I'll get there as soon as I can," I said. "Stay there."

"I am not able to go anywhere else," said Mike.

As I raced out of the house to the car, I thought about Stuart. Was he all right? I turned around and knocked on Tanya's door. Her mother answered. I introduced myself and explained.

Her name was Alice, she offered. Alice Horton. "What'd he say about Stuart?" she asked, removing the apron she wore over a navy blue dress with white buttons down the front.

"He said they're both okay." I took a deep breath. "He didn't say what happened, but they're at the Arlington Hospital, somewhere in Virginia. They've got to be together." Mike said nothing about Darrell. What happened to him?

"Then Arlington Hospital is where I'm going." She grabbed her coat.

Tanya bounded down the hall stairs. "You heard from Stuart?"

"Arlington Hospital," said her mother.

Tanya pulled her coat off the hall tree. "Let's go. I'll drive," she said, running to a Chevy sedan parked on the street. I followed her, glad we weren't all going to pile into Kay's VW bus and relieved someone else was driving. As Tanya started the engine, she pulled a map of Virginia out of the glove compartment. "Navigate," she said to me.

We drove down Sixteenth Street and over to Georgetown to cross Memorial Bridge. It took forty-five minutes to reach the hospital. Tanya's mother, Alice, prayed silently the entire trip, tears running down her cheeks.

Mike sat, head in hands, in the waiting room. His reddened eyes shone through black and blue patches on his face. His coat lay beside him in a pile, bloodied, dirty, and torn.

"What happened?" asked Tanya, running to him. "Where's Stuart?"

Mike's teeth chattered, and he spoke as if it hurt to talk. "Stuart okay, I think. He with doctors now. They check him over. We got beat up pretty bad, but they go worse after Stuart. And Darrell, too."

Alice and Tanya headed for the reception desk before he finished talking.

"Where's Darrell?" I asked.

Mike moaned, holding his head. "They took him, I think," Mike said. His teeth started clicking as if he were freezing. Was he in shock? I took off my coat and wrapped it around him. "What do you mean, they took Darrell?"

"I am too busy being beaten to see. They must knock him unconscious and carry him away, then police come."

"Somebody must have called them," I said.

Mike nodded. "I hear sirens. When those creeps hear siren, they take off." He heaved a huge sigh. "Is what saved Stuart and me. Those guys were gonna kill us."

"On the street?" I asked. "In bright daylight? Why? What were you doing?" This was the United States. Things like that didn't happen to ordinary people going about their business un-less... "Who were they?"

He managed a slight smile. "Mostly OK neighborhood, too," he said. "They were Nazis. What you call Neo-Nazis, but still Nazis. Here in America." He shuddered. "I am strong, but Stuart and me, even with Darrell, we cannot fight those guys. They use clubs."

Nazis. Here in America. I knew such a hideous group lived somewhere outside D.C., but you can find nuts of all stripes everywhere. "What were you doing there?"

Mike shook his head. "Nothing," he said and glanced toward the patient examination rooms. I turned and saw Tanya pushing a wheelchair with Stuart slumped in it. A white bandage wound around the top of his head, and his bandaged arm rested in a sling. Bruises spread across his face, and Alice carried his ripped and muddied jeans and coat. We watched them approach, and I heard Mike say, "I thank God we both okay, not dead."

"But what about Darrell?"

"I ask at desk for him, his name is Darrell Davis," said Mike. "Please, you try again?"

But the reception desk had no record of a Darrell Davis.

"I'll call them tomorrow," I said. "He's probably made it home by now."

Mike shook his head. "I don't think so."

Stuart's mother Alice walked alongside the wheelchair, holding his hand.

"I told you not to go there," she hissed at Mike, "and to keep my son away. They're not worth it. Look what they do."

"Is his arm broken?" I asked, staring at the sling.

"Not broken," Stuart mumbled. His free hand reached up to feel his jaw.

Were they spying on the Nazis? I glanced at Mike for an explanation, but he shook his head and didn't meet my eyes as he wrapped his coat around himself.

Then he muttered, "We make omelet. We break eggs."

Chapter 5

I took the front seat, so Alice could sit next to Stuart and hold his hand. Mike sat on Stuart's other side. We arrived home after eleven o'clock. Tanya crept along on the side streets because every bump in the road elicited an agonized groan from Stuart. Mike gritted his teeth and closed his eyes. He didn't utter a sound.

Alice and I weren't too talkative either, but I finally turned to Tanya. "I'm sorry," I said, "but what is going on here? What were Stuart and Mike trying to do in Arlington?"

"They were on a stakeout," Tanya said. "The Nazis live out on Wilson Boulevard. The neighbors call their place, 'Hatemonger Hill.'"

So they were spying on the Nazis. I sat stunned. "Why? That's asking for trouble. Those creeps are despicable. Ignore them, I say. They don't get much support from anyone, do they?"

"We're not so sure about that," said Tanya. "We don't know what they've got and what they plan. Don't want them interfering now we're so close to getting what we want."

Without thinking, I asked, "What's that?"

Her eyes sparked in the look she gave me. "The Civil Rights Bill. What else? Earlier today, the President signed the amendment ending poll taxes. Now the Civil Rights Bill is on the floor of the House. The Nazis are all white supremacists, along with the Ku Klux Klan and the Southern bloc of segregationists."

"And the devil," said Alice. "They all spit on the bill, given the chance."

"Yeah," I said. "I wrote letters to my representatives about the poll tax. Why should anyone have to pay to vote? Ridiculous. Almost as bad as the fact I can't vote until I'm twenty-one. I have one year to go. Eighteen-year-old guys are being drafted and sent overseas to Vietnam to die, and they can't vote either."

"Kay told us you've done a lot more than write letters," said Tanya. "She's very proud of you. She's been a strong supporter of the NAACP for years."

Another facet of Aunt Kay I knew nothing about. I'd helped behind the scenes in organizing the People's March on Washington last year, but none of the family knew about that. My dad was an electrical engineer, and he moved our family from Massachusetts down to Hagerstown, Maryland, to work with an electronics company there. My parents weren't racists, but they weren't activists, either.

Anyway, it wasn't just me working on the march. I was part of a student group helping out, that's all. It's easy to support a cause when you're with a bunch of similar-thinking people—and you're having fun doing it. I had a shameful record when I was alone. Did I ever stand up against a racist? The answer is no. I even watched my boss tear up a job application from a colored girl last summer and said nothing. Aunt Kay knew how I felt about that incident, and she didn't reproach me, but she would have protested, not stood there doing nothing like the coward I was.

"I'm relieved they didn't kill Stuart," said Tanya. "Mike, too."

So was I, but I worried about Darrell. Where was he? I didn't understand how standing outside the Nazi headquarters might help. Asking for trouble, if you ask me, and they got it.

"We were across and way down the street at a bus stop," mumbled Mike, speaking with an effort. "We watch place. We know about the layout now. We need that. Five guys we saw— they sit on step outside." He paused for a moment. "Only five guys, but we see them, they salute each other with a 'Sieg heil!' Loud, I tell you. I close my ears. Then Rockwell, big man himself, he come out around one, get in car, and drive away. After he leave, the guys sit on front porch. They smoke cigarettes, do nothing."

"Waiting for the revolution," Tanya commented with a grim laugh from the driver's seat.

"We watch place most of the day. There was a cafe around corner. We get donuts and coffee and take them to sidewalk bench. We sit there as if we wait for bus."

I looked at Stuart, sitting next to the window. He seemed to be dozing. Was he going to be all right?

Mike glanced at him, too, as he continued. "We were not, how you say, conspicuous—the bench was down the street, but three of those Nazi guys sneak out the back way, and they come around behind us. They beat up on us. No mercy. I did not think we would get away alive." He stopped talking and withdrew into himself. After a few moments of brooding, he said, "I worry about Stuart, but I cannot do nothing but defend myself." He looked down at his torn clothes and bruised hands. "Not too well, as you see."

"How did you get away from them?" I asked.

"A couple of cars stop and honk horns at us. Then we hear sirens. Make beating stop. We figure someone call police. The Nazis leave, but police take long time coming. Then they question us. They act like it was our fault." He shook his head. "Stuart say some of those police are neo-Nazis themselves. They are not friendly. They do not like my English."

"But someone must have called an ambulance," I said.

"Thank goodness. Once I am patched up at hospital, I call you. I not know about Stuart—how bad he is hurt—until Tanya and Alice find him. Now I worry about Darrell."

"If you hadn't been there," I said, "the police might have left Stuart on the sidewalk."

"I guess so," said Mike, closing his eyes and leaning back against the seat.

Tanya glanced back at him. "You know so," she said, frowning at the road ahead.

"Never mind,' said Alice, patting Stuart's free hand. "Our time will come."

Chapter 6

February 5, 1964.

The next day at breakfast, Ellen nibbled on toast, reading the *Evening Star* newspaper. "Oh, brother," she said and held up an article to show us. "Did you know the Holocaust never existed?"

She wore her usual work outfit, a simple skirt and blouse with a colorful scarf and pumps. Her hair was straight but not wimpy and brown like mine. Hers was blonde, long, and shining. She was pleasant and liked Clark, but she needed to ditch those cat's eye glasses even if they were the current fad.

I stared at her blankly. "Are you kidding?" She'd made a pot of coffee. I needed the caffeine and poured a cup, although I much prefer tea.

"Says right here," said Ellen, holding up an inside article. "According to George Lincoln Rockwell, founder and head of the American Nazi Party, the Holocaust never happened."

"Rockwell the nut. Who would believe such a lie?" That's what worried me. Rockwell seemed to be a man with big plans. How many followers did he have? Not many, I'd like to think, but Hitler had the support of millions of Germans, ordinary people like us. Terrifying to think it can happen in this country, that people are working to make it happen here, that some people would believe anything Rockwell said.

"Sure, Rockwell's an asshole, but he still gets newspaper space." Ellen turned the page. "Even idiots and the insane get coverage, apparently." She munched on her toast, continuing to read the paper. "Did you know he's planning to run for president?"

"Don't be ridiculous." I poured cereal for myself.

Sean walked in. "Everything all right with Stuart and Mike?" he asked. It was after eleven when we returned home last night.

"Are they okay?" asked Ellen.

"We brought them home from the hospital last night," I said. "Probably take Stuart at least a week and a lifetime to recover. If I hadn't seen the damage they suffered, the cuts and bruises, I wouldn't believe what happened. Mike says it was totally unprovoked."

"Mike doesn't start fights. Is Tanya all right?" asked Sean, making his tone casual. He wore a neatly pressed suit and tie. "Exactly what did happen?" He slipped a piece of bread into the toaster.

Then Mike stumbled into the kitchen, wearing a flannel robe and slippers. Black and blue bruises surrounded his eyes. I guessed his body was equally battered and bruised. He saw our startled faces. "I am okay," he mumbled. "I will be fine." He managed a grin. "Didn't lose no teeth, so I was lucky. Anyway, you should see the other guys." He poured out a cup of coffee. "Now we need to find Darrell, that's all."

"Can you tell us more about what happened exactly?" I asked.

"Sure. We act like we mind our business and walk down Wilson Boulevard in Arlington," Mike said, glancing at me, "for the project we work on."

Sean followed Mike's glance at me and nodded. "And...?"

"What kind of project?" I asked.

Mike waved my question aside. He didn't want to tell me about it, but they'd been reconnoitering, he said, for this mysterious project they're working on, which means there's more to this than he talked about last night.

His hands shook, and he swallowed. Tears welled in his eyes.

He dashed them away. "Then Darrell make some comment the Nazis hear, and these three big guys come after him and Stuart. When I try to help Stuart, they beat me, too." He swallowed again. "Thank God someone call police and ambulance come. Those thugs ran, but they drag Darrell with them, and we are taken to hospital."

"I'll call Darrell's parents, said Sean. "See if he made it home." After checking the directory, he made the call. Darrell hadn't made it home.

Mike moaned and clutched his head. "Call Arlington Hospital, too," he asked.

I did. No Darrell Davis.

"They kill him," said Mike. "They kill him and bury him on the twenty-three acres of scrubby woods behind house. I know this."

His words shocked me. "But that would be murder."
Mike nodded.

"Racist bastards," Sean said, buttering the toast. He dropped a dollop of jam on it. "Were they Rockwell's storm troopers?"

"I think so," said Mike, still clutching his head. "We walk past house, you know, like ordinary peoples. Nobody would think we watch house. We go to bus stop."

I saw the effort it took him to talk. I filled in the details. "Mike thinks the three Nazis went out of their house through the back and snuck up on him and Stuart."

Mike looked up. "I know two names. They talk to each other. One name is Leon. Another name is Ted. Remember that. I will fix their gooses."

"What did the police say?" Sean asked.

"They took much time to come," said Mike, gingerly sipping his coffee. "Nazis wave at cops and run back to house."

"The police want to charge Mike and Stuart for disturbing the peace," I said, "but the ambulance came and took them away before the police got their act together."

Mike poured another cup of coffee. I watched the pot shake in his trembling hands and liquid splash into the saucer. "They not like my accent or Stuart's color." He put the pot back on the stove and set the cup and saucer on the table, looking at us apologetically. "I guess I sit here for a while. Think about Darrell."

"The Nazis are in Virginia, you know. The South," said Ellen, glancing up from the paper.

"Maryland and D.C. are in the South, too," I put in.

Ellen shrugged. "Whatever. Stuart and Mike got off easy, I'd say."

Sean nodded. "Yeah, they're alive." He looked at me. "You know what the locals call Rockwell's place?"

I shook my head. "Wait, I think someone mentioned it."

"Hatemonger Hill."

I nodded. "That's right and seems appropriate." Sean and Mike weren't going to tell me anything about their plans. I turned to Ellen. "Tell me more about your project," I asked her. "Why were you studying a map of Virginia?" Did Ellen know what Mike and Stuart were doing in front of Rockwell's house? Were they all working together on one big project?

Ellen put her plate in the sink, washed it, and set it in the drainer. "Gotta go," she said, lifting her cup in a salute. She hurried down the hall to don her coat, pulled the front door open, and disappeared.

I looked at Sean. "Do you know?" I asked, even more curious since no one wanted to tell me about anything going on.

"I'm off. I need to catch the bus." He waved as he left the kitchen, and I heard the front door slam behind him.

They didn't trust me enough to share their secrets. I felt hurt. Even Mike wouldn't explain why they were stalking Rockwell's house. Sean and Ellen liked Mike, which was an endorsement of sorts. He was new to this country. If a professor called his women students flibbertigibbets, Mike probably would think it was okay, maybe even a flattering word. The more I saw of Mike, the better I liked him. I was a blip to him, though. I knew that. I glanced at him, sitting forlornly at the table, sipping coffee with his eyes closed. I heard him mutter, "This was worse even than Hungary."

"How long have you been here in this country?" I asked.

"Four years. Seven years since I leave Hungary. I escape to

Austria, then they send me to England first. Now I live here."

Obviously, there was a lot more to this story. How did he escape? Where was his family? Why Austria? Why England? Why did he come to America? Perhaps this was not the time to ask those questions. It was still hard for him to talk, but perhaps one or two. "What about your family?" I asked.

He managed a smile. "My Mama and Papa live in Budapest. They could not manage the escape I took, but they are okay." He groaned. "Hurt to talk. I think I go to bed now. Rest."

He left the kitchen, and I heard him limp slowly up the stairs. I washed the breakfast dishes and took a book into the living room. I didn't have to drive to class until noon.

Clark trudged down the stairs around ten-thirty, wearing a purple terrycloth robe and shaggy slippers. He sank into a chair and felt his pulse.

"Any job interviews today?" I asked, trying to be friendly. The key to finding a job was actually looking for one, I'd always been told.

"I'll go out later," he said. "Maybe." He got up after a few minutes. "Need some breakfast." He waddled toward the kitchen but paused. "Are Stuart and Mike okay?" he asked.

I filled him in on what had happened, feeling annoyed he was still in the house, but I wasn't his mother. Sean was paying the bills, and Kay was okay with the arrangement. I went back to reading the novel, but I found it hard to concentrate. Something was going on. Maybe this was what Kay felt, or was she part of it? I needed to find out what these people were involved in. The whispered conversations that stopped when I entered a room annoyed me. It wasn't the exclusion and secrecy, I told myself. I was responsible for the house. I should know what's going on under Kay's roof.

Before I left for class, I walked over to the Horton's house to ask about Stuart. His mother Alice came to the door and grimaced when she saw me. This time she wore tailored beige slacks and a cream-colored sweater. Her reply was short. "He's doing as well as can be expected. He was beat up pretty bad yesterday."

"Anything I can do?" I asked.

She stared at me so long without a reply that the message was clear. She didn't hide her anger and resentment. Then she said, "Write your Congressman."

"Yes. Okay," I turned to leave. "Any news about Darrell?"

Alice shook her head. "If he doesn't show up today, his parents are filing a missing person's report."

"Good," I said and added as I turned to leave, "If you need anything, I'll be glad to help." Limp words. No use at all and from a flibbertigibbet.

Mike had gone back to bed after breakfast and didn't surface again until I came home from class. His eyes were swollen shut, and he moaned at each step coming down the stairs. As he passed me to go into the kitchen, he muttered, "Would not get up at all but I am hungry." I heard him banging around in there. Later, he dragged himself back upstairs.

Gail came home around five that afternoon. I took her into the kitchen. She set her books down on the table, filled a kettle with water, and put it on the stove. Clark sat at the typewriter table in the dining room, chomping on his Meerschaum, typing away at his novel, the stack of papers growing ever higher.

"What's going on?" I asked. "What kind of meetings are being held next door that you're a part of?" I knew it had to be something connected with civil rights. "CORE or SNCC?" CORE, Congress on Racial Equality, and SNCC, the Student Non-Violent Coordinating Committee, were two groups fighting segregation and racial discrimination. Of course, the NAACP, the Southern Christian Leadership Conference, and many others were also fighting the battle.

I understood Gail, a Jewish woman, and the Hortons, a colored family, working to further the goals of these groups. Was that the kind of meeting Gail went to the night I arrived? The unprovoked beating Stuart and Mike suffered was a criminal act. Where was Darrell? Was he dead? Murdered? The police were going to charge Mike and Stuart, not the neo-Nazis, for disturbing the peace. I was a white college student, brought up to respect authority and the law, and I was waking up to some unpleasant facts of life for African Americans. Alice's silent reproach stung.

"I joined SNCC a couple of years ago," I said, "at the university. And I helped on the March on Washington last year." Another memory surfaced of an older colored woman beckoning to me outside a restroom built onto a gas station in North Carolina. The manager kept it locked but gave me the key.

"Please," the woman said. "Let me have the key when you're done."

I nodded, and she got the key. The station attendant had denied her the restroom key as they did in the South. He could have been kind but chose instead to turn her down and probably enjoyed the petty grab at power.

Gail got up and closed the kitchen door. She turned and smiled at me as she took her seat again. She nodded at the door. "Clark's out there. Don't want him in on this." She regarded me thoughtfully. "Glad to learn you're a member of SNCC and helped on the march. Good. Kay said you were in the same camp with us, but we were waiting to see what kind of person you are."

"How did you meet Aunt Kay?" I asked. Were they in the same social circle? Stiff, formal Aunt Kay? Nah.

"At church." She laughed at my confused face. Kay was an atheist. "The Unitarian Church down the street," she added. "We're both involved in the women's rights and civil rights activities going on there. Your aunt's a firebrand, didn't you know?"

Aunt Kay? A firebrand? I had no idea. "Women's rights? She has a great job, and she owns this row house."

"Yeah, but she's paid a lot less than men in the same job, and she had to get your dad to cosign on the mortgage loan for this place. The bank wouldn't lend her the money because she's a woman."

"That's ridiculous," I said. Was I going through life wearing blinders? One part of the brain wasn't speaking to the other part? I knew employers relegated women to the typing pool, and I was beginning to understand that because I was female, I wouldn't be treated fairly in the work world or anywhere else. "So she met the Hortons, Mike, and Sean at the church down the street?"

"The Hortons, yes," said Gail. "She met Sean at an art event downtown, and she takes Mike's Esperanto class at the library."

Why did I think Aunt Kay went to work and then spent boring, miserable nights home alone? I'd picked up from my parents, comfortably married, the idea she was lonely and unfulfilled, being single, and probably lived with a cat. What a laugh. With this rooming house alone, she had a lot going on. I looked up to see Gail watching me. "What are you, Sean, Mike, and the Hortons involved in?" I asked. "Does it have to do with civil rights?"

"It's a big issue and a battle, and, yes, we're all involved," said Gail cautiously, studying my face. Obviously she wondered, they all wondered, if I was a friend or an enemy. "Does being a member of SNCC and a believer in your cause," I said, "mean I can join your group?"

"Kay suggested we ask you. She's one of us. She hated having to go overseas when the Civil Rights Bill was on the chopping block, so to speak. We needed to know more about you even though Kay assured us you were all right. Get some kind of confirmation, you know? Volunteering with SNCC and working on the march are good endorsements."

The kettle whistled, and she poured the water into a teapot with three tea bags. "We're trying to help get the Civil Rights Bill passed without being watered down. It will make a big difference to a lot of people in this country. I'm talking about decent people and good citizens."

"I know. I've written my representatives about it."

"Good," said Gail. "If Congress doesn't pass it, things will get terrible for all of us. White people, too, I mean. Colored people are through being patient and waiting for the right time. There will never be a right time for the likes of some people. You know who they are."

"Yeah, but if it gets through the Senate to a vote, the people I've read think it has a good chance."

"Hope so. We passed a law to end the poll tax. That's a step forward." Gail opened the refrigerator door and stared into it. "And the word is out that President Johnson opposes any change to the Civil Rights Bill." She closed the door and looked at me. "No weakening amendments, in other words. An attempt to weaken the bill was defeated two days ago."

"You mentioned that before, but those Southern politicians are sneaky," I said. "Fair play, justice, and liberty for all have no meaning for those guys. They don't have a kernel of human empathy."

"We want the bill passed this year," said Gail, "and Sean, Mike, and I are working on a secret, dangerous project with the Hortons. If the Nazis murdered Darrell, it's more dangerous than we thought." She leaned forward with a gleam in her eyes. "We're keeping Clark and Ellen out of it. They've got their own secret plan. Anyway," she whispered, "Clark's rather a loose cannon, and he blabs."

I nodded. She'd pegged Clark right. Another memory surfaced. I'd driven across the country after high school. At an Arkansas gas station, I encountered a pristine water fountain labeled "Whites Only." Alongside was a dirty bucket with a dipper hanging on the side labeled "For Colored."

After last night, I understood that a lot worse than water buckets happened to Negroes in this country, shameful as it is to say.

"Okay," I said. "What else?"

"If you're as tough as your Aunt Kay," Gail lifted an eyebrow as she smiled at me, "you can join our project. Our group meets next door. If you're interested, I'll take you to the next meeting."

"Aunt Kay is nothing like me," I said as I remembered Alice's reproachful silence. What would Aunt Kay think? According to Gail, she'd be in the front ranks of the battle. This group seemed to know that. At heart, deep inside, I knew that, too. They were waiting to see if I measured up. Did I?

"All right," I said, hiding my misgivings. "When's the next meeting?"

"Next Wednesday, February twelfth. We want Stuart to rest and get better first," said Gail.

"Were Stuart and Mike doing something with SNCC yesterday?" I asked. Would that explain the beating?

She shook her head. "That's, uh, a different project," she said. "I'm not at liberty to tell you about it. You'll find out more if you join us next Wednesday."

"All right," I said. "I'm a resident of Maryland, and I'm not old enough to vote yet. I can still keep writing the Congressmen though, and I'll be at the meeting."

Gail smiled and nodded. She didn't smile often, I'd noticed. She didn't say much either and avoided lighthearted chatting, but she listened, assessed, and dismissed the fools. She picked up her books. "I've got a list with addresses of Congressmen for you. I'll give it to you later." She walked with me back to the dining room and then disappeared into the basement, leaving the kitchen door open as it usually was. I stepped to the living room window and stared out at the street, wondering where Darrell was.

Clark no longer sat at the typewriter, but he'd left his pipe. The dottle had spilled out onto his manuscript.

Ellen hurried in the front door. "Stopped by the Hortons," she said as she took off her coat. "Stuart's doing better."

"I'm relieved to hear it." I watched her go upstairs and knock on Clark's door. The door opened, and she entered his room.

Ellen and Clark were up to something, too. This house was full of plots. Their plot involved a map of Virginia. Vacation? The two of them together? They were too secretive, though. Maybe they thought we wouldn't approve of an unmarried couple going off on their own. Whatever they were planning didn't seem that trivial, but it had to do with Civil War history.

I tiptoed up the stairs and stopped outside Clark's door to listen.

Their voices were low, but I heard Ellen's thin voice. "The problem is it's winter. I don't think this is the right time to do it. The ground's frozen, for Pete's sake."

So frozen ground would matter in whatever they were planning. I mulled that over.

"Absolutely," whispered Clark. "The trees are bare, and we can get a good look at the lay of the land."

"I guess we can spot likely places easier." Ellen's voice had doubt in it. "We have to wait until spring, though, to actually dig."

I heard the floorboards creak. Someone in the room was coming to the door. I sprang away to tiptoe down the stairs. As

Ellen walked out of Clark's room, I turned around and pretended to be walking up the stairs. "I haven't been to this floor yet," I said. "That's your room?"

Chapter 7

That evening after dinner, I answered a knock at the door. The man waiting outside was a stranger. He wore a suede ivy cap and beige trench coat buckled tightly around his stout body. He carried a cardboard shoe box as if it contained a Fabergé egg. His face was square and stolid with red cheeks. He looked at me with surprise.

"Are you a new renter in the house?" he asked. His voice was high and squeaky.

"I'm staying here till June," I said. "Kay's my aunt."

Clark looked up from the book he was reading. "Hi, Horace," he said, then to me, "It's okay. That's Horace Greeley Shaw. He stops by the house now and then."

"Oh." I introduced myself as I stepped aside. He walked in and set the box on the coffee table while he took off his coat and cap. His diffident manner and brown, button-down sweater over shirt and tie with dark brown slacks reminded me of an overfed sparrow.

Sean turned around from his film set-up and shoved his chair back. "Hi, Horace, what have you got for us tonight?" He walked into the living room.

Clark called up to Ellen. "Horace is here."

"Be right down," Ellen yelled back.

Everyone gathered around Horace as he picked up the shoebox, carried it into the dining room and placed it carefully on the table. What can this possibly be about? Everyone knew and welcomed him.

I asked him. "How do you know my Aunt Kay?"

"We met Horace at the coffeehouse on Columbia Road." Sean filled me in. "Kay invited him to drop by when he's in the neighborhood."

"He comes by now and then," added Clark. "He's a medium."

A medium? Really? Aunt Kay knew a medium. "What's in the shoebox?" I asked.

"I can hardly wait to see what you've brought," added Clark.

We all gathered around the dining room table to stare at the shoebox.

Horace smiled and puffed himself up proudly. He bowed to everyone. "This is the result of hours of concentration," he told us. "In this box I placed a plain sheet of paper and a pencil. Then I poured forth all my energy into calling forth a spirit to write a message for us on the paper." He cleared his throat. He was milking every bit of drama out of this.

"We will now see what the spirit has imparted to us." He reached forward to break the tape that held the lid on tight. Then, with a smile all around, he lifted the lid off the box and removed the piece of paper inside. I was skeptical but as interested as everyone else. What would be on the piece of paper?

Horace stared at it with his mouth open. Sean took it and with a blank face passed it around to the rest of us. Everyone took it seriously, it seemed. I was eager to see it, too, but I was the last to receive this important piece of paper and stifled a laugh. The paper was blank. On both sides. None of us even giggled out of consideration for poor Horace, but I wasn't the only one hiding a smile.

Horace was crestfallen. "I don't understand this," he said. "I poured every ounce of energy I had into calling the spirits. I worked for hours." He took the box and laid it on the floor next to an easy chair in the living room before taking the chair himself.

"Glass of wine?" asked Clark, holding up the Gallo bottle.

"Sure," Horace said.

Clark handed him a glass. "Sometimes the circumstances are not right," he said in consolation.

"That must be it," Horace agreed. "My apartment is quiet, but it's in a new building and doesn't have a long history of people living—and dying—there. No atmosphere. I need to find an old church, perhaps, or an old mansion, someplace with history behind it." He turned the paper around in his hands as he thought. After a few minutes, he pulled a book out of his pocket and started reading.

Sean returned to his film project. Clark pulled out a map and stretched it across the dining room table. Ellen followed him, arms folded and a disapproving frown on her face.

Sean eyed the map irritably. "Don't mess with my film," he said, paintbrush in hand.

"Don't worry. Anyway, this is important." Clark looked toward the living room where Horace, Gail, Mike, and I were reading. "Come here, Gail. Take a look."

Gail glanced at their setup and groaned. "Of all the ridiculous ideas," she groused, but I was interested. Maybe I'd find out what was going on around here.

Clark saw me coming. "Wait a minute. I didn't mean you." He snatched up the map.

"It's all right," said Gail. "She's one of us." All of them stopped what they were doing and stared at me. No one paid any attention to Horace, reading quietly in the living room.

"What?" I asked, seeing the doubt on their faces. "I'm harmless, but I would like to know what's going on here."

"She's a member of SNCC," explained Gail. "Kay vouches for her. She's on our side."

"Oh. Well, then, you ought to take a look at this," said Clark, unfolding the map once again.

"I think it's a ridiculous idea," said Gail.

"We don't care what you think," Ellen said. "We know the idea is way out there, but nobody thought Lindbergh could fly across the Atlantic, either."

"What have you got?" I asked, now really curious.

Clark drew himself up. "We're on the trail of Mosby's treasure." He exchanged a triumphant look with Ellen.

A treasure hunt? Was Clark serious? "You mean Mosby of Mosby's Raiders?" I asked. "Colonel John Mosby? The Confederate guerrilla fighter?"

Clark smiled and nodded. "Yep. That's who we mean."

"We like the irony," added Ellen. "Using Confederate spoils to support civil rights."

They were so serious I dared not laugh, especially since my inclusion was still tenuous.

"If we find it, we'll donate it all to CORE and the NAACP to help get the Civil Rights Bill passed," said Ellen. "Churches around the country are preparing to send busloads of their members here to lobby for the bill. They need money for the buses, food, living arrangements."

Gail and Sean looked bored. Sean leaned back and stretched his arms, wiggling his fingers, but buried treasure stories had fascinated me since I was a kid. Now here I was, confronted with an actual treasure hunt. "But what treasure?" I asked.

"Here's the story," Clark began, his eyes gleaming. "Mosby and his men captured a bunch of Union soldiers camping out at the Fairfax County Courthouse in Virginia. Turns out the Union soldiers had looted the home of Confederate Brigadier General Edwin H. Stronghton."

Ellen broke in. "The Union soldiers carried away sacks full of Stronghton's candlesticks, coins, jewelry, silver bowls and other stuff—quite a haul. Mosby and his men took the captured Union soldiers and the booty and headed back south to Culpeper."

"But Mosby was afraid Union troops might attack and catch them. He didn't want the Union to get the treasure, so he buried it in the woods somewhere between the Fairfax County Courthouse and Culpeper, Virginia." Clark pointed out the two places on the map. "Between here and here."

I guessed at the distance between the courthouse and Culpeper. "That's a lot of ground to cover," I said, "and much of that ground is built up now. Shopping centers, housing developments, schools, churches—a lot of changes have happened to that area since the Civil War."

Clark grinned at Ellen, then turned to me. "We know that, but so far, we've found nothing that says anyone has discovered Mosby's treasure."

"And we borrowed my mother's car to drive the back roads from the courthouse to downtown Culpeper last weekend," added Ellen, "and there's still a lot of farmland and woods."

"According to the story," said Clark, "Mosby buried it in the woods between two pine trees and marked them with an "X" so he'd be able to identify them later when it was safe to come back for the loot." He pulled out a chair and sat down. "The trouble is that he and his men got back to Culpeper and stayed around for a few months, and when he thought the time was safe enough, he sent a few of his most trusted men to go dig up the treasure."

Ellen broke in again. "Before they reached the booty, Union soldiers captured and hanged them. That meant only Mosby knew where the treasure was buried, and it was never recovered."

I looked from Clark's eager face to Ellen's. They were true believers, all right. I saw a lot of holes in this story. "Are you sure no one ever recovered it?" Hordes must have searched for it over the years.

Probably Mosby himself returned and dug up the treasure. Who would know? He could have gradually dispensed with it over the years. He'd avoid taxes that way. Or someone else found it and kept it secret. Same reason. Anyway, it's easy to explain candlesticks or jewelry as family heirlooms when you took them to an antique dealer to sell.

What could I say to these two eager beavers? The chance that they'd find Mosby's treasure was as slight as winning a lottery. They frowned at me and waited for my response. Why my opinion mattered, I had no idea, although they'd probably received enough ridicule and wanted no more.

But I had to ask. "The pine trees. Wouldn't they be dead and rotted by now?"

Clark nodded as if he wanted to pat me on the head. "You'd think so." He grinned at Ellen. "We checked on that. Most pine trees live at least a hundred years and often up to three hundred." He held up a hand. "It's possible they're still standing and maybe the crosses carved into them are distorted, but they'd still be there if the tree is alive."

"You've thought of everything," I said. I suppose a little support is better than none. I saw this treasure hunt didn't impress either Gail or Sean.

"All right," I said, as if my opinion mattered. "It won't hurt to try for it. I wish you luck."

The tension broke as Clark and Ellen grinned at each other, then at me.

"Sure, we know our chances of finding it are slight, but can't you see the delicious irony of it? Finding Mosby's treasure to support the Civil Rights Bill?"

I got it, but had they researched the rest of the story? What happened to Mosby after the Civil War? If they didn't hang him or throw him in prison, wouldn't he come back for the treasure?

Horace got up from his chair and came over to study the map. "I can help," he said. "I'm a dowser. A couple of well drillers use me to find water, but there are other kinds of dowsing. Some dowsers also use their skills on maps."

Ellen and Sean had skeptical looks on their faces. I did, too, I'm sure, but Clark was excited. "Anything that will help us narrow it down," he said, glancing at us triumphantly.

Horace reached into his pocket and brought out a length of string tied to a small, lead fishing weight. "I've wanted to try this," said Horace. "I'll work with the map here, and then you can take me with you on your search. I can try again in the field with my dowsing wand."

He suspended the weight about three inches over the map. We watched him swing it in circles as he moved it slowly across the map. He glanced around at us as we stared at the pendulum. Slowly, the pendulum stopped circling. "Mark that spot," said Horace. He waited a moment, then again passed the pendulum over the map. He did this several times, telling Clark when to mark a spot. When he stopped, he wound the string around the weight and returned them to his pocket.

"Now I'll double-check these areas," he said, closing his eyes. He moved his hands slowly across the map. "Ah, I feel a slight sensation here," he said. "Mark where my fingertip touches the map." He tapped a finger. "This one."

He repeated the exercise several times. I didn't believe any of it but hid my skepticism. They were serious.

"That should do the job," Horace said finally. He studied the map with Gail and Ellen. "These places that are marked, they're the likely places to find the treasure."

Clark was visibly thrilled and clapped his hands. "That narrows down the search quite a bit for us. This is terrific!"

"I'm sure it will help," said Ellen noncommittally, watching with arms folded.

"I'll be glad to do what I can." Horace looked down at his hands modestly. "Dowsing has a proven track record, you know."

I'll bet, I thought as I listened to the three treasure hunters make plans for their next search into the wilds of Virginia.

And I wondered what kind of trouble they'd run into searching for Union treasure in Civil War country where the hicks drove pickup trucks with loaded gun racks.

Chapter 8

I mulled over Clark and Ellen's and now Horace's treasure hunt, and more questions came to mind. Anyone might have discovered Mosby's stash by this time, one hundred years later. The whole idea was loony. What kind of shape would silver candlesticks and silver bowls be in after all this time? Corroded and tarnished beyond recognition was my guess.

Before I asked more questions, Clark got up. "We can make that new Hitchcock, Ellen. Wanna go?"

"Sure. *The Birds* is supposed to be really scary. Let me put this stuff away and grab my coat."

"I'll go with you," said Horace, putting on his coat.

Sean, Gail, Mike, and I sat around the living room and watched them leave.

Mike was fussing with his bandages. "What about you?" I asked him. "Were you and Stuart on a treasure hunting expedition yesterday? Why were you spying on the Nazis, anyway?"

Mike laughed and shook his head. Sean got up and drifted to the piano, humming to himself. His fingers picked out the opening bars of Peter, Paul and Mary's hit, "Puff the Magic Dragon." He crooned to himself along with the melody.

Mike watched him, pushing his lips in and out. He hadn't answered my question. I guess he wasn't anxious to please me. I wondered if he had a girlfriend. He probably did. I'd like to meet her. He'd shown little interest in me, but he probably thought I found him offensive. He hadn't understood how obnoxious his professor was in calling the female students he taught flibberti- gibbets. Showed how old the professor was. A dinosaur.

Mike looked at Gail. "What do you think?" He nodded at me.

"Sue's one of us." Gail shrugged. "Kay told us she was okay." Gail studied her fingernails and added, "She's a member of SNCC and helped with the march last year."

"I see. We travel the same path." His warm brown eyes sent shivers down my spine, and he certainly was fit. He was about six inches taller than I, which would make him a little less than six feet tall. He seemed like an amiable guy, too, now that we were clear on the subject of flibbertigibbets. Sure, I'd travel the same path with him.

"You've got to let me in on what you're talking about," I said." What did getting beat up in Arlington have to do with any- thing?"

"Darrell is still missing," added Mike. "They might have killed him."

"It's about civil rights," Gail said.

Mike nodded. "Civil rights."

"I'd like to help the Civil Rights Bill get passed, if that's what you mean," I said. It was all about fairness, after all. Equal rights. Equal opportunity. They should include women, too.

"That's what we're talking about," said Gail. "We're making plans to help."

As if to emphasize the statement, Sean played a loud cre- scendo.

Now I was interested. I wanted something to do beyond writing letters to Congressmen. Maybe this was the test Aunt Kay mentioned. "I'd like to be part of your plans," I said. Depending on what they are, I added silently to myself.

Gail walked to the basement door. "I'll let you know." She disappeared downstairs.

Mike stretched out on the couch. "You might be interested in Esperanto." He yawned. "We call ourselves *samideanoj*. That is, "same idea people." We share the idea that if we can all speak together in the same language, one easy to learn that is politically neutral, then we might be able to communicate better and finally achieve world peace."

"Quite an ideal," I said, but I was thinking a common language didn't prevent the Civil War. Anyway, languages weren't my strong suit, but if it were easy to learn, I might take a crack at it because he was so interested. "You give classes in it, don't you?" I asked. "At the library up the street?"

He started to rise but sank back with a groan, holding his head as he spoke. "I ache all over, and now I've got a headache."

I got up to find aspirin in the kitchen. He stopped me with his hand as I passed. "Our local club holds classes on Thursdays at the library on Mount Pleasant. You should join us."

"Maybe," I said. I got the aspirin and a glass of water and brought them to him. "What were you and Stuart doing in Arlington that got you beaten up?"

Sean stopped playing the piano and looked at Mike. "Go ahead and tell her. We can use her, and she might have some ideas."

"After yesterday, I am even more determined to succeed," Mike said. He stared down at his hands, both of which were closed into tight fists. He didn't speak for a moment, but then cleared his throat and looked beyond me into the distance. He sighed and drew himself up to sit straight with dignity. "I was born in Budapest, Hungary, in 1935. My family was not wealthy, but we were not poor either. My parents owned a grocery store in the Pest section of the city."

He was speaking mechanically, as if he'd told the story too many times and lost interest. I looked at his fists, still closed tightly. He was struggling to be impassive, as if it were someone else's story. I listened closely because now I knew it was important.

"When the Nazis invaded, we lost everything." He looked directly at me with hot eyes, his fists clenching and unclenching. "Everything. We were Jewish, you see. My parents sent me to a farm in the countryside. Those kind farmers kept me and told everyone I was a cousin from the city. In that way, I kept my life but lost my heritage and many of my friends and family. The Nazis murdered them on the banks of the beautiful blue Danube. My Mama and Papa found people to hide them and they survive, but much poorer now. We lived through the German oppression and then Germans leave, but the Russians come in. We suffer more oppression." He shrugged and added, "My sister and I, we escape."

Sean broke in. "Yesterday, Mike and Stuart were canvassing the area around George Lincoln Rockwell's house."

"What does this man Rockwell have to do with anything?" I asked. "I barely heard of him." Oh, yeah. I remembered. He was the neo-Nazi planning to run for president. He had some kind of following, and I'd seen a photo of a bunch of men in front of the Nazi party headquarters in Arlington. Not too impressive.

Sean leaned forward. "I'll give you some background. He was a decorated war hero from World War II, discharged in 1959, I believe, rank of Commander. He loves to sail. He was married and divorced twice and has a daughter." He saw the looks on our faces. "I'm trying to make him more human," he said defensively.

"And he founded the American Nazi Party in 1959," broke in Mike. "Those unspeakable fiends, those..." Words failed him. He sat back, but he clenched his fists, and his eyes blazed.

"Rockwell is not a nice man," said Sean in a bland understatement. "He denies the Holocaust, ardently believes in the inferiority of the Negro race and the supremacy of the whites, and he puts his power behind segregation." Sean spoke forcefully, but now he added with a laugh, "We do not approve of Mr. Rockwell."

"In case you had any doubts, here's what his platform is," added Mike. "You will not believe what I tell you. First, he would publicly hang for treason eighty to ninety-five percent of the Jews in this country for being Marxist Communists. Then he would 'encourage' all the African-Americans to move to Africa. Those who say no would be rounded up and taken to some terrible wasteland in this country. He would strip them of their citizenship, and they must stay on that reservation as...uh...what is word?" He looked at Sean.

Sean supplied it. "Wards." He looked at me. "Wards of the

government. If you think I'm lying about Rockwell's intentions, let me read you this." He pulled a sheet of paper out of his pocket. "Listen to what he said in 1961." Sean glanced at me as he read: "The LAST TIME our leader..." Sean looked up. "That's Adolph Hitler." He continued. "The last time our leader showed the way to victory in one single area of the earth. 'Today Germany!' he predicted. 'TOMORROW THE WORLD! Now it is TOMORROW! Now is the time. White Men! THIS TIME THE WORLD!'" Sean folded the paper and tucked it back into his pocket. "Those are the words of George Lincoln Rockwell."

I shuddered and sat stunned. How could anyone want to keep the horrors of the Third Reich alive? Who was proud to call himself a Nazi? I supposed he'd have to deny the Holocaust to keep his American version of Nazism alive. He had to be crazy, but apparently he'd found some crazy people to go along with him. He must have had a bad, bad upbringing. I sat there dumbstruck.

When I didn't reply, Mike spoke up. "You want to know what we do casing Rockwell's neighborhood?"

"But his ideas are blatantly ridiculous," I said. "He wants to go back a hundred eighty years and set up more reservations? The ones we have never worked well for anyone."

"I agree," said Sean, "but then Nazi Germany was no joke. Hitler had millions of supporters and not only in Germany."

Mike nodded. "He doesn't have many followers here."

"But he worked in advertising," said Sean. "If he had more money, he'd use it to promote his ideas through advertising. How many more supporters would he persuade that way?"

"That's what we worry about." Mike held up the back cover of a magazine. "Promote the Nazis like they sell soap or cigarettes. Cigarettes kill people, too."

Sean smiled. "We have a plan," he said, "to rob him."

Whoa. I felt sucker punched. Had I offered to help them? I wanted to backpedal fast. Did Kay support these wide-eyed idealists? Did she know about their plans? She'd apparently recommended me to them for their little project. I needed to rethink my Aunt Kay. The shock gave way to disbelief. "You can't mean to risk your lives breaking into his house and robbing him." My voice rose to a high screech. "He must have alarms and maybe dogs--Dobermans!"

"You don't have to get involved," Sean said. "You can sit here and enjoy your comfort."

Gail returned from the basement with her blue notebook.

"Yes, yes," said Mike, his eyes flashing. "You can do that, but Gail and I, we cannot tolerate an American Nazi Party."

"The German one murdered our families," Gail hissed. "We say enough!"

"Sure, yes, I see," I said, realizing I was facing steel, not passion. The whole idea was outrageous. They weren't thieves. How would they know how to commit a robbery? But they said they had a plan. "You have a plan?"

"Hold on a second," said Sean, rising from the piano and taking a chair next to the couch. "I don't think we should say any more about this to Sue." He looked at me. "Beg your pardon, Sue. You don't need to get dragged into this."

Gail folded her arms. "We can use all the help we can get." She pointed her finger at me. "Look at her. She's not colored, and she doesn't look Jewish like me. We can use her."

"First, everyone needs to approve bringing a new member into our group." Sean spoke fiercely and directly at Gail. Mike said nothing.

"The Hortons have agreed to include her," said Gail. "I asked."

Of course, the Hortons were in this, too. "That's all right," I said. "Good idea. I need to sleep on it, anyway." I didn't know yet what the plan was, but the whole idea was crazy and dangerous. It sounded like jail if we got caught. I didn't want to postpone graduation and ruin my life because of a jail sentence. No matter how much I admired Mike's eyes.

"If you rob Rockwell," I said, "however you justify it, it's still robbery, taking something that doesn't belong to you. It's theft, and it's still wrong." I don't rob people's houses. I couldn't believe they would, either.

"You're right," Sean replied. "It is theft. We plan to rob him of the money he would use to sway people toward hate and prejudice. The Nazis tortured and murdered their victims. Rockwell and his men, given the power, would do the same. We refuse to allow that to happen."

"They may have already killed Darrell," added Mike.

"And we'd still be committing robbery, even though you think the ends justify the means," I persisted.

"Very well," said Sean. "I suggest you consider our redirection of Rockwell's assets as partial reparation for damages Stuart, Mike, and Darrell suffered at the hands of his men."

"Only down payment," added Mike.

Chapter 9

February 6, 1964.

The next morning, I walked next door to check on how Stuart's injuries were improving. Mrs. Horton, Alice, opened the door. She was wearing a gray, full-skirted dress with a red belt, pearl necklace, and black loafers. With her slim figure, and her hair pulled back into a bun, she looked quite elegant. The other night when we drove to the hospital, her coat was fur. She spoke well, too. She and Cole were educated people.

Did I expect more than a clerical job when I got my degree? I hoped so, but I knew it was a rare woman who got promoted to management, but I expected more than a menial, dead-end job, and I wasn't going to quit working if I got married. My mother still wanted me to learn to type, though, and a lot of the women students I met seemed to look only for an M.R.S. degree. I assumed those women were flibbertigibbets. Or acted like it, following the advice of columnists on how to catch a man. What a waste.

Alice seemed capable and confident. Could she get a professional job if she had a degree? Maybe she did have a degree and a good job. Why would I assume she didn't? I hadn't thought about it before, but even if she did have a degree, the job market would be small and tough for an African American woman. A predominantly colored school might hire her as a teacher, I supposed. The young colored woman who applied for a job where I worked last year would never have gotten the position, no matter how educated and capable she was and how hard she tried. The job market for professional white women was small, too, and often limited to teacher, nurse, or secretary. The same guy who tore up the colored woman's resume told me he would never promote me to manager because I was female. Men, he said, would refuse to work for a woman. Alice broke my reverie.

"I'm off to work, honey," she called to Stuart, then turned to me. "Go on in. He's at breakfast."

I had to ask. "Where do you work?"

"I own a beauty salon," she tossed over her shoulder, "for an elite clientele." She laughed as she rushed out the door. She was a manager and a business owner. Wonderful! I walked in to find Stuart, dressed in jeans and sweatshirt, gingerly eating a bowl of oatmeal. He gestured to another chair at the table.

"Hurts to talk," he said. "Hurts to eat. Hurts to sit and walk, too. Lucky I'm alive."

"You're right." I looked around the clean and cheery kitchen. Bright yellow curtains on the back windows were open to let in the sun, but the day was cloudy, so the overhead light did the job. "I'll do most of the talking," I said. "You can give short answers or nod or shake your head, okay?"

He nodded.

"Who's your mom's elite clientele?" I asked as I sat across from Stuart.

He managed a laugh. "Our people," he said. "Colored women."

"Oh. Okay." At least Stuart was managing to talk, and I had questions. "Mike says you were casing Rockwell's house."

His eyes widened. He winced as his mouth dropped open. I'd surprised him with the forthright question.

"You're not supposed to know about that." He mumbled the words, speaking with difficulty and holding his jaw.

"Whatever you've got planned, it'll never work," I said. "You'll only get beaten even worse." I thought about Darrell. "If you're not murdered."

His eyes turned stony, and he shoved a spoon of oatmeal into his mouth without looking at me.

"I suppose you're part of Clark and Ellen's crazy plan, too," I said, fishing.

"Have no idea about that," he mumbled. "They're not in with us." He looked at me. "And don't you tell them nothin' either."

"Of course not," I said. "I'm wondering how the bunch of you think you can break into and rob a house full of Nazis."

"We've got a plan," he said.

"What kind of plan?" I asked.

"Wait and find out." He narrowed his eyes as he stared at me. It was a dare.

I watched him a few moments as he finished the oatmeal. He wasn't going to tell me anything more. "Can I get you something?" I asked. "I'll be next door most of the day, so call me if I can be of help." I walked toward the door.

"Hey!" Stuart said. I turned around. "Keep your mouth shut."

By the time I got back to the house, everyone but Clark had gone out to work or class. I heard Clark stumbling around upstairs. He came downstairs after a short while, still in his robe and slippers as usual.

"I thought you were searching for a job," I said, more waspishly than I meant. When did he go job hunting? He seemed always underfoot.

He sat back in a chair and took his pulse without bothering to reply.

"How did you find out about the Mosby treasure?" I asked. How credible is this story?

"I heard about it," was the curt reply. "Then I checked on it and read up on Mosby."

"Am I to understand that in the one hundred years since he buried the treasure, no one has found it? What about Mosby himself? He knew where it was, and he would have recovered it for sure."

Clark sat up. "Not necessarily. Grant pardoned Mosby, so Mosby may not have wanted to bring up the loot he stole from a Union brigadier general. He'd barely escaped the hangman. If

Grant found out about the theft, Mosby might face a stiff jail sentence. Better to let it lie."

"What's your next move?"

"We've got it all planned out. First, Ellen and I need to find the exact route Mosby took down to Culpeper. That information has to be in a file somewhere. They can't keep it classified after all this time. Anyway, he was a Confederate. Then I'll have Horace do a map dowsing job as we walk along the route, and we'll check out those spots he identifies. Also, starting now, we'll hike what seems to us the best route and look for those two pine trees and any trees that have depressions in the ground nearby. The depressions could indicate something was buried there."

"Even after a hundred years?" I asked. "Covered with dead leaves?"

He thrust out his jaw. "Maybe. It's another clue to look for. We figure the likely spot will be closer to the courthouse than to Culpeper, because they'd want to unload the treasure as soon as possible. That presents the actual problem 'cause that area's built up."

"It certainly is," I said. "Bulldozers might have dumped tons of gravel on it or contractors covered it with houses and stores. Anyway," I added, "Mosby probably dug it up when he lived in Warrenton. He'd need some money to live on."

"We know we've got a lot to contend with," said Clark.

"Besides that, what would those pine trees look like now, one hundred years later? They probably died, fell over, rotted, and vines covered the remains."

Clark pushed his lips in and out, frowning at me. "You don't have to have anything to do with it." He shuffled to the stairs. "And you can keep your opinions to yourself." He disappeared upstairs for a short while, then came down, dressed in jeans and flannel shirt, and headed for the kitchen. "Need breakfast," he muttered.

Another day not hunting for a job. I listened to him putter in the kitchen, and then he returned to the typewriter during the afternoon as I studied a textbook for class. I heard him sucking on his pipe as he typed. Maybe he was writing resumes for his non-existent job search. He seemed comfortable with Sean supporting him, but how long would Sean keep that up?

Clark and Ellen's foolish escapade seemed harmless if they stayed clear of the good ol' boys looking for trouble. The two treasure hunters might get arrested for trespassing, but that's probably the worst that could happen to them as they pursue Mosby's treasure. I had no faith in Horace's dowsing rod, but having three people instead of two was a safer way to hunt.

The plan to rob Rockwell disturbed me. How much had Aunt Kay been involved? I'd thought of her as a law-abiding mature adult, aligned with my parents, but she was only in her thirties. She must be tough, too, and a visionary. I had assumed I would be treated equally and fairly in life, but if so, why was I haunted by the specter of needing to type if I wanted a job? Why did older women keep repeating this to me? Why were Gail and Ellen the only ones who made coffee in the morning? I didn't because I was a tea-drinker, and the only thing I knew about making coffee involved water and ground beans. Aunt Kay had to get a man's signature on a loan and earned lower wages than a man in the same job. Why were all the good jobs listed under "Help Wanted: Men" and the low-paying ones under "Help Wanted: Women"? Was that to be my reality as an adult?

I did not want to get involved in robbing Rockwell's house. I didn't see how to do it without grave consequences to me and these idealistic roommates I'd acquired. I wanted to support the Civil Rights Bill as much as anyone. I understood the organizations pushing for passage needed money to support their efforts. And there was a delicious irony in robbing Rockwell to support the cause. Mosby's treasure, too. What were Gail and Sean and Mike planning? Their ideas scared me, and now, it seemed, a powerful undertow was pushing me into being part of their scheme.

Was this the test Aunt Kay talked about?

Chapter 10

February 10, 1964.

Nobody talked about the plan to rob the Nazis for several days while Stuart and Mike recovered. I hoped the beatings had sobered them, made them think twice, give up the idea. We'd heard nothing from or about Darrell, and Darrell's parents had filed a missing person report. I suspected Mike was right, and the Nazis had murdered him, too.

My classes were going well at the university. Despite the beatings and the undercurrents I felt at the house, I was less stressed living in a relatively quiet home instead of the chaotic dormitory, but I continued to take a swig of the vodka before entering a classroom to keep the panic at bay. It was a dangerous habit to start, but it worked.

I kept up on the Civil Rights Bill. On February eighth, Congressman Smith, who'd been holding the bill back for so long, proposed adding "sex" to the antidiscrimination title. That interested me, being a woman soon heading out into the workforce. What I heard through discussions at the university, though, was that Smith thought giving equality to women would turn a lot of Congressmen against the bill. He was wrong. Not because discrimination against all women was unfair and wrong, but because people started realizing if the bill passed without including women, it meant colored men and colored women would have more rights than white women.

If the bill passed with the word "sex," I envisioned a huge impact on my life, opening up to me and all women, professional jobs that did not necessarily involve knowing how to type. I'd be able to buy a house and have credit on the strength of my own earnings. And equal pay for equal work sounded pretty good to me.

No one at Kay's house brought up the plan to rob Rockwell, but each evening, I felt as if everyone around the table was waiting. We barely spoke to each other. Maybe, like me, Mike, Sean, and Gail could think of nothing but the job ahead of us. In my mind, I called it the heist. After a shot of vodka, I relaxed enough to call it a caper. Clark and Ellen were too absorbed in their own plans and each other to notice.

Today, February tenth, the House passed the Civil Rights Bill, including the word "sex." Clark opened a new bottle of Gallo wine and shared it around the dinner table to celebrate. I stuck with tea. We all knew the bill would have a hard fight in the Senate. The Southern bloc was organizing a filibuster to prevent it from moving forward to a vote.

That evening after Hannah left, I sat down with Gail and Sean in the kitchen. "I need to know more about how you're planning to rob Rockwell," I said. "I support the Civil Rights Bill and equal opportunity-antidiscrimination laws for everyone in our country. I participated in the March on Washington for Jobs and Freedom last August. Along with thousands of others, I applauded Dr. King's "I Have a Dream" speech there. I'm a member of SNCC, and I'd like to do more to support the Bill. It has to pass."

"But...?" said Gail.

"But I'm afraid of jail. I'm afraid of getting beaten or hosed and not graduating from college. If Rockwell catches us, he might kill us."

"Of course, there's a big risk," put in Sean. "I'd be fired."

"My parents will be mortified if they have to bail me out of jail," added Gail. "I don't want to get killed, either."

"So why plan a robbery?" I asked. "That can't be classified

as protesting or even fundraising. It's plain robbery no matter how praiseworthy your intent."

"I know." Gail studied her fingernails.

Sean shrugged. "Those idiots have gotten little support. They need money desperately to pay the bills. We have a source inside Rockwell's house who says the electricity has been off for more than a year. They use kerosene lamps. No water. The fact is Rockwell has a big mouth, and he used to be in advertising. He knows how to turn a phrase, so the papers report on him, making him seem more important than he is. Gail's parents are on the board of the Anti-defamation League. They told her that the ADL keeps tabs on contributions to Rockwell's group. Their reports show no organization of any size has contributed funds to the American Nazi Party."

"Glad to hear that," I said. "But who is your source inside his house? He'd have better information, wouldn't he?"

"He's Sean's friend," said Gail. "Known him since grade school. He says if they get any contributions, none of the men there see it. The house is a wreck, there's no food, just Rockwell and a few storm troopers rattling around waiting for something to happen."

"No Dobermans, then," I said. A joke.

"No Dobermans," said Mike, "but some real tough hombres out to murder Jews and Negroes. Rockwell distrusts women, too. He insists on women being deferential and keeping to their place in the kitchen or bedroom."

"Nice guys," I said. "But they seem like a weak and powerless bunch. Not worth bothering about. He has nothing to rob."

"Weak and powerless so far, but," said Gail, eyes flashing, "Sean's friend says they are expecting a $150,000 donation from a benefactor in Dallas."

"Wow!" I exclaimed. "That's a lot of money. It changes the picture, doesn't it?"

"Yes, it does," said Sean. "We don't like the possibilities of what he might do with that amount of money."

"And consider this." Gail tapped her fingers on the table. "The money comes from Dallas. President Kennedy was killed in

Dallas about three months ago. Is there a connection?"

I stared at them as my mind conjured up the possibilities. "But this is all hearsay from Sean's friend. Can we trust him? Why is he living there?"

"I've known him a long time," said Sean. "He hates Nazis. I believe he's working for the FBI. Not sure of this, but I think the FBI wants to keep track of Rockwell's activities. My friend is a plant, but he wants to destroy them, not just report on their plans. He's walking a tightrope to help us."

"Are Mike and Stuart still in on this crazy scheme despite the beatings?" I asked. If they wanted out, maybe Gail and Sean would give up, too.

"Yes, even more so." Gail leaned forward. "We need to plan how exactly we would break in, get the money, and escape without getting caught or hurt."

Hurt. The beatings hadn't affected Mike or Stuart's interest in the plan. They were still recovering from the beatings, but Gail says they're anxious to move forward. Mike is ready to go today. Stuart agrees, even if he doesn't talk or laugh much.

I looked at their intent faces. "You're saying all we have to do is break in, get the money, and escape?" Stunned as I felt, the preposterousness of the words struck me as funny. "Piece of cake, no doubt."

I laughed. They didn't.

"We know this won't be easy," said Gail, "but with the inside information about Rockwell's setup from John's friend, we should be able to develop a plan."

"And we have the team to do it," added Sean. "I think it's possible."

"So do I," said Gail, "and he deserves our worst."

Their earnest, committed faces made me feel old. They believed in this project. They believed they could do it. They believed it was right to do it. The idea intrigued me, but I was still scared and doubtful. I'd never done anything daring in my life. The March on Washington last year was as close as I got to political action other than write letters. Until I joined SNCC, that is. I believed in their cause. I felt the Civil Rights Act was essential to the well-being of our country and to a democratic form of government. I thought of the despicable way so many white people had treated colored people and still did.

Gail saw I was wavering. "Think what happened in Germany to the Jews. We need to make sure it can't happen here by protecting the rights of everyone by law. People in the South and the Southern bloc in Congress and men like George Lincoln Rockwell are out to prevent that. We want to make sure Rockwell doesn't have the money to carry out his grandiose but horrifying agenda."

How did robbing Rockwell protect his rights? I wanted to ask but didn't. "Did Aunt Kay know what you're planning?"

Sean nodded as if he'd expected the question. "Yes, yes, she did. She wanted to be a part of it."

"Then she learned she had to go on a six-month buying trip," added Gail. "She told us about you, but none of us knew if you'd want to help."

"When did you find out about this enormous donation?" I asked. "If this donor sends a check, and we steal it, we'll never be able to cash it. The donor will just write another one."

"My informant says it will be cash," said Sean. "Cash, so no one can trace it to him. Cash, so Rockwell can spend it as he sees fit with no accountability. Cash, so there will be no paper trail or IRS questions."

"I see. Laundered money, no doubt." Criminals were behind this huge donation.

Sean smiled. "Kay said you were looking for a way to help and here's a good one."

I nodded, still thinking, still worrying about the consequences should the plan go awry.

"I've got an idea," said Sean. "Tomorrow night there's a talk on a voter registration drive in Mississippi they're organizing for this summer. It's at a church a few blocks from here. Let's go."

I'd heard something about that. SNCC was talking about organizing one, but was waiting for the passage of the Civil Rights Bill. A voter drive in Mississippi sounded dangerous to me. It wasn't only Negroes who got lynched in that state.

"People forget fast," said Gail. "Only three months ago, we were shocked and angry at the President's assassination and horrified such a thing happened here. President Johnson used that anger to push through some civil rights legislation, but the Southern bloc is trying to whittle it down, weaken it to the point of meaninglessness. We've got to prevent that."

"I can write letters," I said. "I can do that." Would much prefer to do that.

Sean smiled. "We're all doing that. Making our voices heard. That's important, too, and maybe you'd be comfortable sticking with the writing part."

They were patronizing me, giving me an exit, but I would then remain an outsider. I liked them all, Sean, Gail, the Hortons, and even Mike. They had happened upon a unique possibility to weaken an enemy to freedom and justice for all. If I joined them, they would accept me as a friend and ally. As I thought about it, I saw some wiggle room. I could join them but stay in the background and volunteer only for the jobs that wouldn't get me into trouble. I could stay out of the action. I'd be a bystander, there to help but not get involved. That's the role I wanted.

"I think of the four little girls killed when their church was bombed in Birmingham," said Gail. "That happened only last September, a month after the 'I Have a Dream' speech."

"The struggle continues, and the battle is heating up," added Sean. "You've got to wonder how many lynchings, beatings, bombings, boycotts, sit-ins, and marches have to occur before African Americans get equal rights and decent treatment."

I joined SNCC because I had some vague notion of helping in the struggle. Now I was confronted with the plan to rob Rockwell and give the money to SNCC or the NAACP. This was a focused and clear goal that might actually help, even though they hadn't worked out the "how" yet. Or maybe they had.

"You've got the plan for robbing Rockwell all worked out?"

Gail and Sean exchanged glances. "No, we haven't," said Gail.

"That's why we're meeting," added Sean, "to see how we can make this idea work."

No plan. Maybe they'd never arrive at a workable plan. "Okay," I said. "I'm interested. Count me in." Inside, I prayed, please if they do come up with a plan, give me only the safe jobs. I put aside the ethical questions. We would be robbing a law-abiding citizen, after all, even if we didn't accept his politics.

What would the American Civil Liberties Union say about that?

Chapter 11

February 11, 1964.

The next evening, I walked with Sean, Gail, and the Hortons to the church where a lively meeting had already begun even though we were fifteen minutes early. I recognized several Negro leaders in the community, but many of the people there were white. The latest copy of the Civil Rights Bill was being passed around with several passages underlined.

The people were signing up to visit various Senators to argue for passage of a strong bill, but pessimism fought with optimism among those present. The passion I saw both awed and exhilarated me. This was truly democracy in action. Ideas flew around me. Organizing voter registration drives to go into the deep South. Sending Negro delegates to the Democratic National Convention. Nonviolent versus violent approaches. Several young Negro men talked about using power tactics to force change. The atmosphere was electric. Everyone knew change was coming.

When we walked home, Alice and Cole Horton didn't say much, but Tanya, Gail, and Sean chattered among themselves, elated by all they'd heard. I didn't say much, either. I was comparing my own weak response to this civil challenge with the fervent commitment I'd heard at the meeting. Those people were serious, dead serious. It was a life and death matter to them and for all of us and for democracy.

I signed petitions, picked up the literature, and talked to a lot of people.

I had never been more aware of the privilege of being white.

After dinner the next evening, Wednesday, February 12, I walked to the Hortons's house next door with Gail, Mike, and Sean. That made eight of us planning the insane robbery of the home of a decorated former Naval aviator who happened to be neo-Nazi George Lincoln Rockwell. My stomach was all butterflies. I felt like someone going to the guillotine.

The Hortons hosted the meeting in their basement. Wall-to-wall beige carpeting lay on the floor. Against one wall was a table with what looked to me like the layout of a train set. No train tracks, though, and no cute little train or town with toy trees. In the center of the layout stood the model of a large house, a dollhouse. They'd set this miniature house back from the road in a grid showing the surrounding woods, houses, and streets. A large blackboard hung on the wall next to the layout. The Hortons had arranged folding chairs in a semicircle facing the blackboard.

Tacked up beside it was a drawing of the plat of land the house sat on. Twenty-three acres of straggling woodland at 6150 Wilson Boulevard in Arlington.

I looked around the room at the group assembled there. Sean and Tanya sat at opposite sides of the room, studiously avoiding each other. I could feel the electricity between them, but no one else seemed to notice. Maybe Mom and Pop Horton wouldn't approve of Tanya and Sean's relationship. Mike sat next to Sean, both of them contemplating the dollhouse layout. There was absolutely no electricity between Mike and me.

Alice nodded toward the house. "Kay bought that dollhouse from an antique dealer and fixed it up to look like Rockwell's place."

No question about it then. Kay supported this insane plan. A cloud of depression weighed me down as I examined the layout. This was the place we hoped to rob. "What about a security system?" I asked.

Alice smiled. "No money for it."

No Doberman, no security system, no fence, no alarm. A bit of the cloud lifted. This robbery might be easier than I thought. We only had to watch out for tough guys looking for a chance to beat up people like us.

"Six men are living there," said Sean. "Five are Rockwell's storm troopers, and they have guns and rifles."

"Our source says every wall in that house is riddled with bullet holes," added Gail.

"No alarm. No Doberman." Mike rubbed his hands. "We make the plan, and we have a secret ally."

"Who's that?" I asked.

Mike smiled at me. "Rockwell himself."

I was sure I hadn't heard that right. "Rockwell, the far, far right neo-Nazi is not our ally," I said.

"You think not?" said Mike. "He is desperate for support and money, and he truly believes that most Americans think the way he does. And so he bring in much money for us."

"I see. I'm sure he planned it that way," I said sarcastically.

Mike grinned. "He expects to be elected president in 1972."

"In his dreams." That possibility was terrifying, but then arch-conservative Barry Goldwater was the frontrunner Republican to run against LBJ in the fall election. Disastrous, but maybe not as disastrous as Rockwell if he won. The current joke about Goldwater was his attitude that if people had any gumption, they'd inherit a department store.

"Rockwell has a vision, you might say," Sean said. "Our informant is a friend of mine, someone I've known for many years. He has papers showing the Army discharged him several months ago, and he has now joined Rockwell's little party. He lives in that house, but he's no Nazi. The Nazis murdered his brother during the war. He hates those guys."

"I don't understand," I said. "He hates them, yet he joined them?"

Apparently, everyone else knew the story. Sean filled me in. "I think he's working for the FBI. Not sure about that, but he wants to take the Nazis down, not just monitor them, so he's glad to feed our little group information."

"But why the FBI?" Gail asked.

"The FBI has their collective eyeballs on Rockwell. They think he might have been responsible for the 1958 bombing of the oldest synagogue in Atlanta." Cole rubbed his hands together as if he were cold. "They want to get a handle on his activities and who's supporting him. Do you know he tried to get on the ballot in the New Hampshire primary this year? That failed because he couldn't get the one hundred signatures he needed." Cole laughed. So did we. It brought Rockwell down to reality. He wasn't as powerful as he thought he was. Most people were too smart to fall for his pile of manure.

"But if your friend is working for the FBI," I said. "Isn't that enough to do it? Why pull us in?"

"I said he wants to take them down. The FBI only wants to know what they're doing and if it's against the law." Sean grinned at me. "He says Rockwell is so desperate for cash he's asked all the men in the house to get jobs and contribute their paychecks to the ANP."

We laughed.

"That's the background," said Gail. "Let's get started." She looked at me. "We're making a list of what we need to do to make this work."

Cole Horton added, "First step in planning Operation Libereco Nun." He smiled and nodded at Mike.

"That is our code name for what we are going to do," said Mike. "It is Esperanto."

Cole spoke up. "It means Freedom Now."

These people are crazy, I thought. What next?

Gail turned to Sean. "When does the money arrive? Have you found that out yet from your ally?"

He nodded. "Next Monday. It will come in a black Cadillac with tinted windows. Around eleven a.m. All the cash will be in an inconspicuous cardboard box. Rockwell plans to hide the box in his bedroom closet."

"Not in a safe?" asked Cole. "Or the bank?"

"My friend says Rockwell's men are true supporters, and they have guns. Rockwell doesn't think he'll have a problem with security, and he'll want to keep the money liquid and accessible without a paper trail."

"I can't see Rockwell," I said, "trusting his bunch of storm troopers enough not to put it in a safe or strongbox."

"I agree," said Sean, "so we have to be prepared for that."

Gail wrote "Safe?" on the blackboard. "And then what?"

"The money will remain with him, and he'll use it as he sees fit. He doesn't have a board of directors or anyone in his organization to question what he does."

Cole smiled knowingly at the rest of us. "All cash. No money trail. It's appalling to think that some Dallas millionaire wants to donate a huge pile of money to this fascist to screw up our democracy."

She turned to me. "One of Rockwell's goals right now is to scuttle the Civil Rights Bill going through Congress. The South. That's where he got most of his money. The Klan loves him."

"Can you imagine donating to a Nazi?" asked Mike. "In this country? I come here because it is land of the free. I hear much about America in Hungary." He shook his head in disgust. "He like to say he make America great like it used to be." He looked at me and added, "He talk about white supremacy."

"But it's not free for us," said Alice. "In some places, it's downright dangerous. If I want to drive down to see my family in Louisiana, I have to map out every step of the way, so I know where I can use the restroom or a restaurant or a place to spend the night." She held up a green-covered book. "This is the 'green book,'" she said. "It lists places that accept us colored folk. It helps."

"Let's move on," said Cole.

I watched them in awe. I had vaguely heard of Rockwell before I moved to Kay's house. I had dismissed him as a horrible nutcase. I was feeling nervous, too, being invited to this meeting. That meant I was a member of this gang of...of outlaws. An image of Billy the Kid rose in my mind. I scrapped that image for one of good guy Robin Hood. In a way, we would rob the rich to help the poor. You can bet Rockwell wouldn't like being robbed. I wasn't sure I wanted to be a part of this dangerous plan. How can they possibly succeed? How can I gracefully withdraw? What will Aunt Kay think of me if I do?

"Remember, a bunch of tough guys hang around outside

the house." Stuart still spoke with difficulty, barely opening his mouth.

"We got to remove them first. They look for trouble," said Mike. "And I got to keep my mouth shut. If they hear my accent, they would get rougher on me."

"And I am colored. White man and colored man, walking together side by side. I don't walk ten paces behind for nobody. That don't work for those guys."

"I got off easy," said Mike.

"I'm still alive," added Stuart, "so I guess I did, too. But I don't think Darrell was that lucky. Nobody's heard from him."

"What we learned from your beating," said Gail as she wrote on the blackboard, "is they are watching the neighborhood with nothing to do but protect Rockwell and to beat up anyone they see walking by."

"Rockwell wants to run for president. I think he'll want to keep his nose clean, but those thugs who beat up Mike and Stuart might be rogue Nazis with their own agenda. Be careful around them."

To me, it was an impossible situation. How can they get by all those guys to rob the place?

"Anything else we need to know?" asked Gail, hands on hips and her eyes flitting from one person to the next. She stopped at me. "What do you think?" she said. "Are you in or not?"

They all turned to stare at me. No humor in any of their faces. They were dead serious. I thought of all the times I'd shirked the right thing to do and said nothing, all the times I'd looked away in the face of bigotry. How much of a coward was I? What was I made of, anyway?

I was a junior at the university and I'd never taken on anything more important than passing tests and turning in papers on time. What these people asked me to do made me question my worth and character and values. Aunt Kay was right. This was a test. If I decided not to take part in this...this challenge, how would I feel about myself?

"You can decide to leave the group," said Gail. "We know our plan is dangerous. You have your own life to live. You don't need to get involved."

"Of course," said Tanya. "If you don't feel committed to our cause, you can leave right now."

"No one will blame you," added Sean. "You're new to all this. You barely know us."

He was right. They all were. If I were smart, I'd get out now. They were making it easy for me to leave. But then I thought of Medgar Evers, NAACP field secretary, assassinated last June in Mississippi. The four colored girls murdered in the bombing of the Birmingham Baptist Church last September. The fight to vote. The sit-ins. The bus boycotts. The lynchings. All this in what we called the "land of liberty." No one would blame me for leaving right now except myself, and I would live with this cowardice for the rest of my life.

I felt tugged by history in the making. If I was ever to stand up for what is right, the time was now. I almost smiled at the irony. What is right is robbing a private home? They were waiting for my answer. I sensed the judgment in all their minds. They think I'll back out. I want to, that's for sure, but the weight of too many times of not speaking up, not doing the right thing, oppressed me.

"So are you in or not?" repeated Gail. No one else said anything. They watched me silently.

My heart was hammering, and my throat felt dry as I gulped and said, "I'm in. What can I do to help?"

Suddenly, smiles broke out all around. They applauded, and I felt good. I am now a member of their team, God help me. The applause quickly stopped, and all eyes turned back to the blackboard.

"What else do we need to know about the situation?" asked Gail.

Alice stepped forward. "We need to know his routine. When he eats, sleeps, and goes out. Does he have a regular schedule? Can we count on him being out when we need him to be out?"

"I'm way ahead of you," Sean said. "I asked our ally inside the house to give us Rockwell's daily schedule, and he passed it to me when we met downtown." Sean held up a sheet of paper.

"Here it is. Rockwell gets up at six a.m., scrounges something to eat for breakfast along with the other men. They told my friend he was lucky he wasn't there when they ate a can of cat food."

A chorus of "ews" sounded around the room.

"Since there isn't much to eat, they just hunt around the kitchen for scraps or leave the house and try to beg a dollar from somebody." Gail wrote "Rockwell up, six a.m." on the blackboard.

"What does he do during the day?" pursued Gail.

"According to my friend, he works in his office in the house during the morning," said Sean, "goes out most days around one p.m., but we don't know what he does then. Doesn't get back until around four."

Gail added, "Leaves at one p.m., out till four p.m."

"What about the evenings?" put in Mike.

Cole laughed. "They sit around and talk about what they're going to do when Rockwell is elected president in 1972."

Sean nodded. "That's about it."

Gail tapped on the blackboard to get our attention. "We know $150,000 in cash is coming to Rockwell next Monday. That means we have to get it that afternoon or Tuesday morning before he has a chance to disperse any of it. We think Rockwell will hide it in a safe in his bedroom closet. Does our contact confirm that? Has he looked?"

"I'll ask him tomorrow," said Sean.

"All right." Gail inserted "probably" in the line about the stash being in the closet. "What about the other men? From what I've heard, they sound like a scroungy bunch of misfits. Why wouldn't one or more of them steal the stash and make away with it?"

Sean rolled his eyes. "Regardless of what you might think, they're confirmed Nazis themselves, and they practically worship him. I don't see them stealing from him. They are gung ho believers in their cause."

"Plus he'll lock it away," added Cole.

"So what do we have on our side?" Gail persisted.

"We know his schedule," said Sean with a smile.

"What else?" She looked at the glum faces in the room. My

heart sank. This group didn't have a plan. It all looked impossible to me, but I needed a clearer picture of the life in that house. "They must be starving," I said, "all the time."

"Yeah," said Sean. Everyone else nodded.

"And what about laundry?" I asked. "Does it go out or do they do it in-house?"

"Cheap laundromat down the street," said Alice. "They don't much bother with that detail, I'm thinking. From all I've heard, they are a grubby bunch. Rockwell tries to maintain a conservative appearance. He takes care of himself. Hair cut neatly. Long-sleeved white shirt. Tie. He looks like a grown-up Boy Scout. It's all public relations. He's a publicity hound for his cause."

"Is he any kind of lady's man?" asked Alice.

Sean shook his head. "Don't see anything like that from him. He expects women to be deferential and homebodies."

Rockwell sounded even more repulsive to me.

"Are there any deliveries made regularly?" asked Gail. "We might be able to piggyback."

"No money," said Mike.

"I don't see how we can get into the place and rob it if the men are hanging around all day," I sensed a window of possibility for giving up this harebrained scheme.

Mike scratched his chin. "They are hungry, half-starved. I know that feeling. All we need is a carrot."

I smiled at Mike's pun. A pun had to be difficult in a second language. "A carrot," I repeated.

"I'm beginning to get a glimmer," said Cole, sitting up with interest.

"Me, too." Sean grinned at Cole, who winked back.

I had an idea, too.

Alice folded her arms and frowned at the group. "Don't forget those guards may not be the smartest pickles in the barrel, but they're mean, they're hungry, and they have guns."

Gail scribbled that list on the blackboard and then stood back as we regarded it.

Sean and Cole looked at each other, grinning. "I think we can do it," said Cole.

"Food," I said.

"Sex," they said.

Sex?

Chapter 12

All of them studied me with calculation in their eyes. I suddenly felt even more afraid. "What do you mean by 'sex'?" I asked with trepidation. Did they think I would do a Mata Hari act and seduce Rockwell's men? Sean and Cole and the rest of them are crazy if they think I can pull that off. I glanced at Sean, wanting to slap the grin off his face.

"Rockwell's neighbors sometimes bring by plates of food," said Sean, nodding his head. He was studying me the way a heron eyes a trout.

Tanya added her grin. "Dad's a pharmacist."

"I don't get it," I said. "Anyway, how do you know this so-called ally in the house is telling the truth?" I asked. "He can be leading you on to trap us."

An ally of ours in that gang of Nazi nut balls sounded iffy to me. Who would voluntarily hang out with guys like that? Wouldn't he worry their hate would rub off on him? I wouldn't last a minute in that place. "Can you trust the man you say is an ally?" I asked again.

Sean nodded. "I think so, especially if I'm right, and he works for the FBI."

Cole interrupted. "That's off the subject at hand. We're beginning to get a glimmer of a plan, but let's take a look at the pluses and minuses we have to deal with first."

All of us stared at the blackboard with the negative factors in one column and beside it the positive factors in the other.

"So tell us your idea," said Gail, standing at the blackboard, hands on her hips.

I spoke first. "According to Sean's informant, if he's telling the truth, they must be starving, and they don't have any money."

"Which means they have little support," added Sean. "Hardly any donations except for the windfall coming on Monday. Rockwell's a big blowhard, and he has the bullshit skills from his advertising background—he came up with "white power," for Pete's sake."

"No telling what he might do with $150,000," said Alice.

"He probably won't pay his bills with it," I said. "I hope he'll feed the men, but he'll probably use it to propagandize his hateful ideas." What a psychological mess the man must be.

"Let's cut to the chase." Sean pounded one fist into the other as he stood in front of the blackboard. "We'll get our ally to bring in some pizzas with extra sauce."

"Supplied by my daddy." Tanya got up and hugged him.

"Special sauce," said Cole, smacking his lips. "My own secret recipe. Enough to knock them out for a couple of hours, so we can do our dirty work, find the money, and get it out without anyone knowing what happened."

"But that will compromise our ally there," said Mike. "If he bring in pizza that knock them out, they blame him for robbery. They'll beat him up like they beat me and Stuart. Maybe kill him. We cannot do that to him."

The possibility deflated all of us. I gave a plus in my mental checklist to Mike for considering the ally's position. The idea was basically good. How else could we get in there and rob the place? How could we administer the drug? Those are the questions now. Sean seemed to be the idea man on this team. I looked to him for a solution, but I found him again staring at me, brows drawn down, pushing his lips in and out.

"What?" I asked as they all turned to study me from head to foot.

Sean's glance swept by each one of us before speaking. "The thing is," he said, "the closest we come to a *femme fatale* in this bunch is Sue." He saw Tanya's expression and added, "No offense, ladies, but our target is violently racist and anti-Semitic. They're all nuts, but I have heard nothing about them being homosexual. Rockwell was married and has at least one kid."

"So I wouldn't appeal to them," said Tanya. "Being colored."

"And I wouldn't either," added Gail, "being Jewish. It would also be dangerous for us to get close to them."

I spoke up. "If you think I'm any kind of *femme fatale*, your head isn't screwed on right."

"All you need to be is a white female," said Sean. "These guys are starving for food and female companionship. Must be."

"I will stay close by to protect you," said Mike.

"Me, too," Sean said. "Don't you have any pretty dresses? All you wear is jeans around the house or boring skirt and blouse to your classes."

I didn't like the way they were sizing me up. "What do you want me to do?" I asked. "I don't know how to vamp." I'd only ever had a few dates since high school. They didn't go well. And my ex-boyfriend was a disaster.

"What we need you to do is saunter by the house and chat with anyone hanging around outside."

Oh, yeah. Sean was full of good ideas. "What do you mean, 'chat'?" I asked.

"Act like you're new to the neighborhood. Be friendly. Wilson Boulevard is a busy place, and one of us will be in a car watching you. You'll be okay." Sean sounded confident about all this, but I wasn't.

Mike stepped forward. "These guys are dangerous. They will have guns, and they will be mean since they do not get much food. We must not forget they buy into Rockwell's Nazi ideas. They insist on women to act like cattle."

"That's right. They're hungry," Sean said. "I want Sue to go by there enough times, back and forth, that the guys get to know her. She should bring any conversation around to food and act sorry for them when they tell her what they're not eating, however they might want to phrase it to save face."

Light dawned. "I get it." It might work, I thought. "They get used to seeing me, so when I show up with pizzas for lunch on Monday, they'll eat them."

"Bingo," said Sean. "You can start tomorrow."

"Tomorrow?" I was stunned.

Gail nodded. "It's a good plan. What about the FBI guy? Should he know what we're doing?"

"No," put in Stuart. His jaw still hurt, but this time he was agitated enough to speak. The words came through with difficulty. "The FBI might stop the whole thing—being against the law, you know. They might even arrest us. We lose control of what's happening, and they take the money. Got to give it back to the man, but no telling what would happen."

"I agree," added Mike. "We know what we want to do. The FBI, they would have other ideas, and then we would not accomplish nothing. I know what I speak. In Hungary ..."

"Okay," interrupted Gail. "You're probably right."

I saw Alice take in our motley group. "It's just us, then."

I looked around at the group. They were all ready to put my life on the line. But they hadn't thought of one thing. "You know what we need?" I asked. Everyone turned their faces to me.

"A safecracker," I said. "In case Rockwell puts the money into a wall safe. I don't see him keeping piles of money without safeguards." Had I already agreed to their plan then? If I only have to walk by, be friendly, and bring them food, I can do it. Sometimes I surprise myself. It wouldn't be dangerous, and nobody will arrest me for giving out free donuts.

The others pondered what I'd said. Alice hadn't spoken much all evening, but she finally stepped forward to address the group. "Sue's right. We'll only have one chance to get the money. We must be prepared."

Gail put her hands on her hips. "This is Wednesday. They're delivering the money on Monday morning, according to our informant. Let's plan on Operation Libereco Nun," she smiled at Mike, "for next Monday noon. We can do this. Agreed?"

"Why can't we call it Operation Stash Stealing?" grumbled

Tanya. "I don't get this Esperanto stuff."

The rest of them poopooed her comment, but I felt as if someone had socked me in the stomach. I gripped my chair with both hands. I would begin taking food to a bunch of Nazis tomorrow so we can rob their place next Monday? So soon? I wasn't ready. And we weren't talking about a quick dash in with pizza and dash out. We were talking about starting tomorrow, Thursday, and repeating this operation on Friday, Saturday, Sunday, and Monday. I'd have to go to their house five times, not once. I don't even know if I want to stay involved in this insane project. The university dormitory was looking like a bastion of sanity, order, and safety. I wanted an ordinary life. I wasn't cut out for heroism. Aunt Kay can't blame me for backing out.

I looked up to see the others were shocked, too. The plan had left the blackboard and become real. None of us were prepared to move forward tomorrow on this crazy scheme, but the momentum of the group's commitment was already at work. We were actually going to rob George Lincoln Rockwell.

After a stunned silence, Cole spoke. "Write down the steps, so we know what we have to do."

Gail began writing. "First, we have to get the food into them."

Cole rubbed his hands together. "I'll prepare a strong sleeping drug, a Mickey Finn, enough for six men, including Rockwell, delayed action for one hour, tasteless, and what I use will keep all of them under for at least four hours. Agreed?"

We all nodded. Mike said, "They'll have to get the pizza around noon to make sure Rockwell gets some."

Gail wrote that down and said, "Next?"

"I'll find a safecracker," said Stuart.

His mother frowned at him, arms akimbo. "How do you happen to know a safecracker?"

"Around the neighborhood." He shrugged and Alice let it go. We needed a safecracker.

"What can I do?" asked Mike.

Alice shook her head at Stuart before turning to Mike. "You can pretend to deliver groceries and take all of us away in a van."

He settled back, grinning. "Good. I can do that." He thought a moment and added. "We will have to rent van Monday morning."

"Wait a minute," I said. "We need the van to be there doing something to keep people away. Delivering groceries won't work. What if a nosy neighbor or Rockwell supporter comes by for a visit?"

"She's right." Sean nodded at me as if he approved.

Mike scratched his chin. "So what will we supposedly do there?"

"What's scary or repulsive, so nobody would want to check it out?" asked Gail.

"Picking up garbage?" suggested Alice, standing behind Cole.

"Funeral home? Picking up a body?" Sean snickered.

"Rat catcher?" I said. "Exterminator?"

Sean snapped his fingers. "Exterminator. That's it. If anyone asks, we can say we're preparing a poison gas to exterminate maybe termites. Or rats. Whatever."

"Rats sounds right," said Cole with a laugh.

We agreed with him.

Cole nodded. "I like that. That'll work. I can get a magnetic sign made for the side of the van."

"Good idea," said Gail. "People see a van with a sign on it, they're more likely to think it's legitimate and not call the police."

"Stuart and Sean need to wear white uniforms, so everything seems legitimate," I said. "Won't they be the ones going in and out of the house?"

Cole scratched his chin. "We'll figure out the assignments later."

Gail turned around. "Is there anything else we need to do for this caper?"

Caper? I shrank in my seat. Now that it seemed we were going ahead, the role I was assigned terrified me. I didn't want to do anything but go back to school.

"We need someone to be at Control Central," Cole said and then laughed. "I mean here. Alice can stay home by the phone."

He glanced at Tanya. "Tanya, too, in case someone needs to drive out and rescue us."

Alice nodded. "If there's any hitch, call here, then I'll figure out what to do or else be here to relay information. That should be simple enough."

"This is Wednesday. We don't have much time," I said, realizing that ready or not, I was being drawn into this plan and would be pulled along till the end. "While I'm in the neighborhood, I'll look for where the phone booths are and anything else that might be helpful."

Sean nodded. "That's why you start tomorrow."

I nodded half-heartedly. He must have known how scared I was. Maybe everyone was scared. People were going to jail in the battle for civil rights. I just didn't want to be one of them. And if the police caught me, I'd be up for theft, not fighting for civil rights. Try to explain that to a future employer.

"I suppose I should play up to the pizza gradually," I said, pondering how to be simpering and girlish enough to lure men to their doom. "Tomorrow, I'll walk by the place and say hello to anyone I see."

"Yeah," said Sean. "Start slow, but not too slow. We only have until Monday noon."

"I'll ask them if they know a place nearby to eat, then later I can bring them hot dogs from a street vendor." Would there be a street vendor in that neighborhood?

"I don't think there'll be a street vendor there," said Mike, reading my mind. "It's more residential, and they're on twenty-three acres that's overgrown with weeds, shrubs, brambles and junk."

I thought for a moment. "I'll get some hot dogs and buns from a grocery store and drop them by. Maybe cookies, too. Friendly neighborhood gesture."

I looked at Sean. "You said the neighbors sometimes drop food by?"

Sean nodded.

"That's the ticket," said Cole. He again took the leadership role. "I suggest that right now we study the layout of the man's house and grounds."

I didn't feel good about any of this. Men had harassed me with catcalls and whistles and rude comments as I passed construction sites. Most women had that experience. What would these Nazis be like as I passed them? Rockwell expected women to be deferential. How could I appear deferential without being victimized?

"Anyone have a black belt in karate?" I asked.

Chapter 13

February 13, 1964.

I spent a restless night worrying about how I would vamp a bunch of Nazi layabouts, probably used to harassing the females they met. I got up early and sat drinking tea in the kitchen as the others made their breakfasts and headed out.

Of course, no one had a black belt in karate, and I would be confronting the Nazis alone. Better that way, everyone but me decided. It turned out Mike, Sean, and Cole all had to work in the morning. This was bolstered by Sean's assertion that "we don't want them to spot anything unusual to tip them off."

"It's broad daylight on a busy street," said Gail. "You'll be all right. If you feel threatened, tell them you're leaving to buy hamburgers for all of them and never go back."

"Daylight and busy street didn't stop them from beating up Stuart and Mike," I said.

"We'll find some other way," said Sean, but he didn't fool me. What other way was there, but for me to worm myself into their confidence, so I could dose them with drugs on Monday.

Did Kay know she was dumping me into a nest of revolutionaries? Most people would call them thieves. I was taking them all at face value. What if they were, indeed, thieves? And now I was helping them. I believed them all. The thought depressed me. What if Kay knew nothing about any of this? She never mentioned Rockwell or exactly what kind of test she meant.

Despite my better judgment, I concluded at last that I did believe them. I did think Kay was part of this scheme. And I was going to go through with it.

The first thing I did after breakfast was put on the nicest dress in my wardrobe. There wasn't much to choose from. I mostly wore unimpressive straight skirts and shirts to class. This dress was royal blue with a full skirt that cinched in at the waist with a wide belt, long sleeves, and a scoop neck. I added a string of pearls. It was quite a flirty outfit and perfect for this caper. Calling it a caper made it seem less scary. I dabbed on lipstick and clipped on pearl earrings.

Then I found a wig shop in the telephone book. Washington is a big city, and wigs were becoming popular, so this task was easy. I bought a blond, curly wig that fit snugly, and if you didn't look too closely, you'd think it was my own hair. It was expensive, but with free room and board and Aunt Kay's stipend, I figured I could afford it. I studied myself in the shop's window and decided I'd done an excellent job in disguising myself. If your focus wasn't too sharp, I might look like Doris Day.

I waited until eleven to drive out to the headquarters of the American Nazi Party on Wilson Boulevard in Arlington. I drove by the house first. It looked rundown, and the lawn in front was patchy and bare, even for February. Two men sat outside on the front steps, smoking. They appeared hungry and bored. Given their poor condition, I could probably outrun them, if necessary. I did feel a little relieved.

I parked the car a couple of blocks away and around a corner, out of sight from the house, then walked casually toward it, fingers crossed. I unbuttoned my coat so my fetching blue dress with the scooped neckline would show. A third man had joined the other two. I stopped and called to them. "Excuse me," I said. "I'm looking for the Hot Shoppes. I know there's one around here." Hot Shoppes was a local restaurant chain specializing in hamburgers.

One of the men walked toward me. I willed myself to smile and not back away. The other two continued to sit, staring at me. "Hot Shoppes, ma'am?" he said. Not menacingly. Listless. His teeth were yellowed, his hair stringy and greasy, and he wore khaki slacks and a shirt that together looked like a uniform. He stank. I was as tall as he was and took heart. Not much fight in these guys. I should learn karate.

"I'm supposed to meet friends there," I said, "but I can't find it."

He took the cigarette out of his mouth, spit on the ground, and stared up and down the street. "I think it's that way about a mile." He pointed down Wilson Boulevard.

I turned to leave. Enough was enough. "Thanks," I said and waved as I walked in the direction he indicated.

"You find it," he called after me, "you bring me back some, y'hear?"

"Okay," I said, holding back a grin. This might be easier than I thought.

I took a circuitous route back to my car, drove to the Hot Shoppes—I already knew where it was—and ordered a Mighty Mo hamburger for myself as a reward, then picked up a box of hamburgers to take back to the guys on the steps. The day was mild for February, and now there were five men outside sitting on the steps.

I handed them the box of hamburgers. Not enough for all of them. They'd have to share. "Thanks for the directions. I would have been lost without them and never met my friends," I told them.

They didn't look up. Too busy eating. I left without incident, but with a lot of relief. Hard to imagine three of these guys had beaten up Mike and Stuart and possibly murdered Darrell.

I came home to an empty house. Even Clark had gone out, but I wasn't so naïve as to think he was job hunting. He was probably at a library or the National Archives researching Confederate trails in Virginia. I took off the wig and changed into my usual jeans and shirt.

By the time everybody had returned home, Hannah was in the kitchen making dinner, so we kept the conversation innocuous. I gave Sean, Mike, and Gail a thumb up when they came in.

That brought grins from them and, glory be, a hug from Mike. While we waited for dinner, Sean idly hopped from one Beatles' tune to another on his honky-tonk piano.

Mike said little during dinner, but he looked at the clock on the sideboard frequently. He saw me watching him. "I have Esperanto class tonight at library," he said. "I will miss it, but I want to run down there before we meet at Cole's. I must give to another person to take charge. I will be late to be with you, okay? Tell Cole."

"Sure," I said. I'd rather be at the Esperanto class. "Let me know when the Esperantists meet next time. I'm interested."

"Bone," he said as he finished his food. "Good."

Esperanto sounded like Spanish to me. Bo-nay. Good.

He took his plate into the kitchen and strode out the door.

Clark and Ellen excused themselves from the table. On the way upstairs, Ellen announced they were going to check their hiking gear. "We're taking along a small camp shovel," she said, giggling. "In case we find a likely spot."

"And I've got a metal detector." Clark added as he bounded up the stairs after Ellen. They had a metal detector and Horace, too. They can't miss.

Most of us heard Clark and Ellen's plans with healthy skepticism, but they, too, hoped to donate their find to the fight for the Civil Rights Bill. How helpful was Horace going to be in their search? Map dowsing? Please.

Gail and I cleared the table and washed up the dishes, so Hannah would be happy. Her attitude made a difference in what appeared on the table. Best to appease. Anyway, we were glad to help out, since Hannah had left an apple pie baking in the oven with cautions on when to take it out.

Once we'd washed and dried the dishes and left the pie on the table to cool, I followed Gail to the meeting in the basement next door.

Sean was already there, and this time he sat on a couch next to Tanya. I wondered if Cole and Alice noticed.

"Mike will be here later," I told them. They nodded. I suppose they were used to his Esperanto classes.

Then Alice turned to me, and pity shone in her face. "How's your assignment going?"

"Surprisingly well," I said, still not believing how easily our plan had worked. "I brought them hamburgers today. They were starving." I'd never seen such a glum group of men. Dirty, too. The water might have been turned off along with the electricity. I suppose the house didn't have any heat either, so it felt warmer outside to them.

"Seems to be going all right so far," I said. "They were polite to me, and I chatted them up, like Sean says."

"So you think they're getting to know you? Like you?" asked Tanya.

I nodded. "Today I brought them hamburgers." I smiled at the memory. "Gone in a flash. Tomorrow, I'll bring them a bunch of hot dogs." I had those guys literally eating out of my hands. Had no idea I could attract male interest this easily. Lesson learned. "Sunday, I'll take them donuts." I couldn't help feeling a bit of pride. So far, so good.

Maybe I should ply Mike with hamburgers. His brown eyes made me tingle all over, but if there was any chemistry between us, I'd yet to feel it from him. He was distracted most of the time and often out of the house. With his work, his studies, his Esperanto classes and meetings, and now the Rockwell campaign, it was understandable. Anyway, unless I wore my Mata Hari outfit, I had no, zero, zip feminine wiles to entice him with. Sadly.

Mike might be a wash, but Sean smiled in approval. "Good start. You are a *femme fatale* after all."

They were flattering words to hear. My parents wouldn't believe it. "I will be when I deliver the pizza on Monday," I said. "Especially the *fatale* part, even though the pizza won't kill them." I hope. What if one of them had an allergic reaction or choked? Would I be up for murder? The idea scared me so much I cut off that train of thought. Think positive, I told myself.

"Excellent," said Cole. "Then when you bring them pizzas on Monday, they won't suspect a thing. The tomato sauce and pepperoni will disguise my magic potion."

I felt proud of myself. "It should work," I said. I'd already lined up a small Mom and Pop pizza shop down Wilson Boulevard. Pizzas were relatively new to the area but catching on fast.

Gail pulled out a sheet of paper listing the assignments, even though they were still on the board. She proceeded down the list.

She turned to Cole. "You have the drug?"

Cole sat with crossed arms, and legs stretched out in front. "I've got it. All good. And I ordered the magnetic sign. I called our company 'CRB Pest Control.' CRB for the Civil Rights Bill, get it?"

We got it.

"Make sure you have more than enough pizza for everyone in the house," Gail said to me. "And they're all eating it. Then you skedaddle."

"Don't worry about that." I planned to triple douse everything.

"Might take up to an hour for the drugs to work," reminded Cole.

Gail turned to Stuart. "What about a safecracker?"

"I've got a lead," he said. "Should have it lined up tomorrow."

Mike bounded in and took a seat, apologizing to everyone.

"You're in time," said Gail. "You're the van driver."

"There is problem." Mike's face turned red. "A driver's license. I do not have one. Car company will not let me take car out no place."

"I've got one," I said, "but there's no way a car agency will rent me a van being a woman and underage. I wondered who had cosigned on the loan to help Kay buy her house. No matter how much money she made or how stable a job she had, she'd find it hard to get credit, too, being a woman.

I totaled all the things I can't do because I'm female, like buy a house or a car or even get credit. Adding sex to the antidiscrimination title in the Civil Rights Bill looked good to me. It gave me a personal interest in the bill. As I sat with this group of plotters, I thought how unfair the laws were to women and at the same time, I perversely hoped something would happen to stop our bizarre scheme to rob Rockwell to support the bill. Instead, all the pieces needed for success fell neatly into place. I was stuck.

"I've got a license, and I'm old enough," said Sean. "I'll rent the van. It'll have to look like a delivery or working van. We won't need it very long, just a few hours. I'll get it on Monday morning, okay?"

"I've been thinking." Cole spoke deliberately, "about our plan. Sean, you should rent the delivery van, but Gail will drive it with you, Stuart, and the safecracker inside. She will stay in the van and keep it running. After delivering the pizza, Sue will leave the house and go to her vehicle, parked down the street out of sight. Then she can bring it close enough to watch what's happening. If Sean and Gail need help, she can run for a phone. Mike will stay with me and Alice to man the phone here. I can take our car down to rescue you or at least be there to help. Be sure every one of you has change for a pay phone and our phone number in case you need to call us."

"Too bad the phones aren't portable," I muttered. "We need radios or walkie-talkies."

"Or a Dick Tracy radio watch," said Stuart. We laughed at this notion while Gail noted our assignments on the blackboard. "What else?"

"I'll go to the door first by myself and knock," said Sean. "I bought a pair of white pants and shirts for Stuart and me, so we'll look official. When I knock, I shouldn't get any response because everyone will be passed out by then. My informant tells me they never lock the front door, but we'll have the safecracker to help if they locked it. I'll take along a clipboard, too, to make our presence look even more official." He glanced at Stuart. "Stuart can act as my assistant. If there's a major hitch, like they didn't eat the pizza and aren't drugged, I'll pretend to have the wrong address."

"What if they get ugly and attack you?" I asked.

"Worse comes to worse, I'll also have an animal repellent spray along and if whoever comes to the door wants to fight, I'll spray him in the face, then call for Stuart to help me tie him up or get out, depending on how many attack us. If all goes according to plan, we'll grab the stash, run to the van, and Gail can step on the gas to get us out of there."

The eight of us sat quietly and thought about this plan. I turned it backwards, forwards, and upside down. It seemed simple enough. We had everything covered. Rockwell and his henchmen would all be out cold. They had no money for an alarm or a dog. We'd grab the stash and Stuart, Sean, and the safecracker would get in the van, and we'd all leave. There would be no clue as to who staged the robbery. I was the only one any of Rockwell's men would have seen, and that was me as a blond, curly haired flirt, not a student with straight brown hair. Unless ...

"Wait a minute," I said. "What if there are cameras on the property? You need to wear disguises in case."

"Did you see any cameras?" asked Cole, frowning at me.

I shrugged. "I never thought of keeping an eye out for them. Those guysm don't have two pennies to rub together, much less to buy cameras."

"Watch for them tomorrow." He glanced at the rest of us. "Everyone wear ball caps and sunglasses or something similar."

"Gloves," added Alice. "Everyone wear gloves." She noticed the stares directed her way. "Don't you people read detective stories?" she asked. "Wear gloves. You don't want your fingerprints all over everything." She held up her hand and waved her fingers. "Fingerprints. It's winter, so no problem. You'd wear gloves, anyway."

Monday seemed too close. They depended on me. They had pushed me into waters beyond my depth, and now I was forced to swim with the current.

Sean got up to stand next to the blackboard. "Here's a quick summary of the plan. At two o'clock Monday afternoon, Stuart, the safecracker, and I will show up at the house in the delivery van I rent that morning. Okay?"

All of us nodded.

"Okay by you, Alice?" asked Cole.

She gazed at us with folded arms, standing tall and strong. "I want to eat at any restaurant I see," she said, "use the restroom in any public place, be hired when I'm the best candidate for a job, and have our colored kids go to good schools. So yeah, it's fine with me to use that $150,000 to pass the Civil Rights Bill instead of electing a neo-Nazi who wants to execute all the Jews and send all Negroes to Africa or remote concentration camps. Yessiree, I am okay with this."

When we returned to the house after the meeting, Clark and Ellen were studying the Virginia map and eager to share their plans with us. "While you tell us your plans," I suggested, "we can sit around the table and eat the pie Hannah left for us."

No arguments with that. We all took a piece of pie to the dining room to listen to Clark outline their latest plan. Crumbs settled in his beard as he spoke.

He beamed with excitement. "We're going to divide the distance from the Fairfax County Courthouse to Culpeper into day hike stretches. Starting point will be the courthouse on Saturday to look for signs of Mosby's treasure."

Ellen chimed in. "In our research," she said, "we've come across several maps of the area printed during the Civil War."

"They give us a clear idea," added Clark, "of the most likely route Mosby might have taken."

"You have researched this?" asked Sean. "I can't believe the treasure will still be there. Somebody in Mosby's raiders or even Mosby himself probably dug it up years ago. What happened to Mosby anyway?"

"President Grant pardoned him after the Civil War," said Ellen, diving into the pie.

"He went to Hong Kong as U.S. Consul and then lived in California," Clark filled in. "He's buried in the old Civil War cemetery in Warrenton, Virginia."

"He never returned to Warrenton or Culpeper or even Fairfax County to live?" Sean asked with cocked eyebrow.

"We-ell, yes," said Ellen, reluctantly. "He did live in Warrenton for awhile after the war."

"But no sign of the treasure ever turned up," added Clark. "It was all identifiable stuff if an auction house or antique store got hold of it, but there's no record showing they did."

"We have as good a chance as anybody else of finding the treasure." Ellen spoke defiantly.

"Will you be taking Horace with you?" I asked.

Clark frowned at me. "I know you want to laugh at Horace, but dowsing has been used for centuries. Successfully, I might add."

"Horace has already identified several possible spots for us. Of course, we're going to bring him along," said Ellen.

"All right. All right," Sean said, but he stared down at his own piece of pie, keeping further thoughts to himself. He was as skeptical as I was, and not just about Horace and his dowsing rod.

Chapter 14

February 14, 1964.

Friday morning, Valentine's Day for most people, came too soon. I barely kept my hands from shaking as I handed the hot dogs to Rockwell's men. This time, they were friendlier. They wanted to talk. I guess they were bored and lonely, and I was the entertainment and the food wagon. The weather continued to be mild, and they hung around the porch outside the house in short sleeves or T-shirts. They all wore camouflage pants, cast-offs from Vietnam or maybe Korea. They might be veterans who enjoyed playing soldier.

I wore my other party dress, full skirt, wide belt, pearls, the works.

"My name's Leon," said a short, squinty-eyed man, looking me up and down as he offered his hand. He was older than the others, but scrawny with tattooed arms. "What's yours, honey?"

I shook his hand and smiled, friendly like, refraining from wiping my hand on my dress. "My name's, uh, Mary Lee." Quick save. I almost said Sue. "I live in the neighborhood."

"It's sure nice of you to bring us these goodies, like you been doing," Leon said.

There was an oily tone in his voice I didn't quite like. Was he flirting with me or was he suspicious?

"I gotta wonder why you're so nice to us." He was studying

me. Suspicious then.

I didn't know what to say. I stammered something.

"Leave her alone, Leon," said a red-haired young man with a missing front tooth. He'd laid aside a rifle to eat the hot dog. He smiled shyly at me. "I'm Calvin, Cal. I'm glad to see you. Hope you keep showing up. Real nice of you, I'd say." He sent a warning glance to Leon.

Another man came forward, waving a hand at me. "Hi. I'm Reg." He seemed more serious than the others. His shirt and his camouflage pants were both clean and pressed. The other two identified themselves in turn. Frank wore a half-buttoned shirt, revealing a heavy gold necklace floating in a nest of black hair. Ted was decorated with tattoos on his neck and arms. I guessed Cal and Ted to be in their twenties. Maybe Reg, too. Leon and Frank were older, forties, maybe. Which one was Sean's informant? And who had beaten Mike and Stuart?

"We surely do appreciate the food you've been bringing by," said Leon, all charm now. "Come have a sit." He moved over to make a place for me on the porch step.

"We do," echoed the others. "Thanks, Mary Lee."

I declined the invitation to stay and walked down the street toward the VW bus parked around a corner, feeling their eyes on my back until I turned out of sight from them. Then I took a deep breath and tried to relax. They were too needy for female companionship and food to harm me, but that could change in an instant if they caught on I'm not what I seem. Leon worried me.

I sweated through the weekend, restless and queasy about what would happen on Monday. I wasn't ready for this. I never stood up for anything. Soon I'd be feeding drugs to the enemy.

On Saturday, I'd decided on deli subs. When I arrived, they were waiting for me. And they'd all showered and shaved and wore clean camouflage outfits. I even smelled cologne. They'd spruced up for me. I was touched and felt even worse than before about this deception. I acted cute and playful, even ditzy for those guys, and they ate it up. Once I got away from them, though, I drove home shaking and sick. They didn't scare me any more, but

I hated the deceit. They were grateful to me and showed it—even Leon. I wasn't made for this.

No one else in Kay's house was talking much, either. On Saturday, Ellen was off work, so she and Clark borrowed her mother's car again, and they picked up Horace to hunt for Mosby's treasure. I'd laugh if I weren't so busy chewing my fingernails. They can't be serious, but I supposed it gave them a project to do together. I looked up Mosby in an encyclopedia and found out he died in 1916. From the end of the Civil War in 1865 to his 1916 death gave him fifty-one years to dig up the treasure. He even lived in Warrenton for a time and was buried there. Why wouldn't he recover it himself?

He wouldn't advertise the fact that he'd retrieved it. It might bring up old grievances against him and, on a practical level, force him into paying higher taxes. Clark said none of the pieces had ever shown up, but did he know that for sure? Canvassing antique stores and catalogs for the stolen loot would be more fun than stomping across frozen fields with a shovel.

On Sunday, I delivered the donuts, which weren't quite the hit the subs and hamburgers were, but I promised to bring pizza on Monday. They were thrilled. I don't understand why they think I'm so generous, but they are Rockwell's men and may harbor the notion this entitles them to such special treatment from women. If they thought I was attracted to any of them, they were crazy. Appalling idea.

On Monday morning, Ellen had gone to work, and Clark was still sleeping when the rest of us met in the Hortons's basement for a last run-through. I wore my blondie disguise. The guys whistled. I guess they thought they had to, since I wore a dress and all.

Cole chaired the meeting. Our assignments still lay out on the blackboard.

"First," he said, "let's study the layout again." We crowded around the model of the house and yard. He took the roof off the house to let us see how the rooms were arranged. The model was simple and without furniture. The rooms were marked out in pen on the thin rectangular plywood sheet that made up the floor on each level. The house was a two-story colonial with an attic and a porch along the front. Four columns reached to the roof overhang, two on each side of the front door. The model looked a lot better than the rundown wreck where the men lived. Nobody had done any repairs on that place for years. There was no fence or gate, and the twenty-three acres were a barren winter wasteland of tangled weeds, thorny brambles, and spindly Virginia pines. It was an eyesore, surrounded by the houses and lawns of a suburban neighborhood, properly kept up and landscaped with shrubs and hedges.

"Sue, you've been at the house," said Sean. "Do you have anything to add about it?"

I shook my head. "I've only been outside, you know. The front porch is in terrible shape, so be careful. Watch your step. That's all I've got."

Cole removed the attic layer so we could examine the second floor. At the top of the stairs, a hall led to a door on the right, which opened into another hallway and then into a large room that spanned the house from front to back. On one side of this hallway was a bathroom and on the other, a large closet. Doors to each opened into the room rather than the hall.

"Oh, man," moaned Sean. "What if we come across locked doors? Rockwell probably keeps his office locked, and that's where the stash will be."

"Your safecracker ought to be able to open them." said Alice.

"I don't think it will be a problem," said Stuart slowly. "The safecracker I found is actually a locksmith."

"A locksmith!" Cole exploded, showing the tension we all felt. "What if it's a safe? What if he needs to use some kind of dynamite to open it? Can he do that?"

Stuart waved his hand. "Yes, he's a locksmith. He has to know how to open all kinds of locks—it's his business. People lose combinations and keys."

"But what if it's a really tough safe?" I asked. I'd been counting on an explosive.

'He thinks he can do it, man," said Stuart.

"But can we trust him?" asked Cole. "He can lose his license."

"Or tell the cops," added Gail.

"He's my friend, too," said Mike. "I know him. His family is from Austria, but he born here. He is true *samideano*, you understand? Okay. We pick him up on the way."

"He knows he'll be breaking the law?" asked Tanya. "If the police catch him, he could lose his livelihood. Is he a citizen now?"

Mike nodded. "Stuart and I meet with him. The Nazis killed his grandma and grandpapa when they take over Austria. He and his mama and papa were already here, but they know what happened. He is no friend to Nazis. He will help us. Maybe he celebrate with us, too. Afterwards."

"I've got three bottles of champagne in the refrigerator," said Alice. "We will celebrate, yessiree." She looked sternly at Stuart. "I'm glad you don't have safecracker friends," she said. "We raised you better than that."

"Hush, Alice," said Cole. "He came through with what we need. I'm all right with that. He's a good boy."

"I never said he wasn't." Alice put an arm around Stuart and gently hugged him. I saw Stuart wince. He still suffered from the beating.

"All right. I've got the Mickey Finn powder here," Cole pulled a blue bottle out of his pocket. "This stuff is tasteless and odorless and easily absorbed." He looked at me. "So after you get the pizzas, you take them to your car and spread three teaspoons of the liquid on each pizza, so it's mixed in the sauce. Get extra sauce, tomatoes, mushrooms, pepperoni to cover traces of the drug. There's plenty of it in the bottle."

"Good," I said. "I'll buy a gallon of, say, lemonade and shake some of the drug into that, too."

He handed the little blue bottle to me. "In about an hour, they'll feel drowsy and then they'll be out for about eight hours. Should work, no problem."

"Should work?" I squeaked. "It better work."

"There's an off-chance the drug will take a little longer for one of them. Don't worry, it'll get 'em in the end." Cole shrugged as if that "off-chance" was of no consequence, but it added to the queasiness I felt.

"What if one of them gets too much?" I asked. The bottle felt hot in my hand.

Cole nodded. "Good question. He'll sleep longer. Not a problem, so you can put as much as you want on the pizza. Then wipe the bottle, get rid of any fingerprints, and throw it away. It's not labeled, so if it's found, it won't raise suspicion."

I breathed a sigh of relief. Eight hours sounded good to me. Especially for Leon. That guy made me nervous. He looked mean. I imagine them waking up in an hour, and all of us still trying to get a door or a safe open.

Alice nodded. "They won't notice a thing." She looked at me. "Be sure you get Rockwell himself, too. He'll be there, won't he?"

Sean nodded. "He doesn't leave the house until one most days, according to my informant. He'll be there all right. He'll want a slice of pizza as much as the other guys."

"One other thing," said Sean to me. "Make sure they never see you in that VW bus."

Cole turned to Gail. "You need to get Sean, Stuart, and the safecracker to Rockwell's house by three p.m."

"Didn't you say two p.m. before?" I asked. I didn't like hanging around that house any longer than I had to.

"Everyone but Sue, who'll park near Rockwell's house, will meet here at two p.m. so we can go through everything again. We arrive at the house at three p.m. That will ensure the targets are in sleepy-time land. Now the van." Cole looked at Sean.

"I'm renting a delivery van as soon as I leave here. Already reserved it," Sean said. "One more thing..." He studied Gail and Stuart's faces. "I didn't think of this before, but Sue has her own disguise. Wait here." He ran upstairs and out the front door. In a couple of minutes, he was back, carrying a large cardboard box. "This stuff might help," he said, opening the box. He pulled out a closely cropped black wig and handed it to Gail. "Try this on."

It wasn't flattering, but it did change her appearance. Sean nodded. "Wear that." Anyone else want a wig or other costume?" He handed the box around as he looked at me, apologetically. "Sorry. I didn't think about this costume box before you went out and bought a wig."

"Why do you have a box of costumes?" I asked.

He shrugged. "I am a filmmaker, you know. And I do have ambitions."

Cole reached back to the shelf behind him and brought out two white signs, each two feet wide and printed with "CRB Pest Control" and a bogus phone number. "These are magnetic. Stick them on the sides of the van."

Stuart pulled a red beret out of Sean's costume box, set it on his head, and grinned. "Suits me fine, man." He added sunglasses. "Nobody recognize me now."

Everyone laughed.

"You all got to remember to wear a disguise in case somebody comes by," said Alice. "Ball cap and sunglasses will be fine. Rockwell might have a security camera installed outside the house."

"I looked for them yesterday but didn't see any," I said. "Still, it's best to be cautious."

"Wear gloves," reminded Alice. "The FBI can get prints off about anything."

"We all got that?" said Cole. "Okay. Everyone except Sue meets here at two, and we'll get this operation underway. Sue, you stay in your vehicle down the street from the house and watch. "You know where there's a handy pay phone?"

I nodded. "There's one in a drugstore two blocks away."

"Any questions? Second thoughts?" Cole sat back and waited.

Nobody said anything. We were all tense, keyed up. Were they as scared as I was? We dispersed. The plan ought to work. It seemed foolproof to me, but I knew something would go wrong. It seemed too simple. We were talking about stealing $150,000 from the American Nazi Party. It can't be easy. What if there's a glitch? If Rockwell found out who stole his money, what would he do to get it back?

But my job was simply to deliver the doused pizza, then get away from the house, watch the operation, and scram. Simple enough. If a problem developed, we'd abandon the plan and get out. Rockwell didn't know any of us.

Chapter 15

February 17, 1964.

I struggled to carry three pizzas and a jug of lemonade, hanging in a string bag off my shoulder, to the house by myself and make it appear easy. I'd been careful to keep my vehicle out of their sight. I didn't want any of them wondering why I didn't take the convenient and normal way of parking my car in front of the house to unload the food.

They greeted me like an old friend. Against my protests, they escorted me into the house, and the men called up the stairs for Rockwell to join us. They insisted I meet the great man. I smiled and even curtsied, hoping they'd be more interested in the pizzas than in me. So far, they've acted like gentlemen, and none of them was at all suspicious of my motives. I hid my nervousness, but I'm not too afraid to be inside with them.

It was the first time I'd seen the interior, and its condition appalled me. As I'd heard, they'd shot bullet holes into every wall. Idly shooting at the walls must be their evening's entertainment. The place stank of sewage, and trash had collected in the corners. They pushed sleeping bags against the walls. I was glad I didn't have to see the kitchen.

They did need an exterminator. And a garbage truck.

The men at the house eagerly dove into the pizzas, but I realized one was missing. "Where's Ted?" I asked.

Leon laughed. "He's feelin' poorly this morning. Too much imbibin' last night." They poked each other with their elbows.

"Oh, but you can't let him miss out," I said. *We* can't let him miss out.

"Teach him a lesson," said Calvin, his mouth full.

I had to be firm. "He shouldn't miss out. He'll be hungry later."

"If you insist," grumbled Calvin. "I'll go roust him out."

"Thank you," I said, acting girlish and pasting on a brilliant smile.

Then all eyes turned to the stairs as the great man descended, followed by Ted and a man I hadn't met before. Rockwell greeted me and offhandedly thanked me for the pizza. He introduced the other man as Matt Koehl, second in command. Was there enough pizza and drug to include a seventh victim? Cole said there was plenty, and I'd bought large pizzas.

I wrenched myself away from my calculations to listen to Rockwell.

"As you can see," he said, waving a hand at the surroundings, "we need a woman's touch around here." His attempt at humor. I said nothing and certainly wasn't going to volunteer. If I were him, I would be ashamed at how hungrily the men—his supporters--wolfed down the pizza. Rockwell ate three slices, too, but pretended he wasn't as hungry as anyone else. Even if one of the men ate only one slice, he'd get enough of the drug to put him out, so I felt I'd succeeded with the worst part of this, uh, caper. Once the men were out cold, it should be a piece of cake for Sean and Stuart.

At first, Leon, especially, and Frank urged me to join them in eating the pizza. Generous of them since I knew they coveted every slice. I was afraid that might happen, so I had my story prepared about the pizza I'd eaten at the restaurant while I waited for theirs. "The restaurant loaded it with so many toppings," I said, "I couldn't remember them all." Then I apologized for not knowing what toppings they like, and how I had to guess. In other words, I verbally tap-danced while they couldn't help themselves from scarfing down all the pizza along with the lemonade I brought.

They didn't want to share it with me, anyway.

I was again embarrassed—and a little ashamed—by the gratitude they showered on me. Leon included. He was probably more cautious than the others rather than suspicious. He still seemed like a snake.

I made my getaway, smiling and nodding at their expressions of gratitude and walked three blocks to the VW bus, then drove it closer to the house and parked where I could watch what happened. I took off the blond wig and replaced it with a ball cap and sunglasses for a different disguise as Cole and Alice suggested. I also pulled a heavy oversized sweater over my blouse. My skirt was dark navy and unremarkable. If any of the men came out and walked down the sidewalk, which was highly unlikely, they wouldn't recognize me. A glance at my watch showed I had a two-hour wait, and I pulled out a textbook to spend the time studying.

At three p.m., I watched Gail drive the rental van up the rutted patchy driveway and park beside Rockwell's house. Sean got out, strode to the door, and knocked. After a minute with no response, Stuart and the locksmith piled out and joined him. The door was unlocked, as we'd expected, and the three of them disappeared inside. Then Gail drove out of the yard and turned the van around. She backed into the driveway for a quick getaway and stayed in the vehicle according to plan.

My hands shook. What was keeping them? This was insane. I sat there silently urging the guys to hurry up. Half an hour passed. What were they doing? We should have left by now. I watched a woman stride confidently to the van. I couldn't hear what she said, but Gail must have wound down the window to talk to her. What did she want? What should I do?

I picked up the clipboard I kept in the car to jot down bright ideas I get while driving. Then I slipped out of my car and walked to the van. I had to get this woman to leave.

She was jabbering away at Gail, who shrank back from her. "Where's Frank?" the woman demanded. "What are you doing here?"

I came up alongside, holding the clipboard to look official.

"Who are you looking for?" I asked.

"Frank, the deadbeat." She put her hands on her hips. "He's supposed to be out here now, giving me my check."

"Everyone's gone. They had to leave. We're here getting ready to exterminate the house."

"About time, too," she sneered. "That place needs to be razed, is what it needs."

She was right about that. "Wait a minute," I said, "I'll see if he left an envelope for you."

She stepped forward as if to accompany me. I took her arm. "I'm sorry, ma'am, you can't go in there. Our men are preparing the house for pest extermination. They spread poison pellets around. Rats, you know. It's dangerous to go inside." I had no idea what real exterminators do to kill pests, but this woman must not go into the house.

"That's fine with me," she said. "The place stinks to high heaven."

"Stay here. I'll see if anyone knows where your friend Frank is." As the woman muttered about Frank being no friend of hers, I walked up the steps, opened the door, and peered inside the house. In the parlor on the left, one of the storm troopers lay on the carpet, mouth open, snoring. Stuart came to the top of the stairs. "What's going on?" he whispered down to me.

"Tell everyone to stay inside," I whispered back. "I'll alert them when it's safe to come out." I pulled my cap down low and adjusted my sunglasses. "We've got a minor problem."

Sean appeared and came down the stairs to talk to me. "The locksmith doesn't recognize the lock on the cash box in the closet," he whispered. "He's trying to open it, but it's tough going. We'd just take the whole thing, but it's bolted to the floor. If you ask me, our locksmith doesn't have much experience."

"We've got to get out of here, ASAP," I said. "We'll start attracting attention."

Sean returned to helping the locksmith. I was about to step to the door, when one of the men groaned and sat up. Through bleary eyes, he noticed me. "What's going on?" he asked. I recognized him as the one named Reg. "It's all okay," I said. Here was the "off-chance" situation Cole shrugged off. Was the drug taking longer to have the full effect on this guy? Or had it worn off too fast? Would the others wake up now, too? I didn't know what to do, but I had to say something to reassure Reg. A quick glance at the other men lying haphazardly on the floor showed they were not stirring. Only Reg.

"Rockwell hired our crew to clean up the place," I said, watching him struggle to sit. I should call Stuart and Sean. I needed help here. Reg tried to heave himself off the floor, but he slowly collapsed as the drug finally took hold, and he became as comatose as the others.

Just in time. That pesky woman was again heading for the porch steps as I opened the door to leave the house. I sprang forward to stop her before she came any closer. "Oh, no, ma'am. You mustn't go in there. Mr. Rockwell agreed that the house would be vacated while we do our work. It's in our contract. For the insurance, you know. The people who live here have all gone out and are staying somewhere else until tomorrow, after the poison has done its job."

I stepped off the porch and took her arm to lead her casually toward the road. She shook off my hand and glared at me.

"Where'd they go, then?" she said. "I want that money."

"We need to get away from the house,' I said, walking her down the drive. She had to come along to keep talking to me.

"I'll wait for him on the porch." She turned to walk back to the house.

"Can't do that, ma'am." I blocked her way. "The gas can leak outside. It's poison, ma'am."

As I led her down the drive to the road, I tried to reassure her. "Talked to the exterminator inside," I said. "Nobody else is there. All the men took off to let the exterminator work, ma'am. I looked around on the tables and desks, but I saw nothing like a check or an envelope with someone's name on it."

"Oh no," she wailed. "I need that money. He promised he'd have it for me today. Now I'm here and he's not."

"Sorry, ma'am," I said. "This was an emergency job. Rats all over the place. Cockroaches, too. Maybe your friend didn't know the exterminators were coming, ma'am. He might have gone to your house. Did you sometimes meet him there or elsewhere?"

The woman shuddered and stopped walking to look back at the house, arms akimbo. "I've dealt with rats and cockroaches. I'm going inside." She again headed toward the house. There was no getting rid of this woman.

Sean came out the front door and down the steps in time to block her way.

"If you don't let me in," the woman yelled, "I'm calling the police!"

"What's going on?" he asked, looking at me.

I explained. "Aren't they through there yet?"

"They've locked up the place." Sean played along. "They're releasing the poison in the house now." He turned to the woman. "They're wearing gas masks."

"Come back tomorrow," I added.

"All right, then," the woman said. "Tomorrow. He better be here." She headed down the drive toward the sidewalk. What a relief.

"They bolted the cash box to the floor," Sean whispered. "We're having trouble getting the bolts loose."

"Doesn't the locksmith have a wrench or something?" I asked. "Maybe a dab of dynamite?"

"Not that good a locksmith, and it's got iron straps holding it in place, too."

Oh God. I knew it. Nothing's ever easy. Sean glanced at the road, and then backed into the house. I gritted my teeth as I waited.

How much trouble could it be to pry or bash open the cash box and put all the money into a pillowcase? They should be out of the house by now. I glanced at my watch. Three forty-five. Rockwell and his henchmen had been out almost three hours. What if one of them is resistant to the drug? What if he wakes early? Like Reg, Cole's "off-chance."

The woman stopped halfway down the block to write something on a piece of paper. She put it in her purse. Maybe she'd leave now. I walked down the sidewalk to talk to her.

"I'm sorry Frank isn't here, ma'am," I said, making nice. "Give me a note for him if you'd like, and I'll leave it at the door." That's probably what she'd been writing.

She frowned at me, eyes narrowed. I realized she was studying me. Now I hoped my ball cap and sunglasses disguise was working. If she were reasonably smart, she'd call the police. A strange van in front of a vacant house said robbery to most people, but she probably knew Rockwell wouldn't want police sniffing around unless they were also Ku Klux Klansmen, of course, which some of them were.

"All right," she said. "When will he be back?" She pulled out a notepad and scribbled something on a page, ripped it off, and handed it to me.

"They'll all be back by tomorrow afternoon," I said. "I'll leave it for him, ma'am." I walked away, too nervous to wonder what she'd written down before. I put on a show of no-nonsense confidence and stepped onto the porch as if I were delivering the note. I pretended to slip it through the mail slot, while I crumpled it in my pocket. Anyway, how did she expect to get a penny from a man who spent his days sitting on a porch and had nothing to eat?

I looked back down the street. The woman gave one last parting glance at the house, kicked a fire hydrant, and disappeared around a corner. She was gone.

Stuart came out of the house first, and then Sean, carrying a rusty steel box covered with dents and scratches. "We've got it," Sean whispered to me, jubilation written on his face. . "We're clearing out." The locksmith followed, carrying his bag of tools.

A rush of relief swept over me. I wanted to get out of here fast. "Must have been tough prying it out of the closet," I said.

The locksmith shook his head. "You better believe it. I ain't never seen nothing like that. Took everything I had."

His language was rough with a vague southern accent. Mike said his family was from Austria, but he had grown up in the States. He grinned at us, revealing a wide gap in his front teeth. "But I won. Yep. I won."

Sean opened the van's back door and shoved the cash box

inside. Then he shut the door, went around to the front passenger door and climbed in. He saluted me and grinned. "We've got it. Let's go!"

Chapter 16

Everything else worked according to plan. Gail drove the van three blocks, then pulled over and stopped. I parked behind her. We transferred the stash to the VW bus first and then huddled outside the vehicles.

"Was everyone still asleep when you left?" I asked.

"Like babies, man. They probably won't wake up till tomorrow morning," said Stuart. "My dad knows what he's doing."

"Can anyone think of anything we forgot or should have done?" asked Sean.

"Sorry it took me so long," said the locksmith. "But all okay now." He grinned at each of us in turn. We congratulated him on his success and gave him our thanks.

"No thanks necessary," he said. "I'm the one who should be thanking you. Wait till this Rockwell Nazi SOB wake up, eh?" He laughed. "Neat job."

I was relieved to be away from that house; I had nothing else to say and felt proud of my role. I was a *femme fatale*, a deceptive poisoner, and a thief, taking money from a hateful man whose goal was to murder and exile millions of innocent people.

Sean shook his head. He opened the van's side door. "Keep your gloves on and wipe off the places you touched. We don't want anyone's fingerprints left in this van, not even mine." After we had given the van a thorough wipe, he closed the side door.

"We're done. Let's get out of here."

Good, I thought, but the memory of the woman who accosted us bothered me. We'd kept her out of the house, and we'd all been somewhat disguised, so even if she'd seen Gail, Sean, Stuart, or the safecracker, she didn't have much to tell Frank or the other men in the house about any of us. She'd describe me as a girl with short brown hair wearing a ball cap, sunglasses, and a heavy sweater. Gail had tucked all of her hair under the wig, topped it with a ball cap, added sunglasses, and put on a heavy frown. I'd never recognize her.

"Thank you for your help, man," Stuart said to the locksmith. "Would you like to come back to the house with us?" He grinned. "We're gonna celebrate."

The locksmith shook his head. "Don't think I can. Got another job ahead of me, and the wife don't like it if I'm late gettin' home." He wiped his hands on his pants and shook everyone's hand. "Anyway, glad to help out. This country don't need no Nazis. Bad people. They deserve the worst, and I'm glad to help give it to them."

We stowed the steel box in the back of my bus, and I drove off with Gail, Stuart, and the locksmith. Sean left to return the van. I dropped the locksmith off at his house along the way and continued on to Kilbourne Place.

We took the cash box over to the Hortons to hide in their basement. Alice had sandwiches and cake ready upstairs. Mike and Tanya were waiting there, too.

"We had the Chevy gassed and ready to go," said Tanya. "I'm so glad you didn't need a rescue."

"Me, too. I don't want to meet up with those guys again," said Mike.

"I kicked all of them before we left," added Stuart with a satisfied grin. "Man, that felt good." Then his grin disappeared. He looked at his dad. "Do you suppose you could give those guys a truth drug? I looked all over the house and didn't see any sign of Darrell. I think they killed him and buried him in their woods."

Cole stared at the floor and shook his head. "I don't know, son. I don't know what to do about that, but his folks have filed missing person reports. That's the best we can do right now."

"It's not enough." Stuart clenched his fists.

"We did succeed in robbing a bunch of low-lifes," said Cole, "so let's celebrate that for now."

I was all for celebrating. We'd done the job and were home free.

Or so we thought.

Alice and Tanya had lined up champagne flutes on the Hortons' dining room table. As Sean walked in the door, Alice brought out the bubbly. "Good job, everyone," she said. I refused the champagne, so Alice gave me a Coke. We sat around toasting each other and eating the sandwiches and snacks for about half an hour. Then Sean said, "We've got to finish the job."

We set the flutes on the table and trekked down to the Hortons' basement to stand around the rusted cash box on the floor. All of us stared at it, silent and awed at what we'd done. Two questions remained. Did we get the right box? Would the money be inside? Rockwell could have planted a decoy.

Sean picked up a crowbar and stooped next to the box as he prepared to open it. I was eager to see the cash inside.

"Now you wait a minute," said Alice. She pulled a slim cardboard box off the shelf behind her, opened it, and held up a bunch of white cotton gloves. "We're thieves now. Don't leave fingerprints on anything." She handed us each a pair, and we put them on.

Sean wielded a crow bar and Cole gripped a hammer. They alternately whacked and pried the cash box open. Inside lay a jumbled pile of crisp, new twenty-dollar bills wrapped in bundles of fifty bills each. The paper band around each pack of twenty-dollar bills was pristine and unbroken. That would be one thousand dollars in each bundle.

We laid the packs onto the floor, arranging them into fifteen stacks of ten packs with ten thousand dollars in each stack.

I stood in awe, thinking like everyone else of how we'd spend the money if it were ours. Graduate school, for sure.

"You know," Cole said pensively, scratching his chin, "that money was earmarked to defeat the Civil Rights Bill or launch

Rockwell into elected office or maybe both."

"And it came from Dallas," said Gail, "which raises a lot of questions."

"There are evil people in this world." Alice stood frowning at the box. Then she looked at our faces. "And good ones. Let's move this money on to do good work now." She pulled three heavy cardboard boxes off a shelf. "Pile it in, everyone." She held the boxes open as we transferred the money from the cash box to the cardboard ones. Fifty thousand dollars in each box. Then she taped them shut and pulled a pen out of her pocket. "I been waiting for you all to get back. I'm ready to send these now. Get them out of the house and into the post office."

"Wait a minute," I said. "Shouldn't we put a note in the boxes, telling them the funds are to be used to support the Civil Rights Bill? That's what we want, isn't it?"

We stood around the boxes, staring at them. Nobody said anything until Alice sighed. "We can't tie strings to this money, anyway," she said. "They'll do what they want with it. All three organizations are committed to furthering our civil rights."

Gail nodded. "We'll have to trust that they'll do the right thing with the money."

"We have to keep this pure and simple," added Sean. "Notes and any attempts to control what happens to the money gives the organizations—and maybe the FBI or the IRS—clues that might point to us. I say we send the money. Period."

"I agree." Alice said. "Let's vote. All in favor of sending the money without a note, say aye." A chorus of ayes filled the room. "Any nays?" No nays. "Okay then, let's go."

Gail glanced at her watch. "It's after five. We can mail them tomorrow morning, first thing."

Alice finished writing addresses on the boxes in large block letters. "They're going to the NAACP, SNCC, and CORE. Gail, Sue, and Stuart and anyone else who wants to go along can take them to the post office tomorrow, while Cole and I dispose of the cash box the money came in."

She stacked the three boxes on top of each other and tied string tightly around the stack. Then she lit a candle and dripped wax across the knot. "I want Gail, Sue, and Stuart to put their initials in the wax. We'll take the string off the stack tomorrow morning, and Sue and Stuart can go together to take the boxes to the post office." She stood back with folded arms. "Making sure we all know no funny business will happen to the money in our basement."

That made sense. I had wondered about someone switching boxes and taking the money. They'd have all night to do it, and how would we ever know? I was glad to scratch my initials with the others into the wax. None of us believed any of us would steal the money, but it was an excellent precaution.

"Why divide the money up?" I asked. "Give it all to one of those organizations."

Alice shook her head. "If we do that and word gets out that $150,000 was donated anonymously to one organization, Rockwell will know what happened to his money. This way, should he ever hear of these donations, he probably won't connect fifty thousand dollars here and there to his missing stash."

"He'd never believe it was stolen for anything but the thieves' own personal use," I said. "He'll think one of his own men used me to set up the robbery."

"Those guys won't wake up until tomorrow morning," said Cole. "The first thing Rockwell will do is check the cash box and find it missing."

"There will be nothing to connect any of us to the robbery," Sean said, "and Rockwell won't report the theft because it will draw too much attention on stuff he doesn't want people to know about."

"What about our ally, the FBI man in their group?"

"He'll know, but he won't say anything."

"There is one hitch," Gail said, studying me. I suddenly felt afraid. "Sue. They'll look for her."

"I thought of that." But I hadn't read Arthur Conan Doyle for nothing. "They only saw me in a blond wig and a dress. I don't think they'll recognize me wearing jeans and my own brown, straight hair."

"Stay out of Arlington," advised Stuart.

"I will," I promised.

"Good," said Cole.

Sean, Gail, Mike, and I trooped out of the Horton's basement and over to Kay's house. Hannah had dinner waiting.

In the middle of the night, I woke up in a cold sweat from a dream about the woman looking for Frank. She'd taken a notebook out of her purse and written something in it. I was the only one watching her, but I was too nervous to pay attention to what she'd written. My dream brought it back to me.

I'll bet she wrote down the van's license tag number. She suspected something was off. I gasped for breath as I fought down the panic. I retrieved the bottle of vodka out of my closet, took a big swig, and tried to calm down. She had no reason to suspect us. No reason to write down the license tag number. It was probably some shopping note to herself.

What if it was the license tag number? What would she do with it? Why would she tell anyone about it?

What if she expected to see one or more of the men hanging around out front? Would she be skeptical about a van parked on the grounds? Of course she would. Would she know anyone can buy a magnetic sign for any kind of business? Would that tip her off?

Even if Rockwell found out the tag number, what would he do? Some police officers were neo-Nazis themselves or members of the Ku Klux Klan. Especially with all that white power rhetoric he tossed around. Would they help him find out who owned the van?

Okay. If they did, it would only lead to the rental office. Then what? They'd bribe the office manager to find out who rented the van, and that would lead to Sean.

The rental office would insist on seeing Sean's driver's license before they rented him the van. They'd write down the information there. None of us had brought up the idea of a fake license with a fake address. We hadn't thought it was necessary. Anyway, I had no idea how to get one. Would anyone else on our team? We never thought they'd be able to trace the van or even know it existed. Rockwell and his men would be asleep by the time it arrived.

Sean was in danger. Once they established that Sean had rented the van, they'd come searching for him and the cash box.

They'd have his address. They'd look here. We were all in danger, unless they decided Sean worked alone with the aid of a blond, curly haired bimbo.

I was wide awake now and had to get up. I dressed, tiptoed up the stairs, and knocked softly on Sean's door. I heard stirrings inside. I knocked again and waited. "Who's there," Sean whispered.

"I've got to talk to you. It's Sue," I said. "It's important."

"Okay." I heard him open a drawer. He was getting dressed. Good.

"Come to the kitchen," I said and left for the stairs.

I turned on the lights and put a pot of water on the stove for coffee and tea. I wouldn't sleep any more tonight, anyway.

Sean showed up in jeans and flannel shirt. "What's up?"

"I've had a horrible thought," I said. "You won't like this, but we've got to consider it and make plans."

"I know you were upset, Sue," he said on his way to placating me. *Poor little Sue, worried about nothing.*

"Yes, I was, but that has nothing to do with this." I told him what happened with the woman looking for Frank.

He sat silently for a moment before nodding his realization. "We may be in a heap of trouble."

"Yes," I said.

"If only you'd told me before I turned in the van." He sat pursing his lips and staring straight ahead.

"What good would that do?" Now he was going to blame it all on me?

"If I'd known, I could have ditched the van and claimed someone stole it. That would clear us of involvement. Or at least given the police—and Rockwell—something else to consider."

Yeah. I nodded. He was right. "What do you think they'll do?" I asked.

"If that woman gives Rockwell the license tag number?"

"I'm sure she will," I said. "Why wouldn't she?"

"He won't want to go to the police and report a break-in. If the police caught us, he can't rely on us keeping our mouths shut. The police will start taking an interest in his house. He'd lose control of what would happen and where that might lead. He needs to keep the police out of it and that means he has to find us himself."

I nodded. "He wouldn't want the police or the public to know about the huge stash he'd acquired. There'd be a lot of questions from the FBI and the IRS, too."

"True. He's also planning to run for office, so he won't want any bad press. What he would do is try to get the money back from us."

"He'll come after you."

"Correct." He stood. "I'm getting out of here. I'll go to a motel somewhere and hole up for a while. I can take a few days leave from my job. Give us time to find out what he's going to do."

I followed him to the stairs. "You pack. I'll call a cab. The faster you get out of here, the better."

Chapter 17

February 18, 1964.

At nine the next morning, Stuart and I took the stash to three different post offices, mailing a box at each one. I didn't want to be associated with an unusual mailing of three identical boxes to civil rights organizations. This way, the postal clerks would have nothing to remember.

Rockwell wouldn't find out about Sean's van rental until later in the day. That is, if the woman had written down the license plate number and given the number to Rockwell or Frank. She was desperate for the money, though, so chances are she knocked on their door early this morning. They were probably awake by now. She would tell them everything.

After I returned, I watched the street, standing back from the windows, so I could survey the passersby and the cars without being seen. Nothing unusual seemed to be happening outside. Still, I was glad to know Clark was sleeping upstairs, and Gail hadn't left for classes yet. I was heading out to class myself but would be back by two. I needed to get away from that house, even if it was to go to the university. I was scared to stay home, worried every minute that Rockwell or one of his thugs would show up at the door. I shuddered whenever I thought of looking into Rockwell's cold blue eyes.

Sean called from his office. "No sense missing work," he

said. "The rental agency will have my address, but that's all. They won't know where I work or anything else about me. Tell everyone there at the house not to answer questions from anyone. Not on the phone or in person. I'll call back tomorrow for the latest."

Around three that afternoon, Clark stumbled downstairs, yawning. He lay down on the couch and felt his pulse as he did every morning. Then he woke up enough to see me in the chair next to the front window. He and Ellen returned from their hike late the night before. Ellen had taken Monday off to stretch their weekend. They weren't around to ask questions about our high spirits on our triumphant return and knew nothing about the Rockwell robbery.

"How'd the hike go?" I asked. "Find anything?" Hard not to sound sarcastic asking that question.

"Long," he said. He sounded depressed. "We never got out of civilization to where someone might dig." He scratched his chin. "Next weekend will be better, though. We'll be getting into farmland."

"Good luck" I said, turning back to my book. "Was Horace any help?"

Clark opened an eye to look at me. "The conditions were not right for the dowsing he needed to do. Too much interference from buildings and power lines."

"I'll bet," I said.

That evening, as we sat around the table for dinner, no one mentioned Sean's empty chair. I had alerted Gail, Mike, and the Hortons to the reason for Sean's absence. Yesterday, we had all toasted to the successful completion of "Libereco Nun." Now we wondered what would happen next. I had explained my fear to the rest of the group. "Sean will call us from work to find out what's going on."

We talked about the Civil Rights Bill, which was read in the Senate earlier that day. We all knew a long battle loomed ahead to get it passed there.

Ellen and Clark, immersed in their own project, talked about plans for the next hike. They knew nothing about our project, but we needed to caution them and explain Sean's absence without revealing our activities. "Sean's okay," I told them, "but he needs to leave for a few days."

"Okay," said Clark absently, not looking up.

"If anyone calls or stops by to ask about Sean, it's important," I paused and repeated, "very important that you not give out any information about him."

"Really," said Clark, looking at me with interest. "What's he done now?"

"Nothing." I needed to think of a good story and made it up as I went along. "I used to date a guy I found out was a criminal. Connected to the Mafia, you know, so I broke up with him and, uh, he didn't like that."

Clark sat up. "So what does that have to do with Sean?"

"He tracked me down to this house, and, uh, saw Sean and me leave together yesterday morning. He called me, threatening to kill Sean, so Sean is living somewhere else for a few days until this blows over. The guy is a criminal and might try to talk to you to find out about who's living here. I'd appreciate your not answering questions about us from anyone you don't know. Okay?" I held my breath. I thought it was a good story and ought to accomplish what I wanted it to.

Gail chimed in. "I know how that goes. I've had the same problem myself. Some guys don't get the hint. They think they own you." She smiled at me and winked.

Ellen agreed. "I had to change my phone number and move out of my apartment because a jerk I dated got ugly." She glanced around the dining room. "That's why I like living here."

Once we cleared the table, it seemed sadly bare without Sean's film equipment laid out across it. Clark sat at the typewriter, staring as usual at a blank sheet of paper. I continued reading my book. Ellen spread a map out on the floor and kneeled alongside to write notes on it. Gail retreated to her basement lair, and Mike had gone out to class. Another quiet, ordinary evening at home. My Rockwell assignment was over and done with. I had gone through with it and succeeded. I was proud of myself. Wait until Aunt Kay hears the story.

I heard a knock on the door and froze. My stomach plummeted. Ellen looked up. "You answer it," I whispered to Ellen. "I need to be inconspicuous just in case."

She got up, turned on the porch light, and peered out the front window. "It looks like a tramp."

"I'm not a tramp. I need to speak to Sean." The voice from outside was loud and harsh.

"He knows Sean." Ellen looked at me, a question in her face.

Clark walked past us to the door and opened it. "I'm Sean's brother. What do you want?"

The man brushed past Clark and walked in. "Where's Sean?"

His hair was as greasy as Clark's, and he reeked of sweat and tobacco. He looked familiar to me, and then I froze. He was one of Rockwell's storm troopers. Which one? Hard to tell what lay underneath all that grime with a baseball cap pulled low over his eyes. His disguise. I couldn't put a name to him. It wasn't Leon or Frank. Ted? Calvin? It could have been Reg, but he was way too neat a dresser, unless this grunge was part of his disguise. I shrank back into the dark kitchen to hear without being seen. I didn't trust that he wouldn't recognize me despite my jeans and short, limp brown hair.

Clark drew himself up and asked with dignity, "Who are you and why do you want to see my brother?"

"You tell him I know he pulled off that stunt yesterday. I don't know what he's doing with the pumpkin, but he's stirred up the yellow jackets. The Commander and his buddy Matt are mad as hornets and suspicious of me and all of us, but especially me. You tell him that." The man glanced around the room, hesitating for a moment, trying to see me in the dark of the kitchen, and then he turned and left.

Clark closed and locked the door after him, but he turned to me. "This guy wasn't your old boyfriend, was he?"

I shook my head.

"That was a cock and bull story, wasn't it?" Clark folded his arms and frowned at me. The others were silent, watching.

"All right," I said. "It was, but Sean has made a powerful enemy, and we all have to protect him."

"You didn't need to lie," said Clark. "Ellen and I won't say a word to anyone about Sean, and we won't even ask what it's about, because, frankly, I don't want to know."

"You will let us in on what's going on when it's safe, though, won't you?" asked Ellen.

"Of course," I said, "but not now." Ellen returned to studying the map.

The tramp was one of Rockwell's men, and he could only be Sean's friend, our ally, and now we'd made Rockwell suspicious of him. I tossed my head. He ought to get away from there, anyway. Rockwell has no money. We've made sure of that.

Again, we heard a knock on the door. I stepped back, not wanting to confront another of Rockwell's men. Clark saw my hesitation, got up, and opened the door to Horace. He was watching the tramp stride down the street.

"What's wrong with him?" asked Horace as he walked in. "He pushed me aside when he came down the steps."

"One of Sean's friends,' I said.

"Oh." Horace nodded as he took off his coat, then he sat in a living room chair, pulled a book out of his satchel, and began to read. I looked at Clark, who shrugged.

"Horace likes it here," he said.

I returned to my book. Later that evening, Sean phoned, and I told him about the visit from Rockwell's man. "He's your confidant, isn't he?"

"Did you recognize him?"

"No. They all look alike," I said.

Sean was silent for a moment.

"Will he be all right?" I asked.

"Probably. He's smart enough to know when it's too hot. He may have to leave Rockwell's group, but he'll probably be put on another assignment. The FBI or whoever he's working for can plant another agent with Rockwell if they need to. We got what we wanted. Wish there were a way to thank the guy."

"Can you get in touch with him?"

"No point, and it might put him into even more danger. He can get out and disappear if it gets too hot for him."

Sean was right. We had no way to help. "What if he doesn't

work for the FBI? You were guessing about that."

Again, Sean hesitated. Finally, he said, "We did what we had to do. He'll have to protect himself."

"I guess so." There was no reason we'd need to go back to that awful place. Sean's friend was on his own. "Now what?"

"You haven't noticed anyone watching your house?"

"No," I said. Not yet anyway, but I'd been looking. Cole and Alice were keeping an eye out, too.

"Maybe that woman didn't write down the van's tag number."

"Maybe."

Chapter 18

February 19, 1964.

I spent Wednesday morning studying and getting ready for class. I heard Clark stirring upstairs and checked my watch. Ten-thirty and, as usual, he hadn't left his room yet. He eventually came down and, as he did every morning, lay on the couch and took his pulse.

"Aren't you supposed to be job-hunting?" I asked, trying not to sound critical, but really. He'd dressed today and wore a yellowish plaid pair of pants with a frilled dress shirt, black bow tie, and cummerbund. Sure, he'd get hired dressed like that. Not even beatniks or the new wave, hippies, would wear those clothes, although maybe Oscar Wilde. It might help if Clark washed his hair and beard, brushed his teeth, and took a shower.

"Do you have an interview?" I asked.

"Today," he said and plodded into the kitchen.

Hallelujah, I thought. I heard him pour a cup of coffee and rattle a cereal box as I stole another peek at the street. Nothing unusual out there.

I finished the book I was reading, grabbed a snack and my flask, and put on an old jacket—not the coat I'd worn in Arlington. I left for the university, trotting down the steps and up the street to Kay's VW bus. It was a pleasure to drive. I eased it out of its parking space and crept down Kilbourne Place between the parked cars on both sides. I studied each car as I passed and saw three with Virginia license places. In one, two men sat in the front seat. They glanced at me as I passed, but looked bored and uninterested. My hands gripped the steering wheel. That was storm trooper Frank, sitting in the driver's seat. The other person was in shadow. I wanted to race down the street and away, but kept to the slow, steady pace as if nothing had happened. I didn't think any of that crew in Arlington would recognize straight-haired brunette me as the blond, curly haired minx who brought them hot dogs and donuts...and pizza.

When I returned after my classes, cars crowded the street, and I had to park two blocks away. As I walked to the house, I again scanned the cars for Virginia license tags but had to be close to see the tag between parked cars. Then I noticed a Virginia license tag and recognized the same car I'd seen earlier. I stopped, pretending to search for something in my purse while I studied it. Ordinary sedan. Rusted. Two men sat inside. As before. The one on the driver's side dangled a lit cigarette out the window. They were sitting there idle, and they were watching our house.

I edged away from the curb and walked faster to get past them in a hurry, keeping my face averted. I didn't think they noticed me other than I was a young female. I heard a soft whistle from one of them. I passed our house and walked to the library at the end of the street.

I hung out in the library for two hours. If Frank and the other guy in the car had any legitimate business in the neighborhood—a huge coincidence—they would be gone by now. If they were watching our house, they'd still be sitting in their car, because I was sure no one had come or gone from that front door since Clark left.

I checked out three books and carried them like a permission slip down the sidewalk, past the two guys still sitting in the car. I zipped around the corner, down the alley, and rushed through the back gate into the house, locking the door behind me. I ran through the house to attach the chain across the front door. With shaking hands, I made a cup of tea. Then I called Sean at work.

"I saw them," I said when he came on the line. "Two guys

sitting in a sedan. I recognized the driver as one of Rockwell's storm troopers."

"That's very bad," he said. "Our worst fears. You're sure it was them?"

"They were parked in front of the house when I went to school, and still there when I came back. I passed our house and walked to the library. I recognized Frank, but the other one kept his face turned away. They're watching our house."

"Okay. Meet with the team tonight, tell them the situation. See what you can come up with."

"Are you all right? You haven't noticed anyone strange, have you?"

His laugh had an edge to it. "Not yet. I'm watching. Living at a motel is boring, though. I forgot my film project back at the house."

"We'll come up with a plan," I said and hung up. The trouble was, the Nazis knew the rented van was involved in the robbery. No other reason for it to be there. They knew that the generous young woman who brought them food was in on the theft, too, and that the food was doctored. I was sure now that, thanks to Mrs. Frank or whoever she was, they had the license number and traced it to our house. They knew we'd stolen the money.

What would they do next? Storm the house? Kidnap one of us? A shiver ran down my spine. It was a terrifying idea. I'd kept back from the windows when I looked out and averted my face when I passed them. Even though my makeover changed my appearance, they'd see through it if they got a closer and longer look. Heard my voice. Noticed how I walked.

Sean was safe so far, but that woman had seen Gail and, of course, me but me in a ball cap and sunglasses and Gail in a wig, cap, and sunglasses. Any description the woman gave would be faulty. We could disclaim knowledge of a van and a young man named Sean. After all, from what I'd heard around school, a fake driver's license with fake name and address were easy to obtain if you knew where to go. Rockwell's men didn't seem like a law-abiding bunch to me. They must know how to get a fake I.D. Why wouldn't they assume the thieves had done the same?

Would Rockwell and his men buy the idea?

Our band of altruistic robbers needed to meet ASAP.

Chapter 19

February 19, 1964.

Wednesday evening. It seemed like an eon since I moved into Kay's house a month ago and met this group of activists. Now I had embarked on a life of crime. I was scared. The car with Rockwell's two Nazis had moved away, but another one had taken its place. Even if I didn't see them, I knew they were out there watching the house.

I had met six of Rockwell's men, and they knew me as Mary Lee. From all I'd heard, Rockwell had many more men involved as neo-Nazis. If he brought in men I hadn't met, used them to shadow me or even pretend to like me or want to date me, how would I know?

Because Sean had to stay away from the house, we decided to meet elsewhere. This posed a problem, because some so-called public places wouldn't allow the Hortons to come in. We had to meet in a place that accepted African Americans. We finally settled on the dining room of a small hotel in downtown D.C. that was open to colored people. No fancy menu, but we all knew where it was, and it was easy to get to.

Mike, Gail, and I left for the Sixteenth Street bus at seven that evening after a hasty dinner. We took the back alley. Clark and Ellen remained at the house to discourage the watchers from breaking in. Neither of them knew anything about what we were involved in, but after listening to the story we made up, they were willing to help. They kept the police phone number handy in case there was trouble, and Ellen called several friends, asking them to drop by. "Make this house look as if hordes of people use it. Horace often comes by, too. That should take the pressure off any one person in particular," she explained.

"Maybe Horace will put a hex on them," I suggested.

Ellen wasn't amused.

The Hortons left their house fifteen minutes later and caught a cab. Sean would meet us at the hotel.

We sat closely around a table in the far corner of the dining room. The few other patrons at this hour were all African Americans. Sean and the Hortons ordered dinner. I ordered dessert but was too upset to eat it.

"What are we going to do?" I asked. "They know we took the stash, and they want it back."

"It's gone," Alice said firmly, "and out of our hands.

"They can't know we took it," added Cole. "They're guessing."

"They know we took it," I repeated, "and they know about Sean. It won't take much for them to finger Gail and me despite our disguises if they see us with Sean."

"I'm staying away from the house," said Sean, arms folded on the table, "but I'm still going to work."

"My own hair is thick and curly." Gail sat quietly, listening and chewing her fingernails. "I tucked it under the wig and then the cap. I'm probably okay."

"The men saw me as a blond." I said. "The woman saw me as I am, but I was wearing a ball cap and sunglasses, so I was still in disguise. Can they identify me?"

Cole sat back and studied me. "Probably not," he said finally. He wasn't convincing, and I wasn't reassured.

Sean shook his head. "You look mousy enough now. I don't think they'll connect you."

The others agreed with Sean, except for Mike. "She doesn't look mousy. She's fine. I do not think they recognize her. How many of us remember people we meet once or even a few times?"

He sat back. "Not many, I think."

I smiled at Mike, pleased that he'd disagreed with the mousy part, but we had a big problem to discuss. "What are we going to do?" I asked. "Sean can't stay in a motel forever." And I didn't want to worry about who'd be waiting for me whenever I went outside.

"I'm okay. I found another rooming house with college kids." Sean grimaced. "It's even cheaper, but more raucous. Hope I can stand it."

"We need to throw their suspicion elsewhere," said Cole. "Away from our houses and away from you--" He nodded at me, "—and you." He nodded at Sean and Gail.

"But how?" That car rental license agreement was damning.

"We need to pull in our FBI ally," said Sean. "I know how to reach him. That is, if he'll still work with us."

"I told you he came to the house," I said. "He's upset with you."

"I'm sorry about that." Sean shook his head. "I'll have to keep him out of this, then."

Cole nodded, pushing his lips in and out, brows knit. "I'm afraid so. Meanwhile, we stonewall. We know nothing and don't understand why Rockwell's storm troopers are hounding us." He thought a moment, and we all pondered this strategy. "Agreed?" he said.

"Agreed," we echoed. It would have to do for the time being. We still had no plan to derail Rockwell's suspicion of us, and we couldn't ask the FBI agent to help. Dispersing to other apartments or boarding houses might be a solution, but none of us wanted to leave Kay's place. Aunt Kay was counting on me to keep an eye on things. Anyway, I liked living there. I wanted to stay.

I agreed not to call in the police. We didn't know what Rockwell might do if pushed by the police. If he had nothing to hide, he would point fingers at us, show them the license number, and let them track us down. No police officers had shown up at our door, so he obviously hadn't done that. This fact alone confirmed our belief that Rockwell didn't want the police entering the picture. Neither did we.

We kicked around a few more ideas, but I wondered about Sean. He was the most affected by our activities, but why was he involved? He wasn't colored or Jewish, but then neither was I. I'd gotten involved reluctantly, but I wanted Aunt Kay's approval, and I wanted to help pass the Civil Rights Bill, especially now that it outlawed discrimination based on sex. Sean was quite taken with Tanya, which might be the motivator.

"Why did you join this group?" I finally asked. "You don't have a stake in the Civil Rights Bill."

Sean grinned. "Hate to sound stuffy," he said, "but I do believe in justice and fair play, Anyway, there's my family history." He spoke lightly and flicked a crumb off the table. "My family is union, union way back," he said. "Solidarity forever, that's my family. We fight for the underdog, the powerless. State police murdered my great granddaddy in the Steel Strike of 1919. The Little Steel Strike of 1937 left my Dad permanently crippled."

He ran his hand over his forehead as if to wipe out bad memories. "You want to get fairness and equality, you got to fight for it, and that means you fight the police, the National Guard, and whoever else the so-called authorities pit against you." He smiled at me. "I've seen how colored people are treated, and it's not fair. No matter how good they are, they're kept out of management and good neighborhoods and good schools." He paused, staring at his hands for a few seconds before looking at me with a smile. "Does that answer your question?"

It did and more. I knew next to nothing about unions. I thought if you didn't like your job, you quit and found another one. No big deal except that it was. Unions fought against exploitation of workers. In the South, the police often colluded with the Ku Klux Klan in crushing Negro efforts for fairness and equal rights. The police sometimes were the Ku Klux Klan, actively involved in lynch parties. I read this in newspapers and books, or I would find it hard to believe, having grown up in a white middle-class neighborhood and taught to respect authority and the status quo.

We left the hotel separately with the Hortons going home by

cab. Sean walked on to his boarding house, and Gail, Mike, and I took the city bus back to Kilbourne Place. When the three of us arrived at the house, I watched for Rockwell's surveillance team but didn't see it. The chain was across the door, and we waited a few minutes before Clark peered out and slipped off the chain. "Thank goodness," he said.

Ellen sat shivering and ashen-faced in the living room. "They came here," she said through clattering teeth. "They tried to beat their way in."

"Solid door. Tough," added Clark. "I yelled at them I was calling the police. And I did."

"They tried the back door, too," said Ellen, pulling a sweater tightly around herself, "but the police came in time."

"What did the police do?" I asked. We didn't want a full investigation.

"They talked to us and looked for signs of a break-in," Gail said, "and then sent a couple of cops to walk up and down the street keeping an eye out for suspicious activity, but they found nothing."

"No signs of a break-in tonight," added Clark. "Nothing suspicious outside."

"Maybe they thought you made up this story," I said. I hoped so.

"But what do those crooks want?" Clark paced the floor. "We don't have any money or valuable jewelry or valuable any-thing. I don't even have a job."

Ellen looked at me. "It wasn't an angry boyfriend. It was a gang." she said.

I shook my head. Calling the police might have saved their lives. Clark and Ellen didn't have to act innocent. They were in-nocent of the robbery, and their own law-abiding plans to find Mosby's treasure immersed them.

"Those thugs don't want to deal with the police," Gail said. "That was George Lincoln Rockwell's henchmen out there."

"Rockwell? The Nazi?" Clark's mouth dropped open. "What have you done? You don't mess with people like that."

"No wonder they were so mean and ugly," said Ellen, "but

why were they after us or you or whoever? Was it something to do with Kay? She's the one who owns the house. Maybe she's a smuggler." Ellen hugged herself. "I'm scared."

"They weren't after you," I said. "And Kay is not a smuggler. They're angry at something I did that doesn't concern you. I'll see they go away." Big words. I didn't know how I would do that, but Aunt Kay trusted me to take care of her house. I had to think of a plan to lead them away from here and from us.

I now knew what Aunt Kay meant about a test. So far, I think I deserved an "A," but I hadn't figured on a life or death dilemma. Rockwell needed the money we stole. How far was he willing to go to get it back? Was he playing for keeps?

Chapter 20

February 20, 1964.

The next day, Thursday, I scanned both sides of the street from the front window, and then slipped out the back door before I walked to Kay's VW bus to drive to class. I felt eyes watching me, but I didn't see anyone who looked like one of Rockwell's toughs. I knew they were out there, though.

Clark stayed home, working on his novel, he said. Through Cole and Gail's connections with civil rights activists, a steady stream of men and women visited the house for most of the day, staying only a few minutes. Several of them later reported attempts by strange men to befriend them at the bus stop or along their walk, but the activists had been told not to reveal anything about the house or its inhabitants. The rest of us stayed with our regular schedules but kept our eyes open and a distance between ourselves, parked cars, the curb, and strangers.

Rockwell had to be going crazy. He had $150,000 in his grasp. It meant the end of his financial problems and the beginning of a real bid for the presidency. Then it disappeared. He's looking for the blond who brought in the poisoned pizza and knows that Sean and the van were all part of it. Sean and the blond have disappeared, too. Would he ever see through my disguise and recognize me? Had he already done so? If he realized the straight-haired brunette at Kay's house was the curly haired blond, his next step would obviously be to kidnap her to find out where the money was or to hold her and demand the money as ransom. Either way, the blond Mary Lee was not in for a good time.

I made it to classes without a problem until I sat in on a philosophy discussion of ethics. I sat near the door of this classroom. An easy exit meant no claustrophobia and no panic. At least I was learning to manage the problem—sit near a door. I couldn't always do that, and so the swig of vodka.

I listened to the ethics discussion, and the doubts and justifications I carried in my mind about the rightness of robbing Rockwell surfaced again. I had plenty of doubts about being personally involved, but a neo-Nazi was fair game, I thought. In black and white terms, the Civil Rights Bill was good, making equality and antidiscrimination practices the law; George Lincoln Rockwell and the Nazis with their goal of white supremacy, murder, and oppression were bad. Absolutely.

But robbery, the theft of another person's property, is against the law and therefore wrong and against civilized behavior. But what if the money we took came from illegal sources like smuggling, drugs, alcohol, prostitution, or whatever? Would stealing it be more wrong if it came from a legitimate source, earned through hard work, and donated to what the donor saw as a good cause?

Were we right to rob Rockwell? Or was it an unlawful act whittling away the strength of a civilization?

I had no answer. The jury was out.

That evening, we began receiving threatening phone calls. I answered the first one. A raspy, deep voice said only six words: "Give back the money or else." Then it hung up. The call scared me. What did Rockwell mean when he said "or else." How much time did we have before he exercised "or else"?

The second call came half an hour later. Ellen answered it. Her face turned white as she listened to the message, then she flung down the phone and jumped away as if she'd stepped on a snake. In a way, she had. She didn't have to tell me who called, but she did demand to know what was going on.

My words stumbled as I tried to think of a plausible story. I could not tell her the true one. Without the context, stealing the money was theft, pure and simple. For all I knew about her, she might go directly to the police. I finally told her I'd dated one of the storm troopers but broke it off when I found out he was a Nazi, and now they were all out to harass me. It was galling to have anyone think I'd get close to those guys, but it satisfied Ellen. "We girls have to stick together," she said. "If they come around here to bother you, I'll tell them a thing or two."

The calls came at half-hour intervals, each with the same message and each hanging up before we responded with denials. Finally, I took the phone off the hook for the night, but someone put it back in the morning. Mike expected a call, and there was the remote possibility an employer would call Clark with a job offer. As I ate breakfast, the calls began again. After the second one, I again took the phone off the hook.

The robbery took place on Monday. On Friday afternoon, I was at class and everyone else was out of the house, too. I was the first one home that afternoon. For once, I didn't see a car with Virginia license plates and two men sitting in it. I kept my eyes open and used the back alley and the kitchen door. I didn't see the cracked front door standing open until I dropped my books on the dining room table. Rockwell's gang had pushed their actions up a notch and broken into the house. It had to be Rockwell's men.

I listened for a moment. The house was quiet, but it didn't mean someone wasn't hiding inside. I heard a slight sound, a swish of something gliding across paper in the living room. I stepped toward the couch and heard a rattle. Clark had left a pile of papers there and on top, coiled and staring at me with flickering tongue, was a rattlesnake.

I freaked and ran out the front door, down the steps, over to the Horton's house, and banged on their front door, hoping someone was home. I was in luck, but it took Alice forever to open the door. Stuart stood behind her.

"Let me in quick," I gasped.

Alice scanned the street and pulled me into the living room.

"What's the matter?"

"They broke into the house." I was shaking. "Ripped open the door and left a rattlesnake in the living room. Did you hear anything?"

"I just got home. Took Stuart in for a follow-up," said Alice. "That's why we're home today." She took another look at my face and shaking hands. "You poor lamb. You must have been terrified. Sit here and I'll bring you a cup of tea."

Stuart stepped past his mother and out the door. "Let's go check out what they did."

Alice grabbed his shirt. "No, you don't. They may still be in there. I'm not taking another trip to the hospital." She turned to me. "Just a minute and we can discuss this." In a few minutes, she brought out three cups of tea.

"Should we call the police?" I asked as I sat shivering on the living room couch and cupped my hands around the hot mug. "Rockwell isn't going to say anything about the robbery if they trace the break-in to him."

"We don't necessarily know Rockwell's thugs broke in," said Alice thoughtfully.

"But who else could it be?" I asked, feeling much calmer.

"I said we don't necessarily know," Alice repeated, "who broke in, do we? Doesn't have to be Rockwell and his storm troopers, does it?"

I saw her point. "You're right. I'm not going into the house until I know it's safe. We need the police to go through it."

"And the ASPCA," added Stuart, "for the snake. I know someone who can handle the problem, and he lives down the block. He'll release it out in the woods where it belongs." He left for the kitchen to make the call.

I nodded. I didn't believe in killing snakes, even rattlesnakes.

"Might need a police report for the insurance company," said Alice. "I'm guessing. Did you see any damage?"

"They smashed in the front door, but I didn't look inside the house. I skedaddled out of there." Did Rockwell leave any messages that would incriminate us? Possibly, but who would give credibility to that bunch? We would disclaim knowing any reason for a cryptic message. Anyway, with five people living there, anything was possible. "It should be safe to call the police and have them check the house. Can I use your phone?" I asked.

She pointed to it on the side table. I made the call.

When the police came, I followed them into the house with Stuart and his friend Albert behind me. The police whistled at the snake, in full view on the couch, but Albert efficiently bagged it, and the two left for a trip to the country.

The police found no one hiding inside. The vandals had pulled out drawers in all the bedrooms, overturned mattresses, shook out the garbage, and kicked it all over the kitchen. Taking their revenge, I guessed. They'd even emptied the refrigerator. Edibles were the only thing they found to steal, and they used the pile of folded grocery bags on the counter to carry away every bit of food from the pantry and refrigerator. They even grabbed the snacks in the cupboard.

The place was a mess, but other than the front door, they'd done little actual damage. Stuart said he'd replace the door and put on stronger locks. He was a born carpenter; it turns out. By the evening, the new door was in place.

Later, after dinner, Gail, Mike, and I met with Alice and Cole and their family in the Horton's basement.

"They ramped up their campaign to find the money," said Cole. "We're lucky none of us has been hurt so far. Was there anything in the house that would confirm to Rockwell we were the ones who took the money?"

"Nobody wrote down Sean's new address, did they?" asked Gail.

"No reason to keep notes or receipts or nothing like that to connect us to the robbery," added Mike.

"Man, I didn't even keep the post office receipts for mailing the packages," said Stuart.

I was quiet but sat with a queasy feeling in my stomach. I'd seen how Rockwell's men trashed my room. They must have found the blond wig and recognized the dresses in my closet. Why didn't I get rid of those dresses and that wig? Stupid, stupid, stupid, but it never occurred to me they'd break into the house and find my disguise. "I'm sorry," I croaked. "The wig was on the dresser, and the dresses were in the closet."

"So they know who you are," said Mike slowly.

I nodded. "Now they do."

No one spoke. They all stared down at their hands. I felt terrible. "I'm so sorry," I said. "I let you all down with that stupid mistake."

Cole cleared his throat. "Can you disappear for a while?"

I shook my head. "Aunt Kay is depending on me to watch over things at the house." I hadn't done too well on that. "And I have classes." I didn't want to leave. I refused to leave.

"You, Gail, and Ellen are the only other women in that house," said Alice. "Gail looks enough different from either of you they would dismiss her as the blond. You and Ellen are essentially the same shape except Ellen does have blond hair."

"Straight blond hair," I said. "Not curly like that wig I wore."

"Still, they might not know for sure which of you was involved," persisted Alice. "Both of you are in danger."

Cole shook his head. "They'll focus on Sue. Ellen's too tall—she really is—and if you have long blond hair, you'd change it to brunette with hair color or a wig, like Sue changed hers to blond. I think they'll figure that out."

I groaned. "I had a picture of my mom and me on the dresser."

Cole nodded. "That nails it. They know what you look like."

"You're only a girl," said Stuart. "and you know they don't think much of women. They probably won't expect you to have any smarts."

Mike nodded. "They'll think you were some guy's stooge."

"They'll think she was Sean's stooge," Tanya said.

She didn't look happy at the idea. She had nothing to fear from me, but to tell her that would acknowledge there was something between her and Sean. If there was, I mean. Anyway, I didn't like being dismissed as "only a girl" or as someone's stooge.

"That may be so," said Gail, "but they'll think she can lead them to Sean."

As demeaning as it was, they were both probably right.

"Now that they know who I am, they'll focus on me," I said, "since they can't find Sean. They'll think I know where Sean is."

"Keep your wits about you," said Cole. He sat back and folded his arms. "We'll all have to be extra careful when we go out. I can see them trying to kidnap one of us. They'll be most interested in Sue, but everyone in your house is a potential target."

"They don't know about us yet," added Alice.

Stuart spoke up. "They saw me when they beat me up."

"And me," said Mike. "But there's nothing to connect us with the robbery."

Gail studied them and nodded to herself. "I doubt they'd recognize either one of you even if they saw you walking along with Sue."

I suddenly felt like crying. I liked these people. I wanted them to like me, but now they'll all want to stay away from me. With Sean hiding out, I became the target. To associate with me made them a target, too. I felt very alone.

I had nothing else to say. I wanted to leave and go home before bursting into tears and making a fool of myself. We disbanded, and Mike caught up with me as we left.

"I'll walk with you," he said, "in fact, I'll take off work and stay with you until you feel safe again."

I was pathetically grateful for this show of support, but he needed the job, and I needed my classes. I thanked him. "I know the score." I said, "You don't need to take off work for me. I'll just be extra careful when I go out. So far, I've done all right."

We all shared in the cleaning up. Aunt Kay had left money for expenses, so the next morning I called a burglar alarm company. They came out Friday morning and installed the alarm. They showed me how to arm it, and I repeated the demonstration for the others. I pasted the alarm company's warning sign on both doors and all the windows.

Gail hung around after Ellen and Mike dispersed for work. Clark went back to his room.

"I'm working on my master's degree in social work," Gail said. "I've had some classes and experience in counseling. Do you want to talk about how you're feeling?"

"Uh, no," I stammered, surprised and embarrassed by the overture. "I'm okay."

"It's all right to feel scared," she said. "You've got a bunch of terrible guys after you."

I suddenly felt like crying, but I blinked away the tears. "Everybody here has the bad guys after them," I said.

Gail studied my face solemnly. "Yes, we all do. We're together in this, you know. You're not alone. You wouldn't be involved at all if we hadn't pushed you way beyond comfort."

"That's right," I agreed, "but I wouldn't have done it if I didn't believe in the cause and why we did it. I'm glad to have helped."

"Good. Now we have to endure Rockwell's attempts to get back at us. He'll move on when he doesn't get what he wants." She reached forward and hugged me.

"I hope so," I said. "There is something you can do."

Gail looked at me. "What is that?"

"Stuart," I said. "He's worried about his friend Darrell. I'm afraid he'll try something stupid, like roaming the woods behind Rockwell's house, looking for signs of a burial. He's convinced the Nazis killed him."

"I've been watching him," said Gail, nodding her head. "He's impetuous and still thinks like a teenager. He's likely to fly off on his own and, like you said, do something stupid. We need to find out what happened to Darrell before Stuart gets into trouble."

"But how?" I asked.

Gail shook her head. "I don't know."

Friday after dinner, we asked Mike.

"Hard to watch what happen to Darrell when they beat me," Mike said. "I thought he got away, but then we would know by now, wouldn't we?"

"Has anyone talked to his parents?" I asked. "They might have heard from him."

No one responded. I had seen Darrell's Dad on the street. I would have asked him, but I was afraid of an emotional scene. Still, he hadn't looked as worried as he had the day after the beating. I hoped Darrell had survived, and we didn't need to do anything about him. He might even be home now.

I heard a knock on the door. My other roommates were dispersed through the house, so I pulled the chain across and opened it to peer out through the crack straight into the icy blue eyes of George Lincoln Rockwell.

Chapter 21

George Lincoln Rockwell. In person. I gasped and stepped back. He knocked again. What was he going to try now?

I had to pretend ignorance. He didn't see much of me when I brought the pizzas to his house. He was polite, but I was beneath his notice. Like the others, he focused on the pizzas. I thought he would sneak a good meal when he drove out in the afternoons, but he also looked too thin and hungry even though he was clean and well-groomed. I suppose it spoke well of him that he didn't make his men suffer more than he did.

His storm troopers must have told him about the blond wig they found, but I pretended I'd never seen him before. I didn't think he could recognize me, so I looked out at him straight in the face. He was wearing a navy blue suit, hair combed; he was quite presentable, in fact. Trying to impress the people he thought robbed him? He looked like a car salesman or a politician.

"Who are you?" I asked. "What do you want?"

"Hello, ma'am," Rockwell said. He spoke politely but with clenched jaw, and I felt the tightly controlled anger radiating off his words and body. "I am sure you know I am Mr. George Rockwell. You also know we have a little problem we need to discuss." He smiled as his gaze passed over me and took in Clark and Mike, who'd heard his knock and stood behind me. "With all of you." His eyes flicked around the room. "And especially with Mr. Sean

Wolfe."

"He's not here. I don't know you, and we have nothing to discuss," I countered. Cole said we should stonewall. I looked behind Rockwell and to both sides outside the door. He was alone. "I don't understand why you need to talk to us. We're not buying anything you're selling." I pretended he was an ordinary solicitor.

"Come, come, you know I'm not selling anything. It's difficult to talk out here. May I come in?" He smiled at me as if this were a friendly visit. He exuded a smarmy kind of courtesy.

"Just a minute. I'll ask the other people who live here. I can't see you having any problem with me, and I don't open the door unless others are here." I closed the door, locking it with the chain still on, and turned to Clark and Mike, both of them now sitting on the couch and listening. Clark's innocence would help. Mike must have had stonewalling experience in Hungary. Gail was in the basement, but she was Jewish and might raise his antagonism and suspicions. Anyway, the woman who waited for Frank's check saw her and must have described her to Rockwell and the gang.

"We have a visitor." I nodded at the door. "Mr. George Rockwell would like to talk to us."

Mike laid aside his book and went to the front window to stare at Rockwell standing under the porch light. He frowned. "Yep, that is him, all right."

"Sure. Let's hear what he has to say," said Clark.

Mike mouthed the word "stonewall." It felt good to have that support in this confrontation.

With Mike and Clark behind me, I felt less intimidated and more curious about what Rockwell was like. I had met him briefly. Now I'd have a better look at this anti-Semitic bigot who had the gall to send out campaign propaganda that the Holocaust never happened. But my real motive was to try to dispel his suspicions about me and Sean if I found an opening.

I unchained the door and invited Rockwell in.

"Thank you, I appreciate it," he said, lowering his head as he came through the door. He doffed his coat and handed it to me, then turned to give Clark and Mike a quick once-over. I surreptitiously felt his coat for a gun and then subtly, I hoped, glanced over his body for any sign of a weapon. I didn't see any. He must feel sure of himself.

"I am George Rockwell," he said as if he expected a trumpet salute

Mike and Clark introduced themselves as they shook hands. They sat down. I saw that Rockwell had already dismissed me to hostess duties, which was fine since I could keep to the background. "Coffee?" I asked to fulfill my role.

They all nodded, and I exited to the kitchen, put water on to boil and hunted for the jar of instant coffee. I didn't know how to make coffee any other way. As kitchen drudge, I needn't involve myself in the discussion at all. Rockwell wouldn't expect me to be of any importance other than as a servant to him and the other men. He showed no signs of recognizing me, and I deliberately acted stupid to be totally unlike the vivacious blonde who robbed him. As the water came to a boil, I stood in the darkness of the hall and watched.

Clark, Mike, and Rockwell sat facing each other. "Are you the George Rockwell in the newspapers?" asked Clark, wide-eyed with awe.

He nodded. "I am that George Lincoln Rockwell, yes, and I am the founder and commander of the American Nazi Party."

Clark's jaw dropped, but Mike sat back, arms folded, face blank, and waited. Neither of them spoke. Rockwell appeared relaxed and comfortable as he gazed around the room.

I did want to hear what they talked about, so I quickly made the coffee and brought it out to them with a bowl of sugar and a small pitcher of skimmed milk. Rockwell didn't deserve cream, I figured. I put on one of Aunt Kay's decorative aprons for good measure and then took a seat myself in an insignificant chair against the wall. They were talking about the weather by that time. I let them talk, wondering what Rockwell would say.

Clark and Mike were ready to discuss the weather until he left, but Rockwell soon brought the conversation around to the reason for his visit.

He sat up, glanced at me, and turned to Clark, probably because Mike was obviously foreign and of no consequence. I smiled at this.

"I have a grave matter to discuss with you," he began and then sipped his coffee, made a face and set the cup aside. He planned to take control. Navy blue suit, six feet, four inches tall, used to the power.

He leaned forward, elbows on his knees. "Someone robbed my home last Monday. They robbed it of the dollars and dimes and pennies donated to my organization from people who believe in America, who believe that my organization would make America great the way it was, the America we grew up in, the way it was before the so called 'civil rights' laws ruined it." He paused to let the rhetoric sink in. Of course he was talking about a white America because African Americans were still trying to make America great at last for them. Rockwell sounded like a politician, all right. I felt like gagging and didn't dare look at Mike, who must have been feeling the same.

"Somebody took away those dollars and dimes and pennies," he went on. "Somebody I suspect may be a Communist, somebody guilty of treason. I want that money returned." His stony eyes stared unflinchingly at Mike and at Clark and then swung around to me. I kept my face blank.

Clark gaped at him. Mike's eyes flicked over at me, but his expression remained neutral.

"What does this have to do with us?" Clark asked. "We don't go robbing people."

"Do you know Sean Wolfe?" Rockwell asked.

Mike forestalled Clark's response. "Sure. Used to live here but moved away awhile back. Why? He's a pleasant fellow."

"He rented the van used to rob me," Rockwell replied, watching our faces.

"I don't believe it," said Clark with genuine astonishment

I willed him not to say anything more.

"He's my brother, and he wouldn't do such a thing." Clark's indignant response was well-played, but that statement put him in danger.

Rockwell studied him thoughtfully. "Where is your brother?" he asked.

Too late, realization dawned in Clark's eyes.

"We don't know," said Mike. "He move out, and none of us see him since. We do not know where, we not even know why. Clark and Sean had big fight, so we think it all connected. You not know where he is, Clark?"

Earlier, during a meeting at the Hortons, we'd discussed whether Sean should tell Clark where he was going, but Sean knew his brother. "If he knows nothing," explained Sean, "he'll have nothing to blurt out to Rockwell and will be of no use to him." We agreed. We kept Ellen out of the loop, too.

Clark shook his head. "No, no, I don't." His doubtful reply made Rockwell study him even more. Clark was our weak link. Then something clicked inside Clark's brain, as if he'd suddenly woken up. "We were mad at each other," he said, following Mike's lead. "I think he got tired of paying for me." He smiled. What an actor. "I'm looking for a job but haven't found the right fit yet. My brother's been helping me out."

I felt like applauding Clark's quick-thinking save.

Rockwell frowned with pursed lips and glanced at me. "They had a woman working with them. It was she who pretended to be a kind Samaritan, bringing my men hamburgers, hotdogs, donuts, and—" This time, he swung his head around to stare intently at me. "And...pizza. Drugged pizza, and while my men were unconscious, your brother and his band of thieves stole the hard-earned contributions of thousands of true Americans."

He was pouring out his bid for sympathy, implying he had huge grassroots support. He might have been convincing if I hadn't seen his place or met his men or known how he really got the money we stole.

Clark gaped at him. "My brother wouldn't have anything to do with that," he exclaimed. "Why would he? He has a good job, makes plenty of money. He's not a thief."

Rockwell calmly sat back. "The attack," he flicked at his slacks, "was politically motivated by Communists seeking to destroy the true America I believe in. A white America."

"You're crazy," said Clark.

Mike stood. "If all you do here is accuse us of bad things,

much better for you to go now," he said, getting up and heading to the front door.

Rockwell also rose to his full six-foot, four-inch height, towering over Mike. "I am serious about getting the money back," he repeated. "I will do whatever I have to do. We have notified the police. We have told the FBI about this Sean Wolfe and his suspected Communist leanings, and I assure you, he will not escape. All of you are under suspicion of being traitorous spies, so it would be best for you to tell me what you know and return the money. Unless the thieves return the money, donated by worthy people to my cause, in full, they will be caught, and when I am elected president, they will be shot."

I glanced at Mike as he looked at me. An unspoken message passed between us. *Bullshit.*

Rockwell waited for a response. There was none. Mike opened the door. "I am sorry for robbery at your house, Mr. Rockwell, but no need to look at us. We are all respectable peoples. Now we are much busy."

"I don't know where you got your information," Clark said between gritted teeth, "but my brother is not a thief or a Communist. He had nothing to do with your robbery." He rose and headed for the stairs. "I've got better stuff to do than listen to this crap."

Rockwell reclaimed his coat. "You will regret this," he hissed. "We are not through with you." He glared at us in a sweeping gaze. "Whatever you think of my politics, I have a right to promote them to all Americans. To refuse me that right is to ignore the principles set forth in our Constitution." He barely acknowledged me and ignored Mike as he swept out the door. Mike locked and chained it after him. My legs felt wobbly. I sank into a chair, wiping a hand across my forehead.

"Was that really George Lincoln Rockwell? The Nazi?" asked Clark from the stairs.

Mike nodded and grinned at me. "Can you believe that guy? He think he some big stuff, all right. We won that round."

I didn't agree. Rockwell now knew that Sean Wolfe existed, and he had a brother named Clark. "He thinks he's the future

President of the United States," I said.

More to come was my thought, but neo-Nazi George Lincoln Rockwell was right. He was an American, and he had a right to disseminate his ideas, no matter how repugnant they might be. On the other hand, I thought, we had not taken away his dubious right; we had merely robbed him of the means to carry out his plan.

Rockwell's threat meant I had to watch every step I took. I didn't want to go anywhere alone, but whoever I took with me would also be in danger. How much of a heroine did I want to be? I worried about Clark, too. He had played his role superbly, even though he didn't understand what it was about, but he was Sean's brother, and we needed to warn him to watch out.

It was near the end of February. Senate Majority Whip Mike Mansfield and Vice President Hubert Humphrey were developing strategies to counter the Senate filibuster under way to block the Civil Rights Bill. Meanwhile, representatives from SNCC, CORE, NAACP and church organizations were meeting with the President and organizing their members for a monumental effort to push the bill forward.

I hope our contribution helped. We were sweating blood because of it. I had to reach Sean.

Chapter 22

After Rockwell left, Mike and I had a serious talk with Clark. "You must be extra careful when you go out," said Mike.

"Is Sean in trouble?" Clark asked.

"Sean is okay," assured Mike, "but he make dangerous enemy in Rockwell. He need to hide for a while, that's all."

"But why?" asked Clark. "And what does it have to do with me?"

I stepped in. "You're his brother," I said bluntly, "and they may try to get to him through you."

"Stay away from deserted or isolated places," added Mike, "and don't talk to strangers."

"What. You think I'm a child?" Clark drew himself up. "I'll talk to whoever I please."

"Only until their interest in Sean blows over," I said. "They'll be looking to find some way to get you to divulge where Sean is living." I was thinking of kidnapping and torture.

"So be careful who you talk to and what you say." added Mike.

Clark scoffed at the idea. "Anyway, I don't know where Sean is right now. You're telling me he's all right, though."

"He's fine," I assured Clark. "I am in touch with him."

"Oh, really," said Clark, studying me. "Sean would rather talk to you than me. So that's the way it is, is it? I thought it was

Tanya all this time."

He'd gotten the wrong idea, but I wasn't going to argue with him. It wouldn't bother him too much to think it was a budding romance rather than a brother boycott. "He said not to worry about him."

Clark hardly ever left the house except for occasional trips to the nearby drugstore, supermarket, or library and his weekend excursions with Ellen. He didn't eat breakfast until he checked his pulse. If he ever had job interviews, I didn't know of them, but it was none of my business. I'd love to get him out of the house more, though.

But for me it was different. I'd been back in school for over a month, and I had to leave the house to attend classes. My nerves were shot by the time I got to the university. I expected Rockwell's men to hijack or rear-end or otherwise attack and kidnap me on the tedious commute to and from the university. It wouldn't take much to bring on another panic attack. Thank goodness I carried the flask with me.

I did see them lurking on our street. I snuck out the back door to leave for school and parked the VW bus a couple of blocks away. I don't think they followed me, but unfortunately, people noticed those red VW buses. They weren't inconspicuous drab-colored sedans.

I hoped my little act as the stupid drudge fooled Rockwell, but they had found the blond wig and the dress I'd worn and knew someone in the house was the blond flirt who brought them pizza. What if they couldn't believe it was me, the drudge, who was the blond bimbo? I felt the conflict. What woman likes to be dismissed like that, especially when she knew she could be a *femme fatale?*

.Rockwell wasn't stupid. He'd only seen me once, though, and hadn't seemed too interested in me when he visited us, so maybe I was safe. Comforting to think so.

I joined Mike at his occasional Esperanto meetings held at Kay's house, but I didn't risk going to the weekly evening classes in the library. The language was easy to learn—all regular verbs and familiar root words that developed into a large vocabulary with prefixes and suffices. The Esperantists were interesting folk with their own eccentric ideas. One of them, for instance, had an extensive library in his home which he categorized by book height. Mike was an adept teacher and got along well with the students who came to his classes.

That evening, Mike returned home from an Esperanto class with a woman about my age, who introduced herself as Sally Ann Bennett from Columbia, South Carolina. She had a soft Southern accent, and she was beautiful with violet eyes like Elizabeth Taylor. Her dark hair was cut in a pageboy style with a pink ribbon and bow across the top. She wore a frilly pink, full-skirted dress with pink shoes. The whole package reminded me of a treacly Snow White from Disney.

Sally Ann showered her charms and attention on Mike. Stacked up against her, I had no chance to interest Mike unless, against my observations, she somehow was not attracted to Mike. I gave up that idea as we sat in the living room after dinner. Sally Ann claimed to be thrilled about learning such a made-up language, hanging onto Mike's every word, and talking about visiting Esperantists around the world. I had said that, too, in earlier conversations, when Mike told me about the Esperanto directory with its international listings of contacts and clubs. Esperanto connections sounded like an appealing way to visit another country—if I learned to speak the language.

At first, she amused me, but then I found her more and more boring as she became a fixture in the living room every evening. Then she started coming earlier, and Mike paid Hannah extra to let her join us for dinner. Her presence and her conversational style annoyed me. They changed the comfortable ambiance we had all established together. She was as Southern and as gushy as crinolines and rattlesnakes. I didn't trust her and hoped Mike used caution in talking to her.

Mike was a tall and handsome man with a good sense of humor and gregarious manner. I liked him, but for her it seemed to be an instant attraction. He lapped it up and forgot I was there.

Mike and I settled into being friends, just friends, which was fine with me, especially since he found Sally Ann so alluring. The man had no taste. Sometimes I caught him staring at me with an odd expression, but that meant nothing. I guess we were both too involved in our own lives. He certainly was.

Walking down the street, even with Mike, was risky with Rockwell's thugs waiting nearby. All they needed was to accost us with a gun and push one of us into their car for a ride to Hatemonger Hill.

Why didn't they try that? They knew Sean and I were connected. They couldn't be sure about any of the others, or how close we were. If they kidnapped me, could they use me to trap Sean when he came to the rescue, or would Sean care?

Clark was Sean's brother. They could reasonably expect Sean to pay a ransom or try to rescue Clark if they kidnapped him. It would be difficult because Clark rarely left the house unless he was with Ellen.

Horace was also a fixture in our living room in the evenings. He arrived shortly after dinner with a book and sat quietly in a chair reading until around ten p.m., when he'd tuck the book into his satchel and quietly depart.

No one reported being accosted on the way to or from our house. I wondered why.

Chapter 23

I relayed the news about Rockwell's visit to the Hortons and Gail but hadn't heard from Sean. As long as he stayed hidden, I hoped he'd be okay. How long that would be, I didn't know, but I had to live under this cloud. Rockwell would never forget or forgive the robbery.

And maybe the ethical dimensions of what we'd done would always bother my conscience.

I varied my schedule and used the back alley to shake off the watchers. I had to attend class, and I had to stay at the house for Kay, so I couldn't hide away like Sean.

Sean found a room in another house, different neighborhood, and I missed his banter and presence at the dining room table. I didn't see much of Tanya. I suspected she was spending her free time in Sean's company. Their romance must be difficult. Where could they go? What could they do without the danger of harassment or worse? What did Cole and Alice think?

A week passed without drama. I became careless. I walked out the front door, absorbed in talking with Mike as we headed down the street to my car. I waved goodbye to him, and he walked on to a bus stop. I climbed into Kay's bus and drove toward the university. In my rear-view mirror, I saw a battered sedan pull out to follow me down the street. Two dark shapes huddled in the front seat. Hard to make out more than that in the car traveling behind me, but I knew they must be Rockwell's storm troopers.

I locked all the doors on the bus as I slowed to turn right down Mt. Pleasant Street to merge onto Sixteenth Street. They scared me. What would they do? Were they planning to rear-end me? Kidnap me? Shoot me? No, they wouldn't shoot me. They wanted the money back. Kidnapping and torture were probably their aim. I had to lose them.

What should I do? Pull into a police station? Fire station? Emergency room? Hospital? Abandon the car and run inside? I didn't know where to locate any of these places in downtown D.C. I never had reason to find out before. Even if I did, parking would be problematic, and I'd have to run from the bus and through the front door before Rockwell's men caught me. If I made it to the university, what then? Once I parked my vehicle in a lot and got out to walk the mile to class, I'd be easy pickings.

I kept my eyes on the rear-view mirror. They were still on my tail. Why didn't they hit Kay's bus in the rear or push me off the road like in the movies? They must be waiting for a better place to do their dirty work. I had to lose them. I began looking for opportunities.

I slowed down as I saw a green light ahead. The car behind had to slow down, too. I approached the light as it turned yellow and slowed even more. As it turned red at Sixteenth and K Streets, I accelerated and turned right. With impatient cross-traffic crowding behind me and between me and my pursuers, they were forced to stop. I had a minute to get lost. I sped down K Street but had to wait for a light at Connecticut Avenue. Their car was a block behind. I took a right turn several streets down and then took the next left into an affluent residential neighborhood and pulled into a parking space. Not the best idea. They were following too close behind and drove up alongside, blocking me in.

They leered at me as they got out of their car, but I had already slid to the passenger seat and spilled out onto the sidewalk, shedding my scarf and coat. Being a distinctive blue and red plaid, the coat would flag me wherever I went. I ran.

I heard their pounding feet behind me. The neighborhood was one of large houses with ivy-covered fences and locked gates.

No place to hide. I looked back to see them gaining on me. I needed to find a cab or a bus stop, but first I needed to lose Rockwell's men. I searched desperately for a way out.

I ran through a barrier for a road construction project, leaped across a puddle, and skidded on loose gravel but didn't fall. The men behind me were out of shape and not as agile. Frank slipped on the gravel and fell. Ted was too close behind to avoid tumbling over Frank. They both sprawled on the sidewalk. I ran faster, dodging into an alley. Trash and garbage cans lined up on each side meant today was pickup day.

Most of the gates into the tiny backyards were closed and probably locked, but one was partly open. I'd lost Frank and Ted, so I slipped inside the gate, closed it, and hid behind boards under the steps leading down from a deck. I sat on an old box, trying to calm my breathing and listening for Frank and Ted. I stayed there for more than an hour, stomach clenched and breathing in gasps, without hearing them.

I was several blocks away from busy Connecticut Avenue where buses and cabs would be plentiful. I walked in that direction, shaking with fear and taking the alleys behind the houses, hoping not to meet Rockwell's men or a mugger. A half-hour later, with no sign of them, I walked on to Connecticut Avenue and hailed a cab to take to the university. Sitting in class would be safe enough, but after that terrifying morning, I headed first to the ladies' room. I felt calmer, but I still drank two swigs of vodka. I feared an out-of-control panic attack and not only from the claustrophobia of feeling trapped in a class.

The vodka helped, but it wasn't the vodka that kept the panic at bay during my classes. I had survived an attack from Rockwell's men. Sitting in class felt safe and even comforting. I relaxed and reflected with pride how I outwitted my would-be attackers. I had a good plan for getting home safely, too. As the vodka took hold, my usual fears ebbed away as I congratulated myself on having survived so far. I enjoyed my classes without the sweating anxiety and compulsion to escape I usually endured. I was ashamed that I suffered the claustrophobia and the panic, so I told no one about them. I hoped they'd go away in time.

When I left the university, I kept my eyes open for a rusting rattletrap or two out-of-place strangers. I hoped they had lost patience by now. I didn't see any odd strangers, but I stayed with a crowd of students until I saw a cab, then hailed it and hastily climbed in.

Were Rockwell's men watching Kay's VW bus? They knew I had to come back for it. I'm sure they noted the license tag number and now would know Kay's bus wherever I parked it. I asked the driver to creep down the street, so I could look for Rockwell's men in the cars near mine. I saw nothing to worry me, and the bus was where I'd left it. As I paid the cab driver, I surveyed the area but again saw nothing unusual. I left the cab and dashed for my vehicle, getting in quickly and locking the doors.

I headed home to Kilbourne Place. My plan was to park on another street a couple of blocks away, then walk down the alleys to the back door of Kay's house. That plan almost worked, but when I walked into the alley behind Kay's house, I saw a man leaning against the backyard fence. Waiting.

I retreated. Where was his partner? Obviously, he was covering the front of the house. I stood on the corner uncertainly, debating what to do.

If they had guns, which I supposed they did, then to call on Clark or Mike or Ellen to come out and escort me would put them into danger. Ditto with Stuart and Cole. Maybe even more so with them since they were colored.

All I needed was a safe way to get through the front door and into the house. I retreated to the corner coffee shop and mulled over the problem until I came up with a solution. I called the house and made sure Clark would be waiting to open the door for me. Then I walked over to Sixteenth Street and hailed a cab. "Kilbourne Place," I said, "I'll show you the house."

I was already inside the cab when he objected to the short distance and low fare. "I'll tip you five dollars," I said, and that settled the matter. "Take the side streets to get onto Kilbourne Place from the other direction." That put me on the same side of the street as the house, ensuring a quick flight into it if Clark did what I asked.

In a few minutes we arrived. I saw one of Rockwell's men standing at the lamppost across the street. Clark waved at me from the door. I paid the driver, ran up the steps, and Clark opened the door. I ran through it, and he locked it behind me.

"Thank you, Clark. It's been a harrowing day." I sank onto the couch. He handed me a hot cup of tea.

"Thought you'd want this," he said.

His thoughtfulness surprised me, but I sipped it gratefully. I was home. Safe.

"What happened?" he asked.

I waved the question away and took another sip of tea. "Be careful," I said. "Dangerous men are after me and your brother and you, too, by association. Keep your eyes open. You should stop going on your treasure hunt until we're through this, and they've given up."

"No way," said Clark. "They don't want me, and with Horace's help, I'm sure we're close to finding the treasure. I'm not giving that up."

Chapter 24

March 6. 1964.

The next day, I feared another threat and debated what to do. I dared not take Kay's bus. I was lucky yesterday, but they'd be watching out for that kind of ruse today. Instead, I called for a cab and when it arrived, ran to the car and climbed inside. "University of Maryland, please," I told the driver. As he sped away, I looked back to see an old car—I recognized the rattletrap—pull out and follow, the shapes of two men in the front seat watching us.

What would they try this time? It wasn't just me now; it was also the cab driver. "The car behind is following us," I said.

"You kidding me?" asked the driver. He glanced in his rear-view mirror. "Let me check this out."

We were driving north on Sixteenth Street. He turned right on Monroe Street, then left on Fourteenth Street for a few blocks, then took a left on Meridian Street to get back to Sixteenth Street. He drove leisurely, so a follower would have no trouble keeping us in sight. When we turned again onto Sixteenth Street, they were still behind us.

"I guess you're right," said the driver. "Like the movies. What do you want me to do?"

"Lose them," I said. Rockwell's men didn't mind being spotted. They followed anyway. It was a case of intimidation until they turned it into...what? I didn't want to give them the opportunity. I felt the growing swell of panic. I needed to get some place safe, like in the middle of the campus.

I tried to sneak a drink from my flask, but the cab driver noticed it.

"Hey," he said, "you're too young to get into that stuff. It's a bad habit to start, young lady."

I ignored him. He didn't know what I was dealing with. I looked behind. The men were still following us. "Can you lose them?" I asked again.

"Who are they? Your boyfriend and his buddy?"

I was so rattled, I gave it to him straight. "They're criminals, and they want to kidnap and torture me because they think I stole their money."

He was still driving as if there were no hurry or problem at all. "Whoa," he said. "That's some story."

"That's right. Can you lose those guys?"

"Did you do it?"

"No." This was technically true, since I only brought the drugged pizza. I didn't take the money out of the house and certainly didn't keep it for personal gain. It was a public service. Really. I had no problem with stretching the truth—all right, lying—to save my life.

"Okay, then, let's go. Hang on." The morning rush hour was long past. We approached a stretch of Sixteenth Street clear of traffic. In the middle of the block, the driver speeded up, and then with a show of skill and dexterity, he executed a perfect "J" turn so we were now headed in the opposite direction and passed the car following us. They tried to do the same, but it's a tricky maneuver, and they didn't have the skill to make it. Instead, they climbed the sidewalk and crashed into a light pole. "Too bad," I said, looking back at the crunched car. "Thank you."

"Used to be a cop." He glanced back at me. "Quit when the stress got to me."

"I've never seen anyone make that kind of turn."

"All in a day's work. On to the university." We arrived on the campus thirty minutes later. I gave him a big tip and my thanks. I would have kissed him.

I thought I'd need a few extra sips of vodka after the harrowing morning, but I felt so relieved at still being alive and well that I left the flask in my purse and sat through even my linguistics class without the crippling panic. If a scary cab ride was what it took to cure me, then maybe I should hope for more.

I expected some trouble on my way home late that afternoon and called Clark to be ready to open the door for me. When the cab pulled up in front of my house, Clark had the door open. I saw no rattletrap, and no one waited outside for me. I ran inside without a threat.

Who should I talk to about the men following me? I couldn't go to the police. They'd start asking questions. Was there anything the Hortons, Mike, or Clark could do? I didn't want Rockwell's' boys to learn I had a connection with the Hortons. No telling what they would think was okay for punishing colored people who had the nerve to steal from Rockwell. The Hortons were busy with their lives. They'd done their part, and that was it for them.

Sean was out of the picture. I shouldn't drag Ellen into this. Gail had offered, but she was busy with her master's degree program at American University. Clark was useful, and I counted on him to open the door for me to dash in from the cab.

The only one I might have told was Mike, but Sally Ann had captured his interest and attention. I did not want to interfere and refused to be jealous. Anyway, he was likely to be patronizing and going to him for help would open that door.

Maybe crashing their car into a light pole put those thugs out of commission for a while. The strategy for getting into the house worked well. I kept their attempts to kidnap me to myself for another day until I saw what happened next. I was proud of myself for outwitting those Nazi storm troopers so far. I was a thief and a *femme fatale*, and I could outwit kidnappers. Kudos to me.

Sally Ann joined us again for dinner that evening. Gail rolled her eyes when she saw her. So did I. Ellen didn't seem to care, maybe because Sally Ann showed no interest in Clark. Sally Ann pounced on me, asking me about my classes and how I enjoyed going to the University of Maryland.

I was noncommittal.

"Must be a long trip from here," Sally Ann said. "How do you get there?"

I hedged. "I take all kinds of transportation. Car, bus, cab, whatever strikes my fancy that day. The trip's not bad, and I'm usually driving against traffic."

"Mike says you take a cab every day," she said. "Must be expensive."

I glanced at Mike. He shrugged.

"Sometimes I do." I saw Clark wanted to butt in. I didn't want him talking about our front door strategy, so I changed the subject. "Are you getting anywhere with your search?" I asked him.

"I think we're on the verge," he answered, fingering his beard, red with spaghetti sauce. "Any day now."

"Horace is a big help," added Ellen, handing Clark a napkin and motioning to his beard.

"Where do you go, exactly?" asked Sally Ann. "What are you looking for?"

"Nothing that would interest you," said Ellen quickly.

Clark wiped his beard and started to speak, but then he saw Ellen's expression and stopped. He repeated her words instead. "That's right," he said. "Nothing that would interest you."

That evening my mother called. I answered the phone and heard a gasp, then silence. Finally, she whispered, "Is that really you, Sue?"

"Of course. What's up?" Mom sounded weak and scared.

"Thank God," she said. "Thank God. Are you sure you're all right? You're not hurt?" Now she spoke fast and breathlessly, the way she did when she was anxious and upset.

"I'm fine," I said. "Are you okay?"

"Someone played a mean trick on us," Mom said. "We received a phone call from a man who said you were critically injured and in the hospital. Your Dad is packing the car now. I called Kay's house to find out where you were. Thank God you're okay, but who would try a heartless trick like that?"

I knew who would do that. "All kinds of jerks out there," I said. "Sorry you had such a scare, but I'm all right. No accidents. No injuries. No need to worry."

"Good thing I called," she said, "before we got on the road."

After a few more reassurances and exchange of news, I hung up. Calling my parents was a warning to me. Rockwell showing he not only knew who I was, he also knew where my parents lived. Terrifying me was bad enough, but to rope in my parents was despicable. He was despicable. No surprise.

My parents lived in Western Maryland, at least seventy miles from the D.C. area but still not that far away. If Rockwell's men couldn't get at me, would they attack my parents? They were desperate and angry and attached a religious fervor to their mission. We thought we were justified in robbing them. The way they were threatening me made me think hijacking, kidnapping, and probably torture were all on their agenda.

Rockwell wanted his money back. I'd been lucky to escape his men so far, but I was angry and scared.

Chapter 25

March 7, 1964.
The next day I took the cab, and no one followed. I didn't trust the euphoria that kept me off the vodka yesterday to get me through classes today—especially after hearing from my mother. I swallowed a couple swigs before each class and sat through them comfortably. I didn't see any threats on the trip home either. No one waited outside the house, but Clark was at the door and opened it for me. I didn't much care for the man, but he had his uses.

What was Rockwell's next move? I didn't believe he'd given up on us, but he might have decided grabbing me on the trip to and from school wouldn't work. I hoped so, but I worried about my parents.

The next morning was a different story. I called for a taxi. It showed up. I searched the street both ways, saw no threat, and ran out to the cab, climbed in, and pulled the door shut. The driver drove toward Sixteenth Street but stopped at the corner. Another passenger tried for the back seat, saw my books cluttering the space, and got in the front seat with the driver. Too late, I recognized squinty-eyed Leon. He turned around to look at me, and he pulled out a gun, pointing it at my face.

"Don't try any tricks," he said. "I've got the gun here, and I'm ready to use it." Another car pulled up alongside. Leon hid the gun. "I can bring it up and shoot you in a flash if I need to," he said.

The cab driver glanced back at me with a grin. Ted. "Got you now," he crowed. "How about some pizza?" He chuckled as he raced down Sixteenth Street on his way, no doubt, to Hatemonger Hill.

At first, I was too stunned to think. Leon meant what he said. I fought down the terror and closed my eyes. I took several deep breaths to calm myself. I had to escape before we got to Hatemonger Hill, but I had no chance if I let the panic take control. Think, Sue, think.

The cab alternately speeded up and then screeched to a halt to stop for red lights or traffic. Leon saw me glance at the door. "Don't even think about it," he snarled.

What could I do? If they got me to Hatemonger Hill, they'd kill me after the torture. Think, Sue, think. I was trapped. Closed in. A panic attack loomed. Could I use it? Could this bane of my life be useful for something? Worth trying. I had nothing else.

I began panting and trembling. I gagged as if I were choking. Crossed my eyes. "I'm panicking," I gasped and grabbed my throat. "I'm gonna die!" Leon shrank back, but he still held his gun on me. Ted at the wheel slowed as he glanced at Leon and then back at me. "What's going on?"

"Keep going!" yelled Leon. "Shit!"

"I'm going to throw up!" I grabbed at the door, feeling for the handle. "I'm gonna die! Help me! Help me!" I dragged my fingernails on the window.

"Shit," said Leon. "Shit, shit, shit." He still had the gun, but he turned it around to use the butt as a club, hitting at me. Rockwell wanted me alive.

I reached over to Ted and pulled at his shirt collar. "Help! Help me! I gasped.

"Get her off me," yelled Ted. He'd slowed down even more as I tugged his head back by the hair. "Ow, ow, ow! She's got my hair!" He struggled to steer the car.

"Air, I need air. Let me out!" I began screaming hysterically and let go of Ted's hair.

"Get her under control," ordered Ted as he hunched over the wheel to get away from my hands.

"You try that!" retorted Leon, shouting above my screams. "She says she's dying. She's grabbing at me. I think she's choking to death."

"Holy shit," said the driver. "What should we do?" He glanced back again. Leon struck out at me with his gun. I blocked his blows with my arms, but they hurt, and I screamed even louder. "Air! I need air!"

"Don't shoot her!' the driver said. "Rockwell needs her!"

"I know!" Leon yelled, still hitting me with his gun, but the angle was awkward since he had to turn around in the front seat to get at me. The blows from the gun kept me from reaching Ted. If I could cause an accident, they might crash their heads against the dashboard. I might draw enough attention to get away. I might get hurt, too, but I had to take the chance.

Acting even more panic-stricken, I dodged the gun and grabbed at the driver's collar, pulling it hard to choke him. The cab swerved from side to side. I screamed, "Help! Help! I'm dying!" I added more heavy panting and gasping. I'd seen an asthma attack once. I mimicked that but added more screams, grabbing, scratching, pulling. I was a wildcat. I'd watched an ordinary house cat attack a large dog once. The cat won. Right now, I was that cat.

With the driver screaming and Leon struggling to get past my hysterics, alternately using the gun as a barrier or a club to push me away, we traveled down the road at an ever slower pace.

Suddenly, I let go of the men and Leon's head hit the dashboard hard. Ted's hit the wheel. I grabbed my book bag and purse, opened the door, and fell out, landing hard on the swale and rolling away from the road. The cab pulled over and stopped, but I scrambled to my feet and ran, hearing them in pursuit.

We'd gone over a bridge, so I was in Arlington, Virginia. I ran for a gas station a block away, dodging the few cars on the road and leaving Ted and Leon gasping for breath behind me. Poor nutrition. Little exercise. They sat on the porch all day. They were way out of shape.

But what kept me alive was the information they needed from me. Where was the money?

When I reached the gas station, I took refuge inside the garage, nodding to the mechanic. From there I saw Leon and Ted return to the cab and rip rubber from their tires as they squealed away. I walked straight to the phone booth outside and called for a cab, but this time, I took a close look at the driver and his license before I climbed in.

As the cab drove away with no sign of the storm troopers, I calmed down. We headed to the university. By the time I arrived an hour later, I found myself chuckling to myself. The panic that crippled me had its uses. Another point for our team, but I'd made fools of Leon and Ted, and they'd have to answer to their boss man, Rockwell. He would not be pleased.

Chapter 26

March 9, 1964.

Despite our cautions to be careful and watch out for strangers, Clark and Ellen drove off every weekend as usual on their search for Mosby's treasure. I wasn't about to let them drive Kay's VW bus, but Ellen's mother's car was now on a month's loan to Ellen to use in the search. With Clark's permission, Ellen told her parents about this treasure hunt, and they were eager to help.

Clark used a metal detector and also maps for the search, and the two intrepid treasure seekers returned on Sunday evenings filthy and exhausted.

Horace now accompanied them, too. Even with Horace's dubious help, they had yet to find the treasure, but the search kept them out of the house, for which I was grateful. I liked the quiet and peace when everyone left the house. That was another reason why the chaotic dorm situation was not for me. Gail was away much of the time, but I barely noticed her when she was around.

The only person I would have enjoyed staying home with was Mike, but he worked through the lunchtime at some restaurant downtown, came home to nap or to study, then left for his university classes most evenings. Once a month he got together with his fellow Esperantists at Kay's house for a meeting, and he held an Esperanto class weekly at the library down the street. I sat in on the meetings even though I had to watch him simpering over Sally Ann's feeble attempts to learn the language.

Kay's stipend for watching the house meant I could afford the cab to and from the university while Rockwell's siege continued. I kept a vigilant eye out for his surveillance team, but if they were there, I didn't see them. I called for a Yellow Cab each morning and checked out the driver and his taxi permit before getting in the car.

Rockwell's thugs may hide, but they were not giving up. The telephone harassment continued, and we kept the phone off the hook now, but it was a great inconvenience for all of us. We put it back on the hook when we needed to make a call, but if we forgot to take it off again, we'd get another harassment call. This was grating on all our nerves. Eventually, they'd grow tired of the harassment and quit, but how long would that take?

Stuart or Cole strolled our street each evening to look for watchers in cars with Virginia license plates. We were careful to make sure Rockwell didn't know the Hortons were involved with the theft. They were ordinary residents and less than ordinary to him since they were colored. Each day they returned from their walk and called us with a negative report.

"No watchers?" I asked. What did Rockwell have up his sleeves now? "No cars with a Virginia license plate?"

"That's right," said Cole. "He's planning something."

"I think so, too."

Rockwell and his storm troopers wouldn't give up the fight for the $150,000. That money represented freedom from debt, a jump start for his campaign, and maybe a few meals for the men. He desperately needed it, so what was he doing?

A sneaky suspicion grew in my mind. The worst student in Mike's Esperanto class was Sally Ann. She feigned an interest, but she didn't put much work into learning the language. Mike was infatuated with her, and she led him on, but she seemed most interested in coming to our house for dinner. Hannah's cooking was good, but not that good, and I was seeing altogether too much of Sally Ann.

Was she a stooge for Rockwell? Why would he stop the harassing phone calls and surveillance unless he had an alternate plan, like maybe bringing in a plant to spy on us? Sally Ann had shown up at the library Esperanto class a couple of days after Rockwell visited the house.

Or was I jealous and wanting a reason to get rid of her? I examined my feelings carefully and decided I probably was a little jealous, but not that jealous. Right now, with all my worries about Rockwell, my panic attacks, and my classes, I was too over-whelmed to add romance or jealousy to the list.

What I needed was evidence, hard evidence she was con-nected to Rockwell. Since I had none, I kept quiet and dropped out of the Esperanto meetings. I claimed I had too much home-work. Sadly, Mike didn't seem to mind, but when the inevitable happened as I was sure it would, I'd be there to pick up the pieces if he let me.

Clark was getting on my nerves, too. He was always in the house, coming downstairs late every weekday morning, flopping down on the couch, and checking his pulse. Occasionally, he ven-tured out to look for a job but wore outlandish clothes together with greasy hair and unbrushed teeth. Why would anyone hire him? He never took a shower, either, that I heard unless it was late in the day when I was in class.

But Ellen and Clark got along fine. I was glad.

I still worried about Sean and missed his presence at the house, but so far nothing had happened. When the House of Representatives passed the Civil Rights Bill on February 10, Alice and Cole held a celebratory dinner at their house. It was prema-ture, but waiting for the Senate to begin the process on the bill seemed interminable.

Spring had arrived, and the forsythia and daffodils cast their yellow blooms everywhere. I felt as if I were waiting for a bomb to go off. Rockwell hadn't shown up again with more threats, but I was sure he hadn't gone away. Meanwhile, I continued to take cabs to and from classes and kept a wary eye on my surroundings.

Today I'd come home from class and was relaxing with a cup of tea as I looked through the front window and scanned the street for Rockwell's men. I saw Mike sprint down the street, climb the front steps, and bounce through the front door. No one else was around. I asked him to grab a cup of coffee and join me in the living room.

"Sure," he said and was back in a few moments, cup in hand. "What's up?"

"We haven't seen Rockwell and his men for days now," I said, starting slowly to test the waters.

Mike nodded as he sipped the coffee. "What will he do next? It is not so easy to give up 150 Gs."

"I wonder about that, too," I said. "I have an idea, though."

"What is that?" Mike sat back with a quizzical look on his face.

"I want you to consider this," I said carefully, "and don't take it wrong, okay? This is only a possibility."

He glanced at his watch. "Lay it on me."

"I don't think he's given up, do you?" I asked.

"No, I do not. He wait his time while his guys search for Sean. You, also, but you outsmart them." He grinned at me.

"Yes," I said, "but here's an alternative idea. Do you suppose he's planted a spy in our group?"

"A spy?" Mike pursed his lips. "But no new people stay here. Who would be spy?"

I waited.

He stared at me. "You do not mean...you do not suggest...?"

"What do you know about her?" I asked.

He thought a moment, started to say something, and then stopped. Finally, he said, "Nothing. I know nothing about her except she like Esperanto. She is like you say, enthusiastic."

"Seems to be enthusiastic," I amended.

"All right. She seems to be enthusiastic." Mike leaned back and stared at the ceiling. "She is a nice person," he said.

I nodded. "And you like her," I said. "Does she give you any opinions about civil rights or current events? Show any prejudices? Tell you anything that might give you an idea of what she thinks?"

"She like all of you," Mike said. "She enjoy coming over here and like to have the dinner with us."

"Have you told her anything about us?"

Mike sat up, his eyes wide. "No, no, nothing like that. Hannah stay at dinner so we don't say nothing much then. After dinner, Clark and Ellen work on their project. They not know much about what we did, so conversation is more general unless Clark bring up Mosby and his treasure. She is not much interested in that."

"Okay," I said, feeling relieved. "And she hasn't tried to pump you?"

Mike shook his head. "You say pump? Like gasoline pump? Like she pretend I am gasoline pump? Not for gas, but for what we do here?"

"I'm probably wrong about her," I said. "Please be careful, though, what you say around her. Just in case. I am afraid of Rockwell."

"I am, too," said Mike. "I will backpedal with her. Not say much. No tip-offs, eh?" He laughed. "Anyway, her enthusiasm is a bit too much sometimes, a bit too much fake, and she does not say nothing about herself. Too gushy, my opinion."

"You know best," I said, keeping my elation under control. "We know Rockwell is desperate for that money. He's tried reasoning with us, threatening us, robbing us, chasing me, and watching the house. He's not going to give up until he gets that money back."

"Which he will never do," said Mike. "because none of us have it. He is up creek with no paddle."

Chapter 27

I felt better after talking with Mike. Maybe Sally Ann was all he thought she was. Maybe she was enthusiastic about Esperanto. Now that Mike was on his guard, and we all made sure the conversation at Kay's house was innocuous, with no references to any robberies, she had nothing to take back to Rockwell.

Since we carried off the theft successfully and had sent the money to the civil rights organizations, we had no reason to speak of it. We pretended to forget about that entire episode. I wished. Rockwell would never get the money back. Now we only talked about and worked for the Civil Rights Bill and hoped that all our contributions, even the illegal ones, helped.

Sally Ann didn't say much during our conversations, but I could tell she listened. Intently listened. It was hard to gauge where she stood on civil rights, but her Southern accent gave us a clue. She continued to appear at dinner, and Mike continued to date her, so I guess she said all the right things—to him. I pretended not to care.

By the end of March, with no new harassments from Rockwell, I was immersed in my classes but also keeping up on the news about the filibuster in the Senate. It was a ploy to prevent senators from acting on the Civil Rights Bill. Somehow, Vice President Humphrey and Senator Mansfield had to find a way to prevent the filibuster from succeeding. I felt pretty glum about their chances for that.

I knew Aunt Kay would approve of my letting two seminary students stay at the house as they lobbied for the bill. They were out all day, coming home to join us for dinner and later camping out in the living room in sleeping bags. In fact, supporters of the bill in the district, Maryland, and Virginia were providing room and board to the people pouring in from all over the country to support the bill. And that included grown working women with high-level jobs who should not have to procure a man's signature on the loan when they bought a house or car or anything else. They deserved equal pay, too.

Rockwell had come by twice to repeat his threats, and no one allowed him into the house. He wasn't as harsh as he'd been before. It was almost as if he'd given up but kept coming by with the threats to intimidate us. I suppose he hoped we would cave, but his appearances were for show. I doubt he'd given up but was relying on his stool pigeon Sally Ann Bennett to find out where the money was.

Ethically, of course, we were wrong to rob him. The news hadn't reported him breaking any laws. His storm troopers had beaten up Mike and Stuart and may have murdered Darrell, but they were acting on their own. Being bullies. Only because we had robbed Rockwell of desperately needed cash had he resorted to criminal behavior himself that we knew of. The FBI suspected him of bombing a synagogue in 1958, but suspicion doesn't convict. Our wrongdoing had a ripple effect of more wrongdoing. On the other hand, our wrongdoing had a powerful result for good by supporting the Civil Rights Bill and diminishing the potential for Rockwell to do tremendous harm to millions of people.

I looked out the front window to see if any of his storm troopers were watching us. I didn't see them, but I did see Mike walking slowly toward the house. His head was down as if he were thinking hard or deeply troubled. What was wrong? I opened the door to him. I knew he'd been out with Sally Ann.

He closed and locked the door behind him and flung himself down on the couch.

"What's going on?" I asked.

"I don't know what to do," moaned Mike. "Sally Ann need money, much money." He heard my sharp intake of breath. "It is not what you think. She is desperate and not know what to do. So desperate she ask me, she beg me for help. Me! I am poor immigrant with no money."

I said nothing.

He looked at me from the couch. "How can I help? I work as waiter for tips. I pay to go to school and to stay here. I have nothing else. Nothing! Why would she think I have money to give her?"

"Why the desperate need for money?" I wouldn't ask anyone else, especially someone I was dating, for money, no matter how dire the situation. Would I? How bad would it have to get to do that?

"Not her. She need money for her parents in South Carolina. Her mom, she not work, and her dad laid off over a year ago. They cannot pay mortgage. They will lose their house if they not pay mortgage. Bad situation. Sally Ann very upset."

"I'm so sorry," I said. "I don't think any of us has the kind of money she's looking for."

"I know. I tell her that, and she get—got angry. Very angry. We never fight before." He sat up, put his elbows on his knees and shook his head. "Why does she think we have money?" he asked me with a hopeless shrug.

Here was another nail in her coffin. He'd figure things out, eventually. Why would she think a waiter-student or any of us would have the kind of discretionary income to bail out her parents? But if she thought she was consorting with thieves who stole $150,000, she might try angling for some of that money. If her story was sad enough, and we did have the money, wouldn't we want to help her out? Mike certainly would if he had the money. If we didn't cough up the money to help, would that convince Rockwell we didn't have the money and to quit threatening us?

None of us offered to help Sally Ann. Mike let her down gently but had no suggestions for her. She still showed up for dinners with us, and she and Mike continued to date, but she had taken on a forlorn air as if weighed down by her parents' dilemma and spoke of it often. She was fishing, but none of us was dumb enough to take the hook.

On the following Sunday afternoon, I had called my parents, so the phone was connected. Even though Rockwell's harassing phone calls had abated, we sometimes kept it off. This time as soon as I hung up the phone, it rang, and I answered it.

"Sue, thank God," Ellen sobbed into the phone.

Fear struck my heart. "What's happened?" I asked. "Are you hurt? Is Clark all right?"

"They took Clark!' she wailed. "They took him!" She gasped out the words as she cried. "What should I do? I don't know what to do. They've got him."

"Who has him? Where are you?" They were on one of their weekend hikes toward Culpeper, Virginia.

"I don't know," she wailed. "These three men stopped their car and called to Clark, acting like they knew him. Clark walked toward them to see what they wanted. Then they asked if he was Clark Wolfe, Sean Wolfe's brother." She sobbed. "He told them he was, and then one of them pulled a gun and told him to get in the car." She gasped, "Why? Why would they want him?"

"Calm down," I said, trying to reassure her. "I'm here. I'm coming out to get you. Did you say they asked for Clark? They knew his name?"

"Yes. Why would they do that?" Sue heard Ellen blow her nose. "We were hiking along a country road," she gulped, "toward Culpeper when this car drove up alongside. They had guns. Guns!" I heard her taking deep breaths.

"Calm down now," I said. "Then what happened?"

"They put him in the car and drove him away." She paused and hiccupped. She was taking deep breaths to gain control of herself.

I kept my voice calm. "Okay. They took him away. Are you okay?"

"I'm okay. It's Clark." Her voice rose. "They've got Clark!"

"Did you call the police?" I asked.

"No," she hesitated. "They told me not to. They said they'd

hurt him bad if I did."

"Did you see who they were?"

"They wore some kind of uniform, but they were dirty."

Storm troopers. Rockwell had Clark. They'd stepped up their game. Doggone it. I told Clark to be careful. Then I remembered Clark pulling out the Virginia map and bragging about his success in finding the probable route Mosby used. We tried to hush him up since Sally Ann was there and listening, but he was too excited. He even mentioned the main road they'd be checking out this weekend. Sally Ann, I remembered, was most interested, and she asked questions. Clark loved the attention.

"Okay. Tell me where you are, and I'll come get you."

"I'm at a pay phone in a country store." She was crying again but managed to give me directions. "I need a ride back to my car," she said. "And help driving it home. I'm so upset and worried, I'm shaking. I'll have an accident for sure. Why did those men take Clark? They didn't ask anything about the treasure or even look through our stuff."

"Is Horace with you?" I asked.

I heard her speak to someone and then come back to the phone. "He's here, but he doesn't drive."

"How do I get to that store?" I asked. "Give me directions."

I wrote them down and glanced at my watch. "It'll take me an hour to get there," I said. "Take it easy. Try to relax. We'll get Clark back okay."

She sniffed up a hiccup. "Okay," she said, her voice quavering.

"I'm on my way," I told her, but first I needed to talk to the Hortons and Mike if they were home. I called upstairs to Mike, but he was out. I didn't know where, work, class, he had a lot going on. I hoped he wasn't with Sally Ann. She heard enough about Clark and Ellen's project at dinner and probably told Rockwell all about it. He knew Clark was Sean's brother, and he saw the possibility. What would they do with Clark? I felt afraid for him. Alice invited me in next door. Cole sat in a chair reading the newspaper. "What's up?" he asked.

"They've kidnapped Clark." As I said the words, a dark

cloud settled on my shoulders. I raised my eyes to look at him. This was terrible, and I didn't see how we were ever to get Clark out of this alive. We couldn't pay ransom, whatever it was, and Rockwell would probably demand $150,000.

Cole put the paper aside. "They've stepped up their game, I see."

"We've got to get Clark away from them." I wrung my hands. "They insist we not notify the police."

"Was he out with Ellen?" Alice asked, taking a seat across from Cole. As usual, her face was impassive. She answered her own question. "Of course he was."

"And Horace. She called me. Mike's out somewhere. Gail's not home either." I hugged myself, feeling chilled all over.

"Okay." Cole stood. "You and I got to go out and get Ellen. You know where she's at?"

I nodded. "Let's go. We can talk on the way."

Cole drove his car. As I'd thought, the drive took about an hour. I felt terrified for Clark, but I worried about Ellen all the way, too. It was cold outside, too cold for hiking, I would have thought, but they were serious about their task.

As we drove out of D.C. and into Virginia, Cole and I discussed actions we might take. I thought we should call the police and put this in their hands. Rockwell had nothing on us, but he had kidnapped an innocent person.

If we brought in the police, what was the likely outcome? Had Rockwell hidden Clark somewhere we'd never find and claim ignorance or harassment? He'd say nothing about the robbery, knowing it would give him a motive for the kidnapping and open the door to embarrassing questions about the money. Would Rockwell kill Clark to teach us a lesson or start sending us body parts until we caved? Of course, we couldn't cave, since we had no money to replace $150,000.

We had to believe Rockwell had hidden Clark in his house. He'd warned us not to call the police and would bet that we wouldn't. We did call the police when his minions broke into Kay's house. It was necessary for the insurance but had no other result. He knew we wouldn't identify the culprits.

How could we give in to their demands? We had no way to return the money. I didn't think even the two-income Horton family had that kind of money to give to Rockwell. He was never going to get that $150,000 back.

Would Sean's friend, our informant, be able to free Clark? He was our best hope if he did work for the FBI. The FBI wouldn't want to take part in a kidnapping and possible murder, would they? Would they help us free Clark? That was the question.

So what were our alternatives? We could possibly exchange Clark for Sean, but that was unthinkable and would place Sean at risk. Was there any way for Sean to claim innocence and be believed? The van rental agreement and the woman's scribbling down the van's license tag number were damning.

What if we simply told Rockwell we stole the money and gave it to three civil rights organizations, so we couldn't give it back? What would he do besides rage at us in frustration and disbelief? Threaten us with execution when, in his fantasy life, he was elected president in 1972? He wouldn't wait that long. He'd enlist his storm troopers, the Ku Klux Klan, and their cronies in the police to kill us in revenge way before 1972. We'd be afraid to walk down the street with Rockwell's vendetta against us. Our saving grace, such as it was with the threats and attacks, was that Rockwell still thought we had the money, and he'd get it back from us if he applied the right pressure.

Another alternative was to rescue Clark. They must be keeping him prisoner in the Nazi Party headquarters we robbed. Rockwell didn't have the money to rent any other buildings. Someone had given him that house and its twenty-three acres for his cause. His minions would have Clark under heavy guard, probably mistreating him as well. I didn't want to use the stark word, "torture," but it stared me in the face.

"We're going to have to rescue him," said Cole decisively.

I agreed glumly, thinking of the old saying: "What a sticky web we weave when first we practice to deceive."

We followed Ellen's directions to the right road, and then traveled at a crawl, looking for her and Horace. We found them sitting forlornly on a log by the roadside. Ellen burst into tears the minute she saw us. "Thank God," she said. "Thank God. I don't know what to do."

We helped her into the car. Horace followed.

"Don't worry," I told her. "We're coming up with a plan to rescue him. We know who did this."

Ellen looked up from her tears. "You do? They said not to call the police."

"This won't involve the police," said Cole.

I looked at him. He made that statement calmly and reassuringly, as if it were a walk in the park. How were we to pull off a rescue? I was scared for myself, for Clark, and for all of us in this...this...adventure.

Chapter 28

I drove Ellen's car and followed Cole back to D.C., dropping Horace on Sixteenth Street. He protested, but we weren't about to bring him home and involve him in the discussion on what to do with Rockwell's latest attack. The less he knew, the better.

I parked her car two blocks away from Kay's house and walked, using the alley to the back of the house. Conscious of Rockwell's surveillance team possibly lurking outside, Cole dropped Ellen off on Sixteenth Street. He then drove to our street and parked in front of his place. Ellen walked down the alley to the house and met me at the gate.

We entered the house by the back door, and I immediately called Sean. A woman answered the phone, and I asked for Sean Wolfe. She yelled his name. The phone must be in the hall for everyone's use. Please be home, I prayed with my fingers crossed. In a couple of minutes, he came to the phone. I breathed a sigh of relief.

I told him the score, and we agreed to meet at a coffee shop near his house in an hour. We had no time to waste. I checked the front porch and door in case Rockwell had delivered a ransom demand. No sign of any such thing. Then I called Cole and told him about the arrangement. Ellen and I left by the back door and walked to Sixteenth Street. Cole picked us up there. Stuart and Alice came along. Sunday afternoon. Tanya was probably spending it with Sean. I glanced at Cole and Alice's stolid faces and wondered if they knew about the relationship and if they approved.

Cole took a circuitous route to the coffee shop to check for a tail. We were all on the lookout but didn't see any suspicious dodging and darting by a possible follower. That meant Rockwell's storm troopers had still not connected the Hortons with the robbery.

We found Sean at the back of the coffee shop in a large corner booth. As I suspected, Tanya was there, too. Only a few customers dotted the tables around the cafe on a late Sunday afternoon, so our booth was as private as it got in a public place.

Cole pulled out several Polaroid photos of the model of Rockwell's house and grounds. "You both know what we're dealing with," he said. "Sean's been in there, and so has Stuart. You have an idea of the lay of the land. How are we going to get Clark out of there?"

Sean looked at Ellen's white face. She was still shaken and scared. "Exactly what happened?" he asked.

She stared at her hands. "We were hiking as usual," she mumbled, "alongside the road, watching Horace with his divining rod, when these three goons pulled over and called to us. We stopped to see what they wanted, thinking they needed directions. Then one of them took out a gun, pointed it at us, and told Clark to get in the car.

"Did they say anything to you?" asked Sean. "Like what they wanted with Clark?"

Ellen took a deep breath. "They said not to call the police. They asked if Clark was Sean Wolfe's brother. Then they said you'd know what they wanted." She shuddered and wrapped her arms around herself. "It's cold in here, isn't it?"

I took off my coat and wrapped it around her. "All right," I said. "We know what they want, and we're going to find a way to handle this." I couldn't stop my voice from trembling, even though I tried hard to speak with confidence. I saw no way to deal with this latest attack on us, much less rescue Clark, who had nothing to do with our problem. And we had no money to return to Rockwell or bargain with him. We didn't even have a receipt to show them, as if that would make a difference. As far as I saw, we had nothing, and I was going to be dragged into this rescue attempt.

"You have to get Clark away from them," cried Ellen. "Give them what they want and get Clark back." She started to cry. "I can't bear it."

Sean reached over to her and took her hands in his. "Ellen," he said. "Clark's my brother, and I love him. I won't stand by and do nothing. We'll get him out of there, but you have to trust us."

I looked at him in surprise. He spoke as if there was no doubt we could rescue him. I had plenty of doubt.

"That's right," added Cole, watching Ellen. "But one thing you have to do is keep it quiet." His deep voice was stern. "Don't talk to anybody about this, you understand?"

"Especially Mike," I said, "or Sally Ann." She was behind this, I was sure. Everyone was so intent on Ellen, they didn't pick up on what I said. I was the only one suspicious of Sally Ann.

Ellen stared at our serious faces. "You're all involved in what happened to Clark? All of you?" She pulled her hands away from Sean and looked at Cole. "What's this about? What do they want with Sean? That's it, isn't it? They kidnapped Clark to get at Sean. Sean moved out, and they don't know where he is." Her eyes swept the table. "What's been going on?"

I looked at Sean and Cole. They should explain this, not me. I waited while the two men debated silently. Then Sean sighed. "We don't like Mr. Rockwell," he said.

"So? I only met him once, that time he came to the house, but neither do I," said Ellen. "He's a Nazi. Nobody likes him. So what?"

"We took something away from him that he wanted very much," said Sean. "And he thinks I'm the one who stole it."

"I see. Now he wants it back." She nodded, pulling the coat tighter around herself. "I wondered what all those secret meetings were about. Now I understand. That's what you've been planning all these weeks. Robbing Rockwell. The answer is simple then. Give the money back."

A glance passed among us. "We can't," I said.

"Why not?" asked Ellen.

I told her. "We gave it all away to a good cause."

"You gave it all away?" Ellen said. Her voice rang. "How much was it?"

"A lot," I said. "And we donated all of it anonymously to the NAACP, SNCC, and CORE."

Sean shook his head. "If word gets out," he said severely, "if you talk to anybody else, we'll lose Clark."

She suddenly laughed. "Rockwell will hate knowing what you did with his money. You should tell him." She looked at all of us, our faces tense and stern. "Okay, yes, I won't talk to anyone about this. If Clark was here and not with those Nazis, I might even applaud."

"We all want the Civil Rights Bill passed," I put in.

She nodded. "But you have to promise me, you'll get Clark back okay." She gripped Sean's hands. "You've got to get him back."

"We'll do that," said Sean before turning to the rest of us. "Now let's think about this situation."

Was it wise to talk in front of Ellen? She hadn't been in on any of our plans before. Could we trust her? I wanted her to leave, but no one else seemed bothered, and she stayed.

"What about your friend in Rockwell's house?" Cole asked Sean. "Can we call on him?"

"I'm setting up a meeting with him." Sean laughed humorlessly. "He's not too pleased with us right now, but I think he'll play. Kidnapping is going beyond their usual repertoire. If Clark keeps his wits and plays along with them, it'll go better for him. Thank goodness we're not Jewish or colored."

"But he knows nothing about this," said Ellen. "And neither do I. How can he play along? It's not fair. If he says the wrong thing or makes a mistake, what will they do?"

None of us wanted to answer that question.

"Can we get a message like that to him?" I asked. "Tell him to play up?"

"Probably not. I'm not even sure he's ever heard of Rockwell," Sean answered.

Ellen's eyes sparked. "Of course he has. That repulsive neo-Nazi grabs headlines." She frowned at us. "Remember? When he showed up at the house that night, he asked if Clark was Sean's brother. You must think Clark is stupid, but he's not. He's...he's brilliant."

I stared at her, dumbfounded at her take on Clark. This must be true love, I figured. She is talking about Clark, isn't she? I turned to the others.

"Okay, then." Cole spread out on the table the photos he'd brought. "Look at these," he said. "These houses usually have a basement, and I'll bet you a dollar that's where they've put him."

"But how are we going to get in there?" I asked. They cast speculative looks at me. I shook my head. "I'm not bringing them any more pizza."

"We've done the food bit," Tanya said and laughed humorlessly.

Even Sean mustered a grim smile.

"That's for sure," added Cole, his eyes roaming about the coffee shop. "Why would someone have to go to that house or get in? Something routine."

We stared at the photos and sat quietly a few moments, each of us trying to come up with an idea.

"Exterminator again?" suggested Tanya.

She was joking, but I wanted to scotch that idea for sure. "We've done that, and it won't work a second time." Then to make sure they understood, I said, "Another thing that won't work a second time is for me to take pizza to them, but somebody, not me, could take them Chinese carryout." A joke, but no one laughed.

"What about a plumber? Electrician?" suggested Alice. "Delivery?"

Then Cole snapped his fingers. "Meter readers. They've got to have meter readers. Those guys go around house to house, read the meters, take notes. I can do that. Nobody knows I'm connected to any of you and, anyway, they can't tell one colored person from another." He nodded to himself.

"Do meter readers wear uniforms?" I asked.

No one said anything for a moment. Then Cole shrugged. "Never noticed, but I'll wear a navy blue shirt with navy blue slacks. I'll have on a coat, too. It'll look enough like a uniform so's nobody'd notice. Anyway, meter readers go around with their notebooks, and nobody pays any attention to them. They're invisible. They might come one day and again the next, and no one will notice." He sat back with a grin on his face.

"So you go down the street checking meters and when you get to Rockwell's house, peer in the basement windows to see what the set-up is like," I thought it over. Seemed like an excellent idea. "Find out if it has a door to the outside. Maybe even see Clark."

Sean blinked. "She's right. It would only take a slight change in position to go from reading the meter to looking in the windows."

Cole nodded. "That's my thought."

"And even to getting into the basement," I said. "But there is one problem."

They looked at me. "What?" asked Sean.

"Their electricity is turned off. Been off for a year or so because of nonpayment."

Cole mulled that over. Finally, he said, "I don't think it matters. They could still send a meter reader to check on the house. If I'm challenged, I'll tell them there were queries about paying to turn it back on, imply they've got a benefactor willing to do that."

I nodded. "That might work."

"Good," Sean said. "Meanwhile, tomorrow morning, I'll check with my informant. He ought to know where Clark is. By noon, Cole will have been by, looked in the basement window, and we should have the situation nailed down. Then we'll plan a rescue operation for the afternoon."

Ellen's eyes had gotten bigger and bigger as she listened to us. "Who are you guys?" she asked. "You talk like you're experienced thieves and housebreakers."

"Don't worry. Cole was joking," Sean said. "We're on the side of the angels. Sometimes the angels need a little help, and that's what we've been doing. Helping the angels."

"This is extremely serious," I told her. "Don't go blabbing about any of this to anyone."

She frowned, still dubious. "But you will get Clark back okay and not hurt?"

"We will," said Sean. "We're not the bad guys here. Bad guys kidnap people; we don't."

Yeah, I thought. We only rob them of $150,000. We're modern-day Robin Hoods, all right.

Ellen shook her head, staring down at the table, pulling the coat even tighter around her shoulders.

"I think we're done for now," said Sean. "It's after six. We'll meet back here at noon tomorrow." He looked at Ellen. "You stay home," he said to her. "Be there when Clark arrives. You can handle phone calls and relay messages."

"When Clark arrives," she breathed. "You sound pretty optimistic."

"I am," said Sean, avoiding looking at any of us.

He was pretending to be optimistic for Ellen's sake, but I wasn't up to pretending. It was crazy to think we could rescue Clark out of a house filled with desperate men who had guns. None of us owned a gun, much less carried one. We didn't even have one pocketknife among us.

"But there's something else," I said. "Sally Ann Bennett."

They all looked at me with puzzled faces.

"Sally Ann?" said Ellen. "Mike's girlfriend?"

I nodded. "Think how she met Mike," I said. "And she wangled her way into having dinner with us and knows a lot about what we're doing. Not about the robbery, but about all of us. I think she's a stool pigeon for Rockwell."

"Yeah," Sean said, nodding his head. "Sue told me about her. She might be perfectly all right, but we can't take the chance." He glanced around the circle.

Nobody said anything, but I saw the idea clicking over in their minds. "And get this," I added, "she told Mike she needs the loan of a large sum of money to help out her parents."

"That's it," said Cole. "She's working for Rockwell. I don't know this young lady, but we can't let her find out what we're doing."

"That means," Sean added, "We keep Mike out of our plans. We can't tell him anything about this."

We agreed. I knew we had to keep Mike out of our plans, but a deep sadness fell over me at breaking up our group, and I worried about Sally Ann. "I had another thought about Sally Ann," I said. "Is there some way we can use her? If she does talk to Rockwell, we can plant a misleading seed."

We mulled over that possibility.

Cole looked at our faces. "That's a good idea, give her misinformation. Tell her Sean's gone to Alaska, maybe. Any story that will get Rockwell off our backs."

Sean laughed. "I like that Alaska idea, but Rockwell probably wouldn't buy it. We'll keep it under advisement. Something may turn up."

Chapter 29

March 30, 1964.

The next day at noon, the Hortons, Sean, and I met again at the coffee shop, seating ourselves in the back booth in front of the restrooms. It was lunchtime, and the tables were filling up. The talk was loud in the cafe. No one paid attention to us. As agreed, we left Mike out of this rescue attempt, since he seemed so smitten by his Southern bombshell, a person none of us trusted. Cole reported first.

"No problem cutting across the backyards to Rockwell's House. Nobody paid any attention to me."

"Were Rockwell's men on the porch out front?" I asked. They seemed to spend a lot of time there doing nothing.

"Two were on the porch, but I don't think they noticed me. I went right to the meter on the side of the house and near the back. There's a door out of the basement. It's in a well with steps up to ground level and a railing around the top except at the head of the steps. The basement also has three windows in wells. They're filled with leaves and trash, but the windows are large enough for Clark to crawl out if he's up to that."

Clark was on the heavy side. I couldn't imagine him climbing anything. "I think it has to be the basement door," I said.

Sean nodded. "He never was athletic. Hiking for Mosby's treasure is a stretch."

Cole turned to Sean. "What does our friend say?"

"Clark is in the basement, and he's tied up, sitting on the floor. Rockwell's men aren't too bright, and they're lazy, so they've organized a sporadic watch on Clark. Somebody goes down there every hour, checks on him, and comes back. Our friend says he will be the one who goes down there at three, and he'll loosen a couple of Clark's knots, unlock the back door, and return upstairs. The rest is up to us."

"Then here's my idea," I said. "Our meter reader can start a blaze on the opposite side from the basement steps, yell 'Fire!' then skedaddle to hide behind the next house. If he's challenged, he can say he made an error the day before, came back to check, and found the fire. He can pretend to look for something to put it out."

"Meanwhile, as soon as you hear 'Fire!' one of us goes down the stairs to the basement and gets Clark out," said Sean. "Then they run to Kay's bus on the side street bounding the property."

"I didn't see anybody around when I walked from house to house," added Cole. "I heard activity in some houses, Moms vacuuming and stuff; men are at work, I guess, and away during the day. Kids are in school." He pulled out the Polaroid photos. "You can see there's a house back here on the next road. I figure one car will park in front of that house."

I piped up. "I'll park Kay's bus there. Nobody can see it from Rockwell's house. I'll bring Sean and Stuart."

"That works," said Cole. "Alice will drive our car and meet you there. I'll get out and act like I'm walking from the next house over to Rockwell's place across the backyard. They don't know our Chevy sedan. It's like thousands around town. No one will notice it."

"What about me?" said Tanya. "I need a job to do."

"You stay by the phone at our house. If anyone needs help or gets separated, they call you."

Tanya pouted. "That's not exciting. I can do more."

"Yes, you can, but we need you and Ellen by the phones." Cole turned back to the rest of us. "I'll bring newspaper and matches, and I've got a few leftover fireworks." He pulled a string of short firecrackers out of his pocket. "Alice will go around the block and park in front of Rockwell's house." Alice objected, but he waved a hand. "Pretend you're looking at a map. Pull over but keep the motor going."

Sean nodded. "So we'll give Cole his two minutes, then Stuart and I will run over to the basement, wait for Cole to yell 'Fire!' and drag Clark out. We'll run to Sue's bus, and she can get us out of there."

Alice cast dubious eyes around the group. "Don't like this plan. Don't like it at all. Those Nazis got guns, and they wouldn't mind shooting the likes of us." She shook her head. "Too much can go wrong."

I agreed with her. "Can't we just report the kidnapping to the police?" I asked. "Rockwell has nothing on us. Not really."

I looked around the group, all of them waiting for someone to answer the question.

"Look," said Sean. "Cole's plan can work. It's quite simple, and we have our informant inside unlocking the basement door for us. If we don't get Clark out, then we contact the police. How about that?"

"Anyway," said Stuart, "we know where Clark is, and we know who the kidnappers are, and we know why. This isn't like the usual kidnapping of a kid where none of the victims or relatives know anything. Dad has a good plan. I think it will work."

Cole glanced at his watch. "We can't waste time debating this. We need to get on our way to be in place by three p.m."

"One more thing," said Alice. "Does everyone have change for a phone call to Tanya if necessary? What about cash for cab or bus fare? None of us know what will happen. Be prepared, I say."

We checked our wallets and quickly reshuffled the cash to make sure everyone had phone, bus, or cab fare plus extra to pay for Clark. Then, with severe misgivings, I trudged out of the coffee shop with the others.

At ten minutes before three p.m., Stuart, Sean, and I in Kay's bus and Cole and Alice in their inconspicuous sedan parked on the side street hidden from Rockwell's house for a last-minute check. I planned to stay there. From previous observation, we didn't expect Rockwell's men to saunter around the neighborhood. I looked between the neighbor's landscaping shrubs and found I could watch the back and side of Rockwell's house. Alice would drive around the block to pick up Cole down the street and in front of the house.

Cole folded the newspaper into a neat square he fit under his clipboard. He also rigged up a long fuse for the string of firecrackers.

"Be a miracle if that worked," he joked, "but if it does, it would add a lot to the distraction."

He pulled his shirt sleeve back from his watch and held it up. "Give me five minutes to walk over there, pretend to check the meter, then get around to the side and start the fire. I'll light the fuse to the firecrackers and set them down. Alice will drive around to stop a little past the house, so I can run from the side of the house to the car. I'll yell fire as I run, and Alice can honk the horn. She'll keep the engine going and move forward to the end of the block, so we can watch your car."

"Meanwhile, Stuart and I will run from Sue's car through the backyard and shrubbery to the basement stairs, get Clark, and dart back to the bus." Sean grinned. "Quick and easy. Sue can keep the motor going and be ready to move when we get Clark out."

Cole pursed his lips in and out before adding, "Alice and I will wait until we see your bus leave. If Rockwell's men spot us and come over to check us out, we'll drive away." He took a deep breath. "After that, you're on your own."

"We'll meet back at the coffee shop," said Stuart. "That way we can organize ourselves for the trip back to the house. You know Rockwell's men will be on our street, somewhere."

"Got it," said Sean. I watched him with misgivings. He thought this escapade was a great adventure. He thought nothing bad would happen to Clark. Not living at Kay's house insulated him from Rockwell's threats and attacks. Nobody had followed or kidnapped him. Rescuing Clark without a hitch would be a miracle.

Cole leaned forward. "Don't be so cocky. We can't let them get a chance at you or Sue. They're onto her despite her brown, straight hair."

If we spot any trouble," put in Alice, "I'll act crazy, like, and keep yelling fire out the car window."

"One more thing," I said. I held up a jar of black soot. "I muddied this, and I'm going to smear the license tags, so we don't get trapped by an observant bystander with pen and paper."

"All right." Cole waved the clipboard. "Do that, then I'm going in."

I smeared the mud on the tags of both vehicles and took the driver's seat in mine. Alice drove away in her car to position herself in front of the house. The rest of us peered through the shrubbery to watch Cole make a show of reading the meter at the house in front of us, then amble across the backyards and patch of woods to Rockwell's house, pretending to refer to his clipboard.

I lost sight of Cole behind the house, but by now he should be approaching Rockwell's meter. Sean had his eyes on his watch, silently ticking off the minutes. We heard Cole yell, "Fire!"

"Now!" Sean said, and he and Stuart ran through the shrubbery to Rockwell's basement door and disappeared down the steps. I stayed in the bus with the engine running and waited. And waited. I heard the commotion on the other side of the house. Why didn't Sean and Stuart get out of there? Maybe Clark wasn't in the basement after all. What if they took him some place else? We'd be sunk. And so would Clark.

I was so intent on watching the back of Rockwell's house, I didn't hear the footsteps from behind. When a voice at my car window barked, "Out of the car!" my knees hit the steering wheel. I whirled around into the business end of a gun. Behind it, the scruffy, squint-eyed man, Leon, motioned for me to get out of the car.

I sighed. I was so tired of Leon.

I obeyed slowly as my mind raced through alternatives. I couldn't get the bus in gear fast enough to speed away before he shot me through the door and window. There was nothing I could do to escape this time, and he looked like he was going to smash the window open. I turned off the engine and got out.

"Walk" he said, pushing me forward toward Rockwell's house. "I thought you was a friend of ours, Missy," he said. "But you ain't, and now we got to punish you, and don't you start pulling none of your so-called panic shit neither. I'm itchin' to beat you up like you deserve."

They must have captured Stuart and Sean, too. They had four of us.

What if they had Cole and Alice? This was bad.

Chapter 30

All I thought as squinty-eyed Leon pushed me forward was what Aunt Kay would say when she heard about this fiasco. I'd giggle if I weren't so afraid I might not live to see the next day. This was very, very bad.

Leon used the gun to push me down the outside steps to the basement door. It was unlocked.

"Go ahead," said Leon. "Open it."

I opened it and blinked as my eyes adjusted to the dim light inside. He pushed me forward into a bare room. The only light forced its way through the dirty basement windows, blocked by piles of leaves outside. The walls and floor were mottled gray concrete, and the place felt damp and smelled of mildew. If I stayed down here long, I'd be sick.

In the gloom I saw Sean and Stuart sitting on the floor next to Clark, their hands tied behind them. Rockwell's men were all in high spirits. "We got 'em," said one. "Just like the Commander said we would."

I understood it now. Clark wasn't a hostage. He was bait, and we fell into the trap. They expected us to attempt a rescue. Which one was Sean's informant? With their grubby faces and clothes, I could barely tell one from the other except for Leon. He was as mean as he looked. He pushed me roughly onto the floor next to Sean, then found another length of rope and tied my wrists and ankles together.

"I have to go to the restroom," I said.

"Tough," he said. All the men laughed. One of them checked the outside basement door to make sure it was locked. He put the key in his pocket.

I was trapped. I felt the panic growing. I gritted my teeth. I could not afford to lose control. I must focus on getting us out of here.

"I think we've caught them all now," another man said. Ted.

Then I heard the inside basement door open upstairs. It squeaked as if the hinges were rusty. Black boots set foot on the stairs. Knee-high boots. Storm trooper boots that pounded the stairs with each step. As the boots descended, khaki slacks appeared, then a white shirt and tie, then the head. There was George Lincoln Rockwell himself, all of him. From my position on the floor, he loomed like Goliath. I didn't have a slingshot. In one hand, he held a thin riding crop, which he slapped across the palm of the other hand like a movie Nazi. He was in advertising and knew about presentation. He was in costume.

He stopped at the bottom of the stairs, and with a slap of the crop he contemplated the four of us, trussed like chickens at his feet.

Finally, he said, "Do you know who I am?"

I ignored the rhetorical question from a puffed-up ego. I kept my eyes on his boots. Had he polished them himself or did one of his minions do it? The boots were run down at the heel—a telling chink in his façade. I glanced up and noticed his fly was open. None of his men dared to mention it. Leon saw it and nudged Ted. They grinned.

Rockwell paid no attention to his men, but his intense contempt rolled over us. He kicked Stuart in the leg as if he were trash in his way. Clark shied back, whimpering. I avoided eye contact for fear of a lash from the crop.

"When I am president," he said, licking his lips and talking directly to Stuart, "I will strip you and your kind of citizenship. Then," he sneered, "you can choose to return to the fetid land of your ancestors or, if you remain here, go to a remote and guarded camp to live as wards of the government, a wasteful drag on our country's resources."

Whew. Man, the guy was bizarre.

"And you," he bent over and swung the crop against my arm. Hard. It stung like the blazes, but I bit my lip, too stubborn to cry out.

"You belong in the kitchen." He laughed. "Taking care of your man. That's what women are made for." He saw the ridicule in my eyes and struck my arm again. I winced. He grinned. "I'm only beginning with you."

"You are a colossal jackass." That's what I wanted to say but didn't. His last strike with the crop stung worse than the first. I didn't need another one.

He stood in front of Sean. "My followers support me and my goals with full heart. They work hard for me and send me gifts," he reached for his pipe in his pants pocket, suddenly noticed his open fly, turned his back on us for a few seconds then faced us again and repeated, "many gifts, contributions to my cause, to help me succeed. You have robbed me of a heavy contribution." He glared at Sean and then at me as he paced back and forth in front of us. "We want it back."

He stopped pacing and bent down to bring his face close to ours. "You must return it." His eyes narrowed as he surveyed us. "You have a most unpleasant afternoon ahead of you unless you tell us where it is and how to reclaim it. If you do not," his voice turned oily. "But of course you will tell us. We will make sure you do."

He folded his arms and grinned triumphantly, leering down at us from his six-foot-plus height. "Your despicable robbery will not stop us. We receive contributions from all over the country, so your thievery is of little consequence."

He paused to let this stilted little speech sink in. I focused on his rundown heels. Then I looked around at the squalid basement, lit only from the filthy windows because he couldn't pay for electricity. I would have sneered, but that dratted stick he carried hurt.

"You can leave this place, alive and well, but first we demand you return the entire $150,000. Not a penny less." He swung the crop down with a crack on a makeshift table wobbling in the center of the room. "We demand this. Do you understand?"

I didn't respond and didn't see any of the others respond either. I had a horrible feeling torture might be next on the program. I wouldn't last long. "We didn't steal your money," I told him, but I couldn't help wincing in anticipation of another swing of the crop. I didn't hold much hope for the lie, but convincing him of our innocence was the only way out I could see.

He ignored me and brought a bar stool from a corner of the cellar, set it in front of us, and then flicked a handkerchief out of his back pocket to dust it. He sat, arms folded, staring at us. "So who will tell me how I may get my money back?"

"We don't know anything about your money," Clark retorted, struggling with his bonds. "Tell him, you guys. He's nuts."

Nobody spoke. Poor Clark had no idea.

"Go ahead, tell the guy," he repeated, looking from Sean to me, then up at Rockwell. "Why would any of us steal your money?" he asked the tall man who sat calmly in front of us, with one hand thoughtfully scratching his chin. Rockwell was thinking how to dispose of us all, no doubt, after we told him where his money was. His men were itching to have a go at Sean, Clark, and especially Stuart.

"I know that you," Rockwell pointed the crop at Sean, "rented a van and you," he nodded at me, "brought drugged food to my men to knock us out, and then you stole the money."

"Go on," Clark laughed. "They wouldn't do that. That's ridiculous."

Rockwell turned to his men and nodded toward Clark. "Shut him up."

One man picked up a pistol.

"No!" shrieked Clark.

"Don't shoot him," I yelled. "I brought you hot dogs and hamburgers and...and...stuff 'cause I thought you were hungry."

"I see," said Rockwell, holding out his arm to stop the gunman. Rockwell looked at me. "We don't have to kill your friend or any of you. Tell me where the money is. Give it back and you may all go."

Despite Rockwell's dramatic entrance and the growing dread I felt, I had so far kept the panic at bay, but they had tied me up in this closed and musty room, unable to move or to leave. No vodka. No exit. The panic would soon take over, and I wouldn't be able to stop it. Then what would happen to me? Would I explode? Lose my mind? What if it played itself out and dissipated? As terrified as I felt, I might learn how much panic I could take and then, maybe, its power over me would go away. If I lived. For a few seconds I was caught up in the psychological possibilities. Then Rockwell came over to me and reached down to my hair. I flinched.

The doorbell rang.

All of us heard it and glanced at each other. I watched Rockwell hesitate, and then nod at one of the men, who ran up the stairs. We heard muffled voices. The man called down the basement steps. "A lady here says she's from the government and needs to show you some papers."

Alice.

Rockwell cursed and bounded up the stairs. I heard someone upstairs yell "Fire!" And then I heard firecrackers. And sirens. Cole must have called the Fire Department. The fire warning galvanized the men watching over us in the basement. They ran upstairs without a glance at us and closed the basement door behind them. I heard a key turn in the lock. We looked at each other. A reprieve. Would the Fire Department insist on checking down here? They hadn't gagged us. When we heard the firemen, we could yell for help, but we'd better not wait for that.

Sean's informant said he'd loosen a couple of Clark's knots. Had he done that? "Clark," I whispered," pull on your knots."

"I am," he said. "I've almost got one hand out. They're tight."

"We're all trying," said Sean. "Ropes stretch. Keep working them."

I heard sounds of confused running and chaos upstairs. We didn't have much time.

Stuart struggled but turned to me. "It's hopeless."

While Rockwell pontificated to us, I worked to stretch the rope binding my hands behind my back. To my surprise and glee, the knots slipped. I would have laughed but kept the fear I was feeling on my face in case Rockwell returned.

What a bunch of losers he'd accumulated. Squinty-eyed Leon didn't know how to tie a square knot. He must have by-passed Boy Scouts. The granny knot easily gave way. My hands were freed, and Clark's were almost free. I finished untying him, and we both worked on Sean's and Stuart's knots. It took a couple of minutes to free them. I heard Rockwell trying to take control to prevent the firemen from entering. We were all free. We raced to the outside basement door. I knew they had locked it, and the key was in the pocket of a man running around upstairs.

What could we use to open the door? Sean was testing it, and the other two men leaned against it to push. I searched the shelves in the gloom for a hammer or a crowbar and found a rusty screwdriver. I ran with it to the door. While the men pushed, I inserted it at the lock to pry it open. Rust, mildew, dry rot, and no maintenance had taken their toll. The lock gave way as the door splintered. We were out of there in a flash and ran to where I'd parked the bus.

But there was no bus. I was astounded, and for a moment, doubted my senses. How could it not be there? I looked up and down the street, but no bus. One of Rockwell's storm troopers must have driven it away and hidden it. Where would they take it? I didn't have time to puzzle about that now. We were miraculously free, and we had to get away from here fast.

To make things worse, it started to rain. I glanced back at Rockwell's house and saw the fire trucks leaving. Rockwell and his men may have been kept busy while the firefighters tracked down signs of fire, but they would all be gone in a moment. Then the storm troopers would come after us.

Chapter 31

I scanned the street for Cole and Alice's car, hoping they were cruising the neighborhood looking for us. I saw no sign of them. They might have headed home. If they didn't see my bus, would they assume we'd rescued Clark and all gotten away?

No. They must have seen the Nazis capture me. Alice had to be the one at the door with papers, and Cole called the fire department. They were around somewhere. They wouldn't leave without knowing Stuart was safe. Even if they picked up Stuart, they would be back for the rest of us. But there were four of us. Not easy to hide four people.

"Split up," Sean said. "Stuart, you and Clark run behind the houses till you find a bus stop or a cab. Keep hidden until you can get on the bus. Sue and I will run across the street and behind the houses there. Meet at the coffee shop."

Instead of running like he had brains, Clark stood on the sidewalk and protested. "Why don't we call the police? They kidnapped me. That's against the law."

It wouldn't take long for the storm troopers to spot him.

"No time," Sean said. "Go! We'll explain later. Run! Don't let them find you."

I heard shouts behind us. There was no traffic on this side street. Sean and I bolted across and hid behind a modest frame house. Peeking around the side of the house, I saw one of the storm troopers looking up and down the street we'd crossed. Clark and Stuart had disappeared.

Keeping the house between us and the storm troopers, Sean and I crossed the backyard and crept behind the shrubbery to pass through the next yard and onto the street beyond. We crossed that street but had to run along a chain-link fence confining a German shepherd. The dog immediately set to fierce barking, his mouth dripping saliva. The hound from Hell. We might as well have sent up flares. I had nothing to throw to him to shut him up.

We dashed to the next house and slipped behind it as a black rattletrap of a car crawled down the street. The car was all too familiar, having spent days parked in front of our house. Peering around the corner, I saw two men, dirty and unshaven, in the front seat, swiveling their heads from left to right. Leon was driving. I wasn't close enough to recognize the other man. Rockwell's men were searching for us. Behind them, on the next street, I saw Cole's car cross and disappear. They were searching for us, too. If only we could get to them, but we didn't dare risk the exposure. Would Alice or the Nazis find Clark and Stuart? Did they get away?

I held my breath. Leon stopped at the house with the German Shepherd. He and his buddy got out and snuck around to the back. We ran in the opposite direction across the backyards behind the shrubs and hedges. Luckily, the dog made so much noise, it covered the rustling of our feet, stirring up dried leaves and sticks as we ran. I took a quick peek back to see Leon draw a gun, but the homeowner had come out and yelled at him. As Leon turned to leave, he spotted me and shot in my direction. It missed by a mile, but he'd seen me and sprinted towards us, his gun still drawn. His buddy ran back to the car.

The homeowner had seen Leon shoot at us. He'd gone into the house. He should be calling the police.

We darted across another backyard, Leon still in pursuit, but we hid behind an ancient oak tree and let him pass. Then we doubled back to reach a street three blocks away from Rockwell's house. We kept behind the shrubbery to case the area before crossing open spaces. Good thing we did. Rockwell's thugs again drove by. I had spotted two different cars; one was the old rattle-trap with Leon as the driver. Ted drove the other, a white Dodge dart sedan with a large dent across the front. The rattletrap was coming our way.

We waited until it passed and jogged more than a block before we dashed across the street and almost collided into the Dodge Dart. Ted and the other man inside shouted at us as we sprinted behind another row of houses, searching for a place to hide. Neither of us looked back, but we heard Ted and his pal panting behind us. Both Sean and I were winded. I couldn't keep running much longer.

We rounded a corner to find a garden tool shed. The door was unlocked, and we scurried in. It had no window, and the place smelled of mildew, dead leaves, and chemicals. We tried not to pant while catching our breath and listened for sounds of our pursuers outside. Looking around inside as my eyes adjusted to the dark, I saw fishing poles and a pile of fish netting as well as garden tools.

We stayed there for about fifteen minutes before I cautiously opened the door and found myself staring into Calvin's eyes. He was as startled as I was. He grabbed at me, but Sean picked up a hoe and pushed him back with it. Then he swung it hard at the thug's solar plexus and downed him. Sean threw the hoe aside and picked up the fish netting. I grabbed the opposite edge, and we threw it over Calvin. We left him groaning and clutching his stomach as he sank to the ground enmeshed in the web of rope. We hurried across the yard, jumped over a narrow stream, and landed in a school playground. It was barren of anything for cover. We darted across and hoped we'd lose them on the other side.

Calvin had to untangle himself from the netting, but his buddy Ted wasn't far behind. School had let out, and several kids played on the swings and jungle gym. We couldn't endanger the kids. We needed a crowd of adults, maybe a parade, as a buffer, but we didn't have that. I wished Sean had kept the hoe, so we'd at least have a weapon. We crossed the street in front of a school bus, which blocked Cal's buddy on the other side and gave us time to disappear behind another house and head away from the school. We doubled back to the garden shed.

Where was the thug who had drawn a gun? Were they all searching for us with guns? Maybe they were, but aside from Leon's wild miss, we hadn't heard any shots so far. Maybe Clark and Stuart got away. I listened for police sirens but heard none.

As we crossed the street a block from the school, the Dodge Dart sped up and came alongside as the Horton's black sedan arrived from the other direction and slowed to our pace. Sitting in the back seat was Cole. He opened the door and pulled me in while Sean jumped into the front seat as Calvin and Ted realized what was happening. They were too slow. Alice gunned the car away from them, turned a corner, then the next corner, and lost them. Then we were out of the neighborhood.

"Where's Stuart?" asked Alice anxiously.

"He's with Clark," I said. "Stuart knows what to do. Run to a bus stop and get the first bus or cab out of here. They were supposed to hide till a bus came."

We had to hope that Clark and Stuart were okay. As we drove away, Cole said the thugs were still circling the area looking for us.

"What about Kay's bus?" I asked. "I left it on the street hidden from Rockwell's house, but it's gone now. Where did they take it?"

Alice drove, keeping her eyes on the road. "I'm praying Stuart and Clark got away." She glanced back at me. "That's all I'm interested in right now."

"Me, too," said Cole. "If they catch him, they'll probably kill him this time." He stared out the window and shook his head. "As a lesson to us."

Alice made a right turn at the next corner. "I'll see if I can find Stuart. You and Sean keep down. They don't know about me and Cole even if they saw this car. It's a common make and color. They won't connect it to you unless they see you in it."

We did as she said while she drove up and down the streets in the neighborhood.

"They're still looking for you," said Cole after a moment. "We passed two of them driving an old wreck. Didn't give us a second glance."

"That's a good sign," said Alice. "You're sure Clark knows to meet at the coffee shop?"

"That's the plan," said Sean. "He's with Stuart and Stuart knows."

Alice pulled over at a stop sign and tapped her fingers on the wheel as she slowly surveyed all directions. "They'll start noticing if I pass by again." She frowned at Cole. "Stuart suffered enough when they beat him up last time."

I didn't say what I was thinking. Calvin and Ted had seen us get into this car. Were they so intent on grabbing Sean or me they didn't notice Cole and Alice enough to recognize them? Would they put the Hortons and the fire alarm together? I had smeared enough mud mixture on the license plates to make them unreadable. I hoped that was enough.

Alice slowly moved forward. "We'll have to go to the coffee shop and hope he's there."

Cole nodded but stared out the window. This must be terrible for them, I thought. Stuart is their only son. If Rockwell's men caught him, they would beat him up and kill him or maim him forever. "I'm so sorry," I began. The missing Darrell crossed my mind.

"Don't be," Alice said through gritted teeth. "Stuart is fighting for our rights. He won't be the first or the last to die in the battle."

"Let's see if they made it to the cafe," added Cole, "before we start any eulogies." He glanced at me, still crouching next to him in the back seat. "We're out of the area. You can sit up now."

"I'll stop at the next pay phone I see," said Alice. "We'll call Tanya. Maybe she's heard from Stuart."

But Tanya hadn't heard from either Clark or Stuart. We headed for the coffee shop.

"Rockwell's men were waiting for us," said Sean.

Cole nodded. "Do you suppose your informant tried to save his own skin?"

Sean shook his head. "That's possible, I guess, or they might be on to him. He stuck his neck out for us."

"Can you still get in touch with him?" I asked. I recalled the seven men I met when I delivered the pizza. Leon, Calvin, and the others. Who was the informant? Certainly not Leon or Calvin, but who else? I'd met Sean's informant. He must have been the man who came to the house looking for Sean, but he was dirty and wearing a cap and heavy army jacket—hard to pin him down for sure to any of the men I met at Rockwell's house. Except for Leon, they all seemed to look alike. Would it matter if I could?

"Don't know if he'll risk it now." Sean clamped his lips shut. He looked grim. "Rockwell's no dummy. He'll be wondering how we got freed so easily."

"It wasn't because your informant loosened Clark's knots," I said. This would be a good joke after Clark and Stuart were safe. "Leon tied granny knots."

Sean groaned. "Oh, brother. What a bunch of losers."

At the coffee shop we took the booth in back and waited. Alice found the pay phone and called Tanya with an update. None of us felt like eating, but we ordered sandwiches for the right to stay there. After an hour, sandwiches gave way to coffee and tea. There was still no sign of Stuart or Clark. I worried about both of them. Stuart was young and impulsive. Clark was a naïve twit. Would they have the sense to keep hidden until they found a bus or cab?

"I'll go back to Rockwell's neighborhood for another drive-through," said Alice. "They've probably given up searching for you by now."

We all stared glumly at the door as six young, colored men entered, all in good spirits. Behind them, as if they were part of the group, came Stuart and Clark.

"Oh, thank God," whispered Alice, grabbing Cole's hand. They rushed forward to hug Stuart and drag him to the table. Clark followed behind. Their clothes were wet and muddied, and they looked exhausted.

"What happened?" I asked. "Did you get a bus?"

"Took four transfers," grumbled Clark. "We missed a couple of buses because we had to hide when those guys came by."

"Tried to hail a couple of cabs," said Stuart, "but they saw me and speeded away. He laughed. He sat straight, and his eyes sparkled. He seemed proud of himself. "We outsmarted them every time, man. Them and their white supremacy wasn't so supreme against us."

"Yeah," said Clark. "We won."

Sean looked up. "Not quite," he said. "Not yet."

"What do you mean?" asked Clark. He was in a jubilant mood. "We got out of there. Hey, by the way, thanks for the rescue." He glanced around. "Where's Ellen?"

"She's okay," I said. "We picked her up, and she told us you'd been kidnapped. We thought it best that she not be part of our rescue operation."

"Good. I worried about her," he said, "when I wasn't anxious about me. That place stank, and so did those guys."

Alice stood. 'Excuse me, I'll phone Tanya and tell her the news. She can tell Ellen."

"Tell Ellen. She's probably upset about me," said Clark. "What did those guys want? They kept asking me about some money. I thought at first they knew about Mosby's treasure and somehow figured I'd found it, but it wasn't that."

"Never mind," I said. "We're glad you're safe." I turned to the others. "There's one thing..."

"Your bus," said Sean. "We've got to go back there and retrieve it."

"With any luck," added Cole, "they won't have connected the rescue operation with me and Alice and our sedan yet. Even if those guys saw us when we picked up Sean and Sue, they won't recognize us. Probably won't even recognize Stuart, even though they were close enough to beat him once and several weeks later, tie him up in their basement. They won't notice us driving around their neighborhood."

"And thanks to Sue's mud job on the license tags," added Sean, "they won't have any license numbers, either."

Glad I thought of that for our cars, but by now the rain had washed the mud away. They knew I drove a VW bus, but those vehicles are common, and I kept it out of sight of Rockwell's house when I delivered the food. They caught me while I was waiting for Sean and Stuart to rescue Clark. The keys were in the ignition, and the doors were unlocked. I had Kay's bus all ready for them to drive away.

"It's after eight and dark outside," I said. "I'll take a cab over there and try to find the bus. I'll be quick about it."

"Nuh-uh." Cole wiped his mouth with a napkin and laid it beside his plate. "I'm ready to go. I'll take you all home and then drive Sue over to look for her car so she can bring it back."

The drive through D.C. was smooth. Rush hour was past. Cole let everyone out on Sixteenth Street, but Sean insisted on coming along on the ride out to Arlington. I harbored a dim hope I had made a mistake and simply missed seeing Kay's bus where I parked it, but when we returned to the street, the bus still wasn't there, nor was it on any adjacent streets. I didn't see it in Rockwell's driveway either. The house didn't have a garage. My bus was nowhere.

"You're sure this is where you parked it?" asked Sean. "It's dark. Maybe you got confused."

I shook my head as we searched both sides of the street and then drove down the side streets around the Rockwell house. "It's not here," I said finally. "They stole it." What would Aunt Kay say? Now I'd have to deal with the insurance company, try to call Aunt Kay, and take the city bus everywhere. I felt a headache coming on.

We drove back to Aunt Kay's house. I felt too depressed to talk.

"You'll have to call the police and report it stolen," said Sean.

"I guess so." Even more depressing.

Parking on Kilbourne Place was tight in the evenings, but Cole found a spot a block away. As we walked home, I saw a VW bus like Kay's, parked on the street across from our house.

Like Kay's? The VW bus was a popular vehicle. It didn't have to be Kay's. I left Sean and Cole on the house steps while I crossed the street. The bus was unlocked, and I recognized the car keys hanging from the ignition. It was Kay's car.

I opened the glove compartment. They'd rummaged through it but it was intact except for the registration certificate, which was lying on the dashboard. I expected a message from them left on the front seat, but there was no message except for the blatant display of the registration certificate. They hadn't ripped the up-holstery or damaged anything on the inside or outside of the bus.

Rockwell and his thugs had brought it back in good shape. But why?

Chapter 32

"It's Kay's car," I called across to Sean, then I checked under the bus seats for any clues how it got from Arlington to Kilbourne Place.

"Anything of interest?" asked Sean.

I shrugged. "Rockwell and his men must have driven it here." I guess the bus itself was the message. They added this stunt to their terror campaign against us, but I was glad I didn't have to call the police or the insurance company or Aunt Kay.

"They know where we live," I said. "They know my bus, and now they have Kay's name and address from the registration certificate. They'll think it's my name."

Then I noticed the glance Sean and Cole threw each other.

"What's their next move?" asked Sean.

"Don't drive that car for a day or two," said Cole. "Leave it there, and let's see what develops."

I had no intention of driving Kay's bus. The car chase was scary enough, and after what happened today, driving such a recognizable vehicle would make me an easy target. Besides, I looked forward to the calm comfort of taking a cab or riding the city bus and sitting in class, even if it was one that brought on claustrophobia. When they tied me in that moldy basement, I was too worried about being tortured or shot or watching the others get killed to let the claustrophobia bloom into panic. What would happen to me if I let the panic go the full course instead of staunching it? Next time I went to class, I'd try leaving the flask at home.

Anyway, I had flesh and blood enemies now, not mental ones. I needed my wits too much to drug myself with alcohol.

Hannah had been and gone, leaving a huffy note for me. Only Gail was there to eat dinner, but Hannah put the rest in the refrigerator for heating and eating when we got home.

Rockwell and his men could show up anytime, and they were more terrifying than claustrophobia. They'd had my keys. They could have copied them. That meant they could get into the house at any time. I called Stuart. "Can you get hold of your locksmith friend?" I asked. "I need to change the locks on this house immediately."

"Sure," said Stuart. "I'll phone him. He gets calls late at night a lot. He's used to it."

Two hours later, we all had new keys to the house.

I worried about Kay's bus. Had Rockwell's thugs tampered with the brakes or engine some way to bring about my demise? Except why would they want to hurt or, I gulped, kill me before they found out where their money was? It wouldn't make sense. They might damage it so it would break down as I drove to class, and then they'd capture me. That was the most likely scenario. Or they might go back to posting someone to watch the bus and house.

We met again late that evening in Kay's living room. All of us, including Sean, who moved back because Rockwell now had a much bigger pond in which to fish.

"Is Tanya home?" I asked. "She ought to hear this." I saw Sean perk up at Tanya's name.

"I'll bring her over," said Alice, getting up. "Be right back."

Since we learned Rockwell knew Sean and I were the thieves he sought, the Hortons had taken to entering and leaving by the back doors of our houses to minimize their connection with us.

Mike was in Maryland working with a catering company, which was a relief for the rest of us. We included Clark and Ellen this time because they needed to know what was going on for their own protection.

"Rockwell knew we'd try to rescue Clark," I said. "and used him for bait."

Sean nodded. "Get at me through my brother. They found out where we live. They identified Kay's car, and they know about Clark and Ellen's treasure hunt. But how did they get all that information?"

"We know how," I said, biting my lip. "Sally Ann."

Clark gasped. "Sally Ann. But she's a nice girl. I like her."

"And I don't believe it," added Ellen. "Why would she associate with men like Rockwell?"

Clark frowned at me, pushing his lips out. "You're jealous. We all know you like Mike."

"Enough. I agree with Sue," said Sean. He got up restlessly and paced the floor.

"So do we," chimed in Cole and Stuart. "Rockwell knows too much about us, and none of us are on speaking terms with him."

"Did Mike tell you her sad story?" I asked. Cole and Alice shook their heads, so I repeated it for everyone. "Sally Ann asked Mike for a lot of cash to help her parents."

"She wouldn't do such a thing," said Clark. "I don't believe it. She's a nice girl."

I shrugged and deliberately misinterpreted his response. "I didn't believe her story either."

Ellen's scorn was palpable. "Who would fall for it?"

Sean stopped pacing the room. "Obviously, it's another of Rockwell's stunts to get the money."

"If Mike did pony up the money for Sally Ann," added Cole, "it would confirm that we'd stolen his money and still had it. Rockwell would know for sure then and make even more demands."

Alice returned with Tanya. "What did I miss?" Tanya asked, taking a seat on the couch next to Sean. If anyone objected, I didn't see any signs of it.

We filled her in.

"What's their next move?" asked Cole. "That's the question."

"We can't sit here and let them victimize us," I said, "but how can we avoid it?"

"I don't see the problem," said Clark. "Give them back the money. That will get rid of them."

He saw the way the rest of us looked at him. "What?" he asked.

"We can't," said Alice.

"What you did was wrong," said Ellen belligerently. She sat close to Clark and held his hand. "Clark almost lost his life because of it."

Cole cocked an eyebrow and folded his arms as he frowned at Clark. "We don't have the money. We've moved it on."

"Moved it on?" said Clark. "You didn't keep it?"

"It's serving a better purpose." Cole said.

I filled Clark in. "We donated it to the NAACP, SNCC, and CORE."

"Oh." He pondered this idea a moment, but shook his head. "It was still stealing," he said, "and that makes all of you thieves."

"Whatever you think," Cole said, "it's done now." He turned to the rest of us. "I for one am proud of what we did. Any ideas on how we deflect their next attempt?"

"I will try to contact my informant in their house," said Sean. "I'm not sure we can still trust him, but he may have some explanation of what happened and what Rockwell plans next."

"Get what you can out of him," added Gail, speaking for the first time. "Then tell him to get away from there. They've got to be suspicious of him by now."

"That's right," I added. "And trying to protect him ties our hands."

"I'd like to say," Stuart nodded at Sean and me, "we've done a great thing so far in diverting $150,000 from Rockwell's Nazis to the NAACP, SNCC, and CORE to help them get the Civil Rights Bill passed. Hooray for us."

Clark and Ellen exchanged wide-eyed glances. "So that's what this is all about," said Clark. "I'm glad. You get those guys. After what they did to me, they deserve it." He raised Ellen's hand, "and they scared Ellen half to death."

"It's all right," said Ellen. "What you did was stealing, but from a terrible man and for a good cause." She smiled at Clark.

We all cheered. Clark and Ellen joined in. "But this doesn't mean I approve," Ellen added.

Gail was right. Sean's informant had to get out of that vipers' nest, and we had to keep Rockwell's thugs from killing us. Rockwell wanted the money. He probably wouldn't kill us until he got it back. Was there some carrot we could hold in front of him to make him think he'd get it back?

We kicked that idea around a bit, but no solutions presented themselves. We broke up for the night. For now, we were all safe and unharmed.

At midnight, I had finally calmed down enough to fall asleep. Suddenly, a window-shattering boom shifted my bed and shook the floor. Window glass sprayed across the room. The lamp rattled on the bedside table. I shook broken glass out of my slippers before donning them, grabbing a robe and running to the front window. Jagged glass fragments clung to the frame. I stared in shock at Kay's beautiful VW bus, now a charred hulk engulfed in flames.

.

Chapter 33

March 31, 1964.

I dressed to go out and mingle with the growing crowd, gawking at the flaming wreck. Both Sean and Clark had stumbled down the stairs and stood at the window, watching the chaos outside.

The bus quickly became a blackened frame silhouetted against the dying flames licking around the remnants of seat cushions inside the vehicle. People up and down the street had come out onto their porches. Charred metal fragments and bits of car upholstery lay on the street and sidewalk, igniting small fires down the block. The cars in front and back of mine suffered extensive damage. In the distance, I heard fire engines.

Some neighbor called the police. As I stepped out onto the porch, a white envelope taped to the door fell onto the porch floor and landed at my feet. I picked it up. The outside of the envelope was blank, but it was unsealed. Written in large block letters, the message inside said, "GIVE BACK THE MONEY OR YOUR HOUSE WILL BE NEXT."

I showed it to Sean and Clark as I stumbled back inside and collapsed on the couch. "They won't stop until they get their money back or kill us," I moaned. I felt like crying. Would this nightmare never end?

Sean and Clark sat on each side of me, staring blankly at the note in my hand.

The police arrived and a minute later a fire truck. Mike came home as we straggled out to join the chaos in the street. He was as shocked as the rest of us.

The firemen doused the flames, inspected the wreck, and left. One of them came in a separate car and remained to examine the situation. The police had kept the onlookers back but now began a systematic interrogation. After a quick consultation with Sean and Clark, I came forward and identified the wreck as belonging to my aunt, who was out of town. I disclaimed all knowledge about why or how it exploded. I was an innocent victim.

If the police searched my background, they wouldn't find anything, but since Aunt Kay registered the car in her name, they'd probably search her records, too. I hoped the police hadn't caught her smuggling or committing some other crime. Aunt Kay? Nah.

Had I ever called the robbery a caper? It was becoming deadly serious, deadly being the operative word. The bombing was more of Rockwell's work. A warning of what he planned to do with us if he didn't get the money back. It was imperative that we implement some kind of plan fast to get us out of this fix before Rockwell carried out any more destructive stunts. He threatened to target our house next, probably with us in it.

We didn't get much sleep the rest of that night. Sean called in sick at work. Not a lie. He looked as frazzled and ill as the rest of us. Mike left for work again in the morning, but no one else went to school or work the day after the explosion. We were all too tense from being up most of the night and worrying about what Rockwell planned to do next. We needed to defuse the situation with Rockwell, and we all wanted to be part of the plan. We could not let Rockwell blow up Aunt Kay's home.

We had to think of something.

My legs felt weak, and I couldn't stop shivering. Early that morning the Hortons came over, and all of us, even Ellen and Clark, sat in the living room staring at the rug. With Mike at work, he was out of the way. As long as he was dating Sally Ann, we couldn't include him in our plans.

"They'll never give up," I said, my teeth chattering.

Cole nodded, brows drawn, pushing his lips in and out. "We're dealing with the aftermath of a few serious mistakes," he said. "Sean's informant is the only ace in the hole we have."

We sat quietly, mulling over this fact. Then an idea occurred to me. "We can still use him, can't we? I've got an idea." I began to smile. "I think I can get us out of this situation."

"I'm glad somebody does," Ellen said. "You got us into this mess."

I certainly did not, but I ignored Ellen's remark and nodded to myself. My idea might work.

Everyone turned to me. "Tell us," said Alice.

"I say we pin the robbery on Sean's informant," I said.

Sean sputtered his objection.

"Wait a minute." I held up my hand. "First, Sean meets with him, finds out everything the informant can tell us about Rockwell and his thugs and their plans."

"Okay, so far," said Gail.

"Then he disappears." I looked at Sean. "It's too hot for him there now, anyway. Rockwell and his second in command—what's his name?"

"Matt," said Sean. "Matt Koehl."

"Okay. Matt Koehl. That's right. I met him when I brought them the pizzas. Rockwell and Koehl probably suspect all the men there and will watch them too closely for your friend to be effective, anyway. I'll bet he's already noticed they're treating him differently. They have to be suspicious."

"But even if he disappears, it won't change our situation. Rockwell knows we stole his money, not my informant," said Sean. "We're still in the hot seat."

I smiled. This was the beauty of my plan. So simple. "I go visit the house to talk to Rockwell."

"No, no, no," said Cole. "We can't allow you to risk your life like that."

"I can do this without involving any of you," I said, "and I don't think they'll harm me once I'm through."

"So far so good," said Sean. "How will you do that?"

"I'll act deferential and dumb, like they expect women to

be," I said, "maybe do some crying about my car."

"You think they'll buy that?" asked Alice skeptically.

"Hope so," I said. "Then I'll apologize for what happened--I won't know too much, something about money being stolen, how I had nothing to do with it. I'll say I often visited friends in that neighborhood, and they told me they thought you all were very poor. I thought I was doing a good deed for all of them by bringing them hamburgers and hotdogs and donuts. People in the neighborhood did that. Brought food for the men. They looked so hungry, and I was sorry for them."

"Oh man," said Clark. "You did that? You all were in on this stunt?"

I ignored him. "Here comes the tricky part. I'll tell them one of the men there suggested I bring pizza. I'll pretend to look around and ask where he is because he could explain everything to them. I'll insist I only wanted to help. They looked so hungry. It was my good deed for all of them, especially for a future President of the United States."

"He'll love that," said Sean with a laugh.

"But how will you explain the van in the driveway?" Cole asked.

Sean whistled, folded his arms, and thought a moment. "I'm thinking our friend, the informant, loaned me some money and to repay him, he asked me to rent the van and come out to the house, so he could pick up a box of papers and deliver it to a storage place on Fourteenth Street."

Cole pursed his lips and nodded his head. "If they buy that story, they'll make the leap that the same man who wanted the van stole the money. It's logical."

"Is there such a place?" asked Clark.

"I've passed by it, so yeah," said Sean.

"I think they'll buy it," I said as we put into place the pieces of strategy. "They'll look for the informant, and he won't be there. Naturally, they'll think he took the money. They didn't find it at our place and despite their threats, we haven't returned it. In fact, we've told them repeatedly that we don't have it. And that's the truth. They'd love to have an answer to where it might be.

They'll leap to the idea that it's in storage."

Sean nodded. "I agree. Does anyone have a lock with two keys or a combination lock? We need to supply our own lock for the storage unit."

"I have a lock we can use," said Alice. "Two keys, too."

"Great. We'll use the lock, and I'll give one of the keys to my informant to drop in his room for them to find."

It seemed a workable plan. "Can you meet him this morning? Give him the key?"

Sean nodded. "I'm sure I can."

I turned to Cole. "Can you rent a storage unit this morning?" I stopped a moment to consider. "Put it in the informant's name and bribe the manager to write down a date on the contract to show he rented it a couple of months ago. Before the robbery, you know," I said. "So it'll look like he planned the robbery awhile ago."

Alice suddenly looked up. "I'll go to the bank and withdraw a bunch of twenty-dollar bills, enough to include the wrapper, and I'll ask the teller to keep the wrapper on. Then we'll leave the wrapper and maybe a twenty in the storage unit."

Sean nodded. "They'll find all that when they use the key my friend will leave in his room."

"Great idea," I said.

Sean nodded. "You think this plan will work?"

Cole shook his head. "It's too risky. I don't like it. I'd hate to see you get hurt."

"We won't let Sue go alone," said Sean. "I'll go with her."

"And we'll stand by," said Cole. "In case they try something."

"All for one," said Stuart, "and one for all."

I shook my head. "I don't think so. It would be good to have people outside, but it should be Gail, Clark, and Ellen." I turned to Cole to explain. "A colored family waiting outside will be like a red flag to a bull. It would mark all of us as the enemy and might lead them to speculate about you and the money. They are ready for violence."

"I suppose you're right." Cole scratched his chin. "White people see us, they think we're out to rob them."

"I meant that with the Civil Rights Bill in Congress and all it means to you, they might make a connection. On the other hand, Gail, Clark, and Ellen look like the kind of doofus college kids--"

"Wait a minute," put in Clark. "I resent that."

"Hush up, Clark," said Gail. "College kids are the right sort who might do something stupid but would never dare to rob a guarded fortress like Rockwell's house."

"That's right," I said. "And that's why Gail, Clark, and Ellen will wait in front of the house for me to come out. If I don't return in a reasonable amount of time, they'll get to a phone and call the police."

"I'll tell you what," said Cole. "Gail can take my car and park close by. If she gets a signal from you, she'll find a pay phone and call the police." He looked at Ellen. "You still have use of your Mom's car, so you and Clark stay in your car to watch Rockwell's place and make sure they don't take Sue away and hide her before the police can get there."

"All right," said Ellen.

"Wait a minute," said Stuart. "Man, you ain't gonna leave me outta this. I'll drive Dad's car and be a chauffeur. The more people the better, I say."

Cole was about to object, but I supported Stuart. "He'll be okay as long as he stays in the car," I said.

"That's right, man," Stuart said. "I got me a cap that'll be perfect."

"If I run into problems, you and Gail find a phone and call the police. With two of you, one can stay in the car in case there's no parking place."

Cole stroked his chin. He finally said, "Okay, but get out if there's any trouble. Rockwell's men don't like you."

With that settled, I thought of another detail. "I'll smear the sooty goop on the license tags like I did before," I said. "We don't want either car associated with this operation."

Sean got up. "I'll set up a meeting with my informant now."

"I hope this plan works," said Tanya.

So did I. It was risky, and the whole idea scared me, but I didn't see another way to get out of the frying pan.

We adjourned the meeting at ten a.m. with the plans made. We would start immediately and carry it off today. We were running out of time.

Chapter 34

By noon, Sean had met with his friend the informant, and Cole had rented the storage unit. Inside the unit they left a pile of clothes the informant had worn as a storm trooper, a twenty-dollar bill, and a bill wrapper.

Sean confirmed what I'd suspected. Reg was Sean's informant. Reg was the one with the pressed khakis, which indicated the kind of rigid uptightness I'd expect from a "G-Man." Maybe he wasn't. Sean didn't know for sure, and other organizations were interested in the resurgence of a Nazi group and wanted to keep tabs on them.

Reg was now on his way to the airport. By tomorrow I guessed he'd have a new name, new background, and new address, and Rockwell would have one less storm trooper. Even Sean didn't know any details, but we were free to blame this anonymous man for everything without consequences to him. We planned the visit to Rockwell for two that afternoon. The sooner the better. I couldn't rest or relax thinking the house might be the next to go. With us in it.

We gathered in the Horton's basement for last-minute instructions before we left. We were all tense. Cole reminded the group one last time, "None of us knows anything about the money, and we are as puzzled as they are about what happened. We didn't want to get Sean's informant in trouble until he explained what was going on. The fact that he's missing should be enough to make them look in his direction. Our line is we know nothing."

"I don't know anything," said Ellen.

"That's right," I said. "Neither do any of you and neither do I. One thing we do know is we don't have any of their money."

As he insisted, Stuart drove the Hortons' car, wearing a jacket and an ivy cap. To an observer, he might seem to be a hired chauffeur, especially since he was colored. Sean sat in the front seat with Stuart, and Gail and I sat in the back. Clark insisted on going with Ellen as she followed in her Mom's car. None of us said much on the way out to Rockwell's place. Stuart and Gail's job was to call the police if necessary, but each of us knew where to find the closest pay phone.

We didn't let Mike in on the plan, of course, and fortunately, he was at work or in class during the day. Sally Ann would be working. She had said nothing to the rest of us about her pressing need for cash to help her parents.

The trip was all too short. I was becoming a nervous wreck. Why did I volunteer to be the spokesperson for the group? Sean could do this job by himself. Worse, I hadn't brought my flask. As long as I was able to leave Rockwell's property, I was okay, but anything might happen. I was afraid.

I took a deep breath, trying to calm myself as Stuart swung in front of Rockwell's house, A tremor of fear raced down my spine. They didn't call it Hatemonger Hill for nothing. As usual, patches of mud and weeds spread out across the ugly yard, and the house still needed paint and repair. It looked as depressed as I felt. Sean squeezed my hand. He had to be even more frightened than I was. I trembled at the thought of what they might do to me, but what would they do to him if things turned ugly? They were angry, violent men. They'd beat him to death and think he had it coming.

"Give us fifteen minutes," I said. "We'll either come out, and we can leave, or the thugs might insist that you come into the house. If that happens, you and Gail leave, find a phone, and call the police. Rockwell already knows about Ellen and Clark, but probably not about you two, so if there's any trouble, you need to get away. You're both Rockwell targets for hate and violence. Remember, none of us knows anything about the missing money. Okay?"

"Okay," said Stuart. "Got it."

"Our story is that if there's missing money, Sean's informant took it all." I looked at Sean.

"That's right. Reg has a new name and address by now," said Sean, "and he's far away from here."

I looked at Sean and took a deep breath.

"Showtime," he said.

No one lounged on the front porch. Sean and I walked up the rickety step and across the porch to the front door. I knocked.

I heard scrambling inside, and a moment later the door opened. Squinty-eyed Leon peered out at us, a gun in a holster hanging from his belt. He yelled back into the house. "Looky who we got here!"

"We want to talk to Mr. Rockwell," I said politely.

"I know he'd like to talk to you," the man answered with a mock bow and stepped aside to let us enter. This would be harder than I thought. I needed to stand tall and strong to avoid harassment from these guys, but act like a silly ninny in front of Rockwell.

One of the men ran up the stairs and banged on the door to Rockwell's study.

"You got any friends with you?" Leon asked, hands on the gun holster, ready to draw. Other thugs stood behind him and carried rifles, pointed at the floor but ready to raise them to fire. They'd love to shoot the lot of us.

One of them pointed out the front door, which still hung open despite the forty-degree temperature outside. "There's a car out front," he said. "Got two people in it. A colored driver and a lady."

"No kidding." The others crowded at the door to peer out.

"There's another car out there, too," I pointed out, "to go for help if there's any trouble."

Leon grinned. "Trouble? What makes you think there'd be trouble/"

I didn't reply, just stood there waiting. I heard the heavy boots first, and then turned to watch Rockwell in military khaki descend the stairs, knee-high, polished black boots advancing one deliberate step at a time. He stared at me the entire time.

He came into the room and stopped, frowning at us with arms akimbo. "I'm surprised to see you," he said deadpan.

"You and your buddies have terrified me and my friends," I said. "We want to know why."

"You know why. You stole my money."

"This has gone on long enough, and it's time we got things straightened out," I said.

Sean stepped forward. "We don't know what you're talking about. We didn't steal any money."

Whew. Lying came easily when your life was at stake. And it was.

"Why would you think that?" I asked Rockwell. "You keep harassing us about this. You kidnapped our friend. And now you've blown up my car. You've even ransacked my house and know we don't have any cash hidden away. Who told you we stole your money?"

Rockwell looked me up and down, a frown of contempt on his face. "You set it up. You and your hamburgers and hotdogs and–." He came closer and pointed his finger at me. "And pizza. Drugged pizza."

Here I gaped in astonishment. Audrey Hepburn or Shirley MacLaine couldn't have acted more convincingly. "What do you mean, drugged pizza?" All innocent. "That was good pizza. I bought it from the sub shop down the road. Ate some of it myself. If you fed the men here properly, they wouldn't need hamburgers and hotdogs and handouts from your neighbors."

Rockwell's eyes narrowed. I'd never seen anyone look so much like a snake. "What would you know about how I feed the men here?"

"Nothing. But it's common knowledge in the neighborhood that your men are starving, and anyway, one of your men told me when I chatted with him outside." I pretended to look around the room as if searching for someone. "I don't see him here now, but he'd tell you. He's the one who suggested pizza, and he took them all when I got to the yard outside. I wanted to help you guys. Then you started scaring me, talking about missing money. I didn't have anything to do with it. Now you've carried this stunt too far."

"What did this man look like?" Rockwell asked. "The one who took the pizza."

I was ready for this question. "He was tall and had black hair, blue eyes, I think. He took care of himself. Better dressed than most of these guys." I pretended to study each of the men around the room. "I don't see him here, though."

"That's Reg." Rockwell turned to the man standing next to him. "Matt, where is Reg?"

Matt glanced at the men. "Any of you guys know where Reg is?"

"Haven't seen him since last night," said one of the men. "But he left with a bag of laundry."

"Go search the house for him and his things," Matt commanded. "All of you."

The men disbanded. Several for the stairs, one for the basement, and another for the kitchen.

"I knew Reg casually. We were in school together years ago," said Sean. "He asked me to rent a van and bring it here to the house. I owed him a favor. That's why I did what he asked and left the van here for him. He said he needed to move some things out."

"Why did he need your help for that?" Rockwell was visibly skeptical.

"Said he didn't have any credit and couldn't rent the van without it." Sean shrugged. "He was a nice guy. Glad to help him out. He returned it to the rental place okay, didn't he?"

Rockwell paced in front of us, scratching his chin. "So you expect me to believe you had nothing to do with the robbery here." He glanced sharply at me. "Is that right?"

I was ready with our story. "I picked up Sean when he dropped off the van. We could see how poor you are, and how hungry. Say, how come you've got all this money you're worried

about, when this place is a dump, and you don't have any food?"
I heard the men mutter among themselves. A couple threw disgruntled looks at Rockwell. Maybe that idea hadn't occurred to them.

"That's what Reg told me," added Sean.

"That's right," I said. "I thought you'd appreciate my dropping by with hotdogs, hamburgers, and stuff. One of you told me you'd even had to eat cat food. I felt sorry for all of you. Why would I steal money from you, when you obviously needed it?"

Leon turned away from me and advanced toward Rockwell. "Was you going to feed us with that money?" Everyone's eyes were on Rockwell.

Rockwell clenched his jaw and flicked his eyes at me before glowering at the men. He drew himself up. "We are on a mission," he blustered. "The stolen money was for us and our mission. Now it appears one of you is a traitor."

"He told me about it," I said. In for a penny, in for a pound. "I thought maybe I'd find out more about your mission. He said you're going to run for president. I never met anyone that important before. I listened to Reg and felt proud to bring food for you. I could help out, you know, to make America better, although..." I added doubtfully, "it seems pretty good already."

Matt snickered. Rockwell frowned at me. "We don't have women here unless it's for cooking and cleaning."

"Let's me out then," I said, trying to keep the relief from my voice. I'd gone a bit too far that time. "I can't cook—that's why I brought you hotdogs and hamburgers instead of home-baked cakes—and my Mom would tell you I know nothing about cleaning." That's the truth. I learned that from my Mom. She didn't want to iron, so she never learned how. A basic survival skill, she told me.

As we talked, the men staggered back from their search. "No sign of him," said one of them as he stepped down the stairs. "He is cleared out."

"He cleared out?" asked Sean, striving to look astonished. "I still owe him a few bucks."

That had the ring of truth in it. Kudos to Sean.

"I found this key on the floor." Ted held it up. "Look here. A label's attached to it with an address on it." He peered at it. "And it says 'Unit 124.'"

"But he seemed like such a nice person," I said. "Maybe he had to leave for a few days.

Matt grunted. "Not if he has our 150 Grand."

"Oh, my God," I said. "You mean he stole $150,000? That's why he wanted the van? I can't believe it."

"You've got to be kidding," added Sean. "I don't believe he would do such a thing."

Matt stepped forward and poked Sean in the chest. "Then where is our money?"

"We had nothing to do with any of this," I said. No acting lessons, but I felt I was putting my point across. "Leave us alone."

"If you had nothing to do with this, why didn't you call the police when we took your friend?" Rockwell was still suspicious.

"We did," I lied, "but we're college students. They didn't believe us."

"Thought we were stirring up trouble," added Sean. "Lumped us in with the student activists." He snorted. "As if we would get involved in that stuff."

"I'll take care of that when I'm president," said Rockwell. "Student activists are all radical Jews. Treasonous spies. Communists. I'll take pleasure in executing them when I'm elected."

That chilled me. He must be demented.

Leon came forward. "And why was you dressed up in blond curly hair and a dress? What was that about?"

"My hair's straight as a board. Sometimes I like to dress up and look pretty," I said, thinking fast. "I did it for...for fun." I turned to Sean. "I do that sometimes, don't I?"

"You sure do. Like to see you in a dress now and then," he said, catching on.

Rockwell studied me for a moment, pushing his lips in and out. Matt snickered.

With a sneer of contempt, Rockwell muttered, "Women are all alike." His eyes turned mean as he flicked them from me to Sean. "However that is, your friend stole money earmarked for getting my message across to the American people. It is a setback, but a minor one. I have a broad base of support and can find more where that came from. Bet on it."

Not likely. "You think the American public will go for your ideas?"

"They will once they understand the Jewish conspiracy and the overwhelming evidence that the Holocaust is a complete fabrication. The supremacy of the white race is beyond question. I am the voice of the right kind of people. The white race. They will vote for me. My year will be 1972.

He was definitely insane. I edged toward the door. "You do understand that we had nothing to do with the robbery," I said. "One of your men duped us, obviously."

"He must have taken your money. The scoundrel." Sean took my hand, and I reached for the doorknob. "Good luck in reaching your goals," I said, fingers crossed. No way. The man was nuts. I was glad we'd stolen the $150,000.

"Insurance will take care of your car," said Rockwell. "Anyway, we had nothing to do with it." Now who was lying?

"That wasn't even my car. I'm staying with my aunt. It was her car," I said. Sean and I walked out the door, feeling Rockwell's steely eyes on our backs. His men had itchy trigger fingers on the guns, too. They all wanted to blast us into oblivion, but we had four witnesses in two cars waiting outside.

"Did they believe us?" I asked Sean in a low voice.

"They seemed to," Sean said. "With Reg's disappearance, they would naturally suspect him."

We resisted the urge to run and strolled hand in hand to the car. We slipped into the back seat, keeping our faces blank. Sean whispered without moving his lips, 'No questions until we're away from here." Stuart stepped on the gas and drove us toward home. Only then did I heave an enormous sigh of relief.

"How'd it go?" asked Gail.

"They bought it," said Sean. "I think we're done with that gang."

Gail grinned. "You mean we got away with it?"

I smiled. "I think so."

"Wonderful," breathed Gail.

Suddenly, Sean started clapping. Gail and I joined in, startling Stuart into crossing an intersection against the light. No traffic, so we made it safely. We all felt relieved to exit Wilson Boulevard as we speeded toward the Memorial Bridge and Washington, D.C.

"I never want to see Hatemonger Hill again," I said.

"We have one more problem to solve," said Sean, "then we're home free."

"What's that?" I asked.

"Sally Ann." Sean glanced at me.

"Sally Ann," Gail said. "We've got to get Mike out of her clutches."

I said nothing, still miffed Mike fell for such a phony. "It doesn't matter now, does it?" I said cautiously. "If she is Rockwell's stooge, she'll disappear because we're off the hook."

"If she does disappear," Gail said, "it will mean we're right about her being in Rockwell's camp."

"If she doesn't," Sean added glumly, "we'll be stuck with her."

"Maybe Mike will wake up," said Gail. "We'll have to wait and see."

We arrived home in record time, and Stuart parked the car down the street. "Staying away from where your car exploded," he said. "Just in case."

As we walked up the front steps, Stuart stayed on the sidewalk and waved goodbye. "Gotta tell Mom and Dad what happened." This time, instead of going around to the alley to access his home via the back door, he whistled as he sauntered to the Horton house next door. We could go back to using front doors again now.

Chapter 35

I'd been living under the threat of Rockwell's reprisals for weeks, and I still wasn't quite sure we'd derailed his suspicions. An hour after we returned from Rockwell's house, I scanned the street for a rattletrap or a white Dart. I didn't see either car, so I hopped down the front steps with a letter to mail. I still kept away from the curb and looked for Virginia license tags, but I didn't see any, and no cars idled in the street. I thought I was safe. Why would they want to harass us now they knew we didn't have their money?

Then I heard footsteps walking quickly behind, and an arm gripped mine.

"Come along, Missy," a familiar voice said. "I've got a gun in your side."

Squinty-eyed Leon. I became angry. "What are you doing?" I asked. "We don't have your money. Leave me alone!" I tried to twist away from him as he pulled me to the curb. The Dodge Dart that had searched for us in Virginia drove up alongside. They must have parked around the corner. Ted drove.

Leon gestured with the gun. "Get in the car." He yanked the back door open, pushed me inside and climbed in after me. "Go!" he yelled at Ted.

"I told you," I said, "we don't have your money. Rockwell knows that now. One of your buddies stole it. Not us."

Ted glanced back as Leon laughed. "The Commander is too soft. Maybe he believed you, but we don't, Missy. We think you got the money. Maybe not all of it. Maybe ol' Reg took half, but we think you got the other half, and that half you can give to me."

He picked up a pair of handcuffs from the floor. "You're gonna let me put these on," he said, "Or I'm gonna hit you so hard on the noggin, you'll have a headache for weeks." He waved the gun at me. "Or maybe I'll shoot you in the knee. And don't pull any tricks, neither."

I shuddered. "Okay. Don't shoot." I held out my hands in front.

"Oh, no, you don't. Hands in back, if you please. I don't know how the bunch of you got out of those ropes, but I'm not taking any chances now."

I slid forward and put my hands behind my back. Rats. He wasn't going to take chances on a rope this time. The handcuffs felt snug around my wrists, but as soon as I turned my back away from him, I started working them. It was like a tight ring on a finger. If only I had some soap. I didn't see any way out of this, but as terrified as I felt, I could not afford to panic. Anyway, if I tried that, Leon would shoot me in the knee. I looked out the window to see where we were heading. Apparently, it was back to Hatemonger Hill.

We bypassed the house and drove about a block farther. I didn't see a break in the bushes, but Ted knew how to zigzag onto a hidden and rutted dirt road cut through the scrubby woods. He drove about a hundred yards and parked the car next to a wooden shack. Unless you knew it was there, you wouldn't see it because of the shrubs, fallen trees, and vines disguising the road to it and the shack itself.

"The boss, he don't know this place is here," said Leon, grinning. "Somebody gave him these twenty-three acres, but I found this shack, and I fixed it up for me and Ted here." He stepped out of the car and gestured for me to get out, too.

"Home sweet home," he snickered.

I shivered and felt sick. I wasn't going to get out of this. I twisted my wrists in the handcuffs. I could move my hands, but the cuffs were too tight. Leon pushed me inside and made me sit in a straight kitchen chair with my arms behind the back of it. He lit a kerosene heater, and the place began warming up. It was still March, and the weather was chilly, but the shack was so drafty, I didn't need to worry about carbon monoxide poisoning from that heater.

Leon glanced around the single room with satisfaction. They'd furnished it with a cot, a table, and four chairs. A pile of sheets and blankets lay rumpled on the cot. They'd set a few dishes, cups, flatware and a pot on the table. Leon and Ted, two slobs, couldn't help messing this Spartan living space with trash and empty beer bottles, carelessly tossed in the corners.

"Nobody's found this place yet. It's all ours," Ted crowed.

My heart sank as I assessed my chances for escape. They hadn't tied me to the chair, so if they'd leave, I could easily stand up out of it and get away. If they left me alone, that is.

When would Sean and Mike at the house notice I was missing? What would they do? We all figured Rockwell bought our story and let us off the hook. They wouldn't think his minions would question their autocratic leader and make other plans. After a couple of days, Sean or Mike might notify the police. They might mention Rockwell and his gang. Rockwell would deny all knowledge, and there'd be nothing to show I was there.

Who knew about this shack? According to Leon and Ted, no one.

I was entirely helpless against them, and they bore a grudge against me. I didn't have any money to give them, but how long would they torture me until they gave up? What would they do with me then? I knew one thing. They couldn't let me go. They would use me and then dispose of me. These men were ruthless, angry, and sadistic. I saw no way out, but it was no use dwelling on the hopelessness of my situation. I needed to think how to survive and escape instead.

Maybe I could pretend to faint. Have a heart attack? That might buy a little time, if it didn't enrage them into treating me

worse. Could I try my *femme fatale* persona? I didn't have the costume, the food, or the heart for that. Play on their sympathy?
Shed a few tears? Possibly. I felt slightly cheered by what I did
have in my arsenal, meager as it was, considering Leon and Ted
were brutal sadists. I'd have to wait for the right moment to try
any of these gambits, but they gave me a wisp of hope.

Leon and Ted pulled beers out of a cooler I hadn't noticed
before. They were rocking back as they sat in the kitchen chairs,
contemplating me. Leon saw me watching him.

He grinned. "We got plans for you, Missy, so you better be
thinking about how you can give us your share of 150G and make
us happy."

"We gotta go, Leon," said Ted. "We got a meeting.".

Leon checked his watch. "You're right."

My hopes leaped. They had to leave. I had a chance.

Leon scraped the kitchen chair back as he got up and slipped
out the door. I heard the car trunk open and close, and then he
came back with an armful of nylon rope. "Gotta make sure you
don't get away, don't we, Missy."

My heart sank as Leon and Ted wrapped one piece of rope
around my body, and then tied my legs to the chair with it. They
wound another piece of rope tightly around my arms and the
handcuffs to secure them to the chair. They tied the rope to the
heavy table. I couldn't move. Ted made the knots, and they didn't
look like grannies. They placed a gag in my mouth, so I couldn't
yell for help. They'd thought of everything.

"Don't worry. We won't be gone long," said Leon. "You can
work on that rope all you want to, you're not gonna get free."

They left. I heard the car back down the dirt road. All was
quiet. I pulled at the bonds and could stretch them a tiny bit. I
kept working at them, but I would need hours to get them loose.
Even if I did, I would still be handcuffed. I couldn't stand or even
move the chair. I sobbed.

Outside, the sun had gone down, and the kitchen had no
light. I felt more scared than ever in my life; I was hungry, and I
needed to go to the bathroom. There was no way out, and they
would be back soon.

Chapter 36

I sat in the dark, quietly crying and listening with dread for Leon's return. As I shivered and wept, I felt the floor shake, and a light suddenly appeared in a tiny crack in the floor next to my feet. The crack widened, and a trapdoor opened slowly. I saw two eyes appear, and then a hand threw back the trapdoor. A young colored man climbed into the room from a cellar beneath the floor.

"You're Sue, aren't you?" he asked. "Miss Kay's niece?"

I nodded, shocked that he knew my name. Who was he and how did he know me? It didn't matter. I didn't care. He'd come to my rescue. He untied the gag and worked on the knots.

"Who are you?" I asked, unable to believe what was happening. I had given up hope.

"Darrell. Stuart's friend," he said as he untied the gag.

"Darrell! Am I glad to see you," I gasped. My mouth felt dry and gritty.

Darrell pulled a penknife out of his pocket and cut the ropes. "If you stand, I can pull the chair out from under the handcuffs, and we can get out of here."

My legs were wobbly, but I did as directed, still dazed at this miraculous rescue. "We thought you were dead," I sputtered. "Stuart said the Nazis had taken you away and beaten you to death. Your parents filed a missing person report."

Darrell opened the door and pushed me out into the darkness. "Let's get out of here. We can talk later."

I began running down the dirt road.

"Not that way," Darrell hissed. "I'll show you. Just a minute."

He went back inside the shack, but I heard a car turning onto the dirt road. I ran after him. "They're coming back," I whispered to him. We both heard the car then.

"All right, let's go." Darrell led me along a trail through the brush, using a bushy evergreen branch to erase our footprints in the sandy soil. The trail twisted and turned, but we eventually arrived at a side street to Wilson Boulevard. I was reluctant to leave the safety of the bushes. "They'll drive around this area looking for me," I whispered.

Darrell listened. We both heard faint sounds of thrashing and cursing in the distance. "You're right," he said.

We retreated to the trail and found a small clearing. He helped me contort my body, so I could bring my hands under my feet to rest in front of me rather than in back. That was much more comfortable. We listened for sounds of pursuit as we sat close together on the ground. "They're no woodsmen," I said. "One of them ties granny knots, but the other one tied me up. He knew knots."

Darrell chuckled softly.

"Do your parents know you're okay?" I asked.

He nodded. "I told them, but I couldn't come back. Not after that."

"What do you mean?"

He was silent a long moment, staring off into the woods. "I've finally made peace with myself," he said. "And maybe rescuing you adds a couple points in my favor." He glanced at me. "While those guys were beating up Stuart and Mike, I ran. I didn't stay to help them. I ran. I was the worst kind of coward, and I couldn't face myself or anyone else. That's why I chose to disappear for a while."

"We worried about you. Stuart was really upset," I said. "Your parents, too."

"Is Stuart okay?"

I nodded. "You didn't need to run away. We understood the situation." I shivered. I was still wearing the jacket I'd left the house in, but sitting on the ground was chilly and damp. We couldn't hear Leon or Ted, but it was still too soon to leave the protection of the woods. "Thank you for rescuing me," I said. "Were you living under the shack? Did that place have a basement?"

Darrell chuckled. "Nah. Some farmer built the shack over an old springhouse years ago. You know, a large, deep hole dug to use for cold storage before refrigeration came in. A lot of farms had those around here. It had a roof, but somebody removed the roof, put in a floor, and built a shack on top. Don't think it was those two guys who tied you up, because they didn't seem to know about the cellar. I lived there off and on these past two months. Ready to go home now, though." He glanced at me. "Maybe Stuart will be glad to see me."

"You bet he will," I said. "They know nothing about your running away. They thought the Nazis had beaten and maybe killed you."

Darrell mulled this idea over. Then he said, "Can't go back to the shack. Not with the hatch open. They'll see that first thing. Too bad."

"Why too bad? Why would you want to go back?"

"My specimens," he said. He turned to me. "I'm studying botany at Howard U. I've been combing these woods for survival. What plants to eat. What not to eat. What's toxic to humans. What will kill and what will make people sick. I've used these two months well." He laughed. "It's been a study project."

"You can get more specimens. Maybe better ones, now that you know what to look for," I said. I was not going back to that shack.

"That wasn't my concern," said Darrell. "I have food in that cellar along with roots, berries, and nuts, some deadly toxic, some not so deadly. I know what to eat and what not to eat. Most people have no idea unless they study them, like I do. Especially not those two Nazis."

"I'm really glad you were there," I said. "You saved my life."

Darrell held a finger to his lips and listened. I heard voices. Leon and Ted were still searching for me. We scooted back from the clearing to hide in the undergrowth. We heard their soft curses as they passed, and their flashlights beamed into the woods but missed us. A few minutes later, they came by again. We listened for them another hour by Darrell's watch but didn't hear anything except after a very long time, the faint sound of a car.

"They're leaving," I whispered.

"Let's stay here another hour," Darrell said. "In case they're driving the streets looking for you."

"Good idea." We waited in the dark for a long time, listening for Leon and Ted. Then Darrell set out ahead of me to emerge onto the side street. "All clear," he whispered back to me.

I followed him to Wilson Boulevard and a cab, and we returned home by ten that night. After such a grueling evening, I would have sworn it must be after midnight. The ride home was stressful, too, because I had to keep the handcuffs hidden. Darrell wrapped his jacket around my wrists, and I held them close under the jacket, pretending I was cold.

I said goodbye to Darrell on the steps. He was glad to be coming home at last and waved as he walked to the Hortons' house.

Leon and Ted, two hungry neo-Nazis, would come back to the shack, find the hidden cellar, its stash of canned food, and a miscellaneous assortment of nuts, berries, and roots, some toxic, some benign. What would they do with it all?

I knew the answer.

Eat.

Chapter 37

I walked in on Sean, Gail, and Mike, who was sitting disconsolately on the living room couch.

"Where've you been?" asked Sean. "We've been worried." He eyed the handcuffs. "And what's that about?"

I told them the story, ending with Darrell's rescue.

"Darrell's okay?" Mike asked.

"He's fine," I affirmed. "He'll tell you all about his adventures later."

Sean shook his head. "So we still have to worry about those neo-Nazis."

"I don't think so," I said. "I think the problem will resolve itself. Anyway, if they come after us again, we can bring in the police without qualms. Everyone knows we had nothing to do with the heist."

"I guess we'll see what happens," said Gail. "For a while, you'd better keep your eyes open."

"So how are you getting rid of the handcuffs?" asked Sean.

"Darrell's telling Stuart to call his locksmith friend," I said, sinking onto the couch next to Mike. "Why so glum?" I asked. "Where's Sally Ann?"

Mike moved over an inch. "You may have been right." He picked up the bottle of Gallo and poured wine into a coffee cup.

"Right about what?" I asked.

Mike sipped the wine as he brooded. "She was so nice, and she seemed interested in learning Esperanto." He leaned back against the cushion. "Women confuse me."

I thought of a few things to say but kept them to myself. I wasn't particularly jealous of Sally Ann. Mike and I had never dated, but I was attracted to him, and I didn't like or trust Sally Ann. "What happened?" I asked.

"I walk with Sally Ann on Sixteenth Street." He shook his head. "Where the Baptist Church is. Even now, I cannot believe this."

"I'll get some glasses," said Sean, eyeing the Gallo.

"Tell us what happened," Gail moved to a chair across from Mike and waited.

"She thought I was not looking, and I was not. I see friend of mine down the street, and I turned to tell Sally Ann about him when I saw her on purpose..." He heaved a heavy sigh. "On purpose, she meant to do this, she step on bright, patent leather shoes of little girl waiting for the bus with her Mama and Papa. The Papa wear yarmulke. You understand now? The little girl cried. Sally Ann laugh, then she see I am not laughing, so she act sad."

He held his head in his hands. "You are right. Sally Ann is not what she seem. She is not a nice person."

"I'm sorry, but what did she do then?" I asked. "Any other insights?" Stepping on the little girl's shoe was probably an accident. Some people laugh when they're upset.

"She say she sorry and did not mean to step on little girl's foot," Mike lifted his head and looked at me.

"I'm sure that's true." Who would deliberately hurt a little girl? Other than white supremacists bombing churches, I added to myself.

"Then she tell me, no, she lecture me about Holocaust." Mike's eyes blazed. "That it was fake. That it never happened. She say this to me. Me!"

"That's what Rockwell says." Sally Ann picked up that lie listening to Rockwell, and she swallowed the party line. I was right. I was even more sure she was in cahoots with him. That's why he had pared down the harassment and surveillance. He was hoping Sally Ann would find out for him where Sean was hiding or, better, what happened to the money.

"So I tell her what the Nazis did to my family." Mike glared at me. "And she tell me I lie!"

He lapsed into some Hungarian words. I didn't understand what he was saying, but I knew what he meant.

"She ask me if I am Jewish. I say yes, yes, yes. And yes again."

He sat back, the anger dissipating. He stared at his hands for a few minutes. I said nothing. Finally, he looked at me and grinned. "I do not think she will be good Esperantist. I am sure I will not see her again."

He was probably right about that. Rockwell had tired of using her to find out about us and getting nowhere. She stopped pretending, became herself, and picked a fight with Mike for an easy exit. Good riddance, I say.

Now that Rockwell had fixed on Reg as the thief, I hoped we wouldn't hear from him again. I'd still have to watch out for Leon or Ted, but I'd be on my guard now. A fleeting thought of the maybe toxic, maybe benign, nuts and berries Darrell left in the shack crossed my mind. How toxic?

Chapter 38

I hadn't realized how low our spirits had sunk as we struggled through the Rockwell affair. With Darrell's return and the continued success of the Humphrey-Mansfield strategy to outwit the Senate filibuster, the Hortons came over the next night after dinner with several bottles of a French Bordeaux and a platter of desserts with a bowl of pretzels. We were ready to party! We even invited Ellen and Clark to join us.

But first we congratulated ourselves on our own success. We had robbed the American Nazi Party, such as it was, besting George Lincoln Rockwell and his storm troopers, and contributing $150,000 to the battle for justice and fair play. Kudos to us!

Cole and Alice wanted the full story of what happened when we went to Rockwell's house on "Hatemonger Hill." They were as amazed as we were that our scheme worked. "You mean they believed you?" asked Cole several times as I told him of Rockwell's bluster and threats with his armed stooges surrounding us.

"And they think Sean's informant stole the money?" asked Alice as if she needed to make sure she heard it right.

"Rockwell did," I said. "Two of his neo-Nazis still thought we'd stolen it and wanted their share." I repeated the story of Darrell's rescue. They'd already heard Darrell's version. "We probably won't be seeing any of them anymore."

"I'd like to make a special toast," said Cole, raising his glass.

"To Sue. Without her ideas and her courage in this...this...heist, we couldn't have done it." He smiled at me. "To our *femme fatale*."

They all raised their glasses to me. I stared down at mine, which was actually orange juice. I still thought I was a coward and, frankly, on the plain side. Yet the group of us outsmarted a man who expected to be elected president in 1972, and I'd played the part of a *femme fatale* who lured seven men to their doom. Okay, not doom, exactly, but I'd accomplished our goal. Unbelievable. I finally raised my glass, feeling I had a lot to sort out in my understanding of myself. "Here's to me," I said and emptied the glass.

Sean sat at the old piano and banged out a succession of tunes from the Beach Boys. Tanya stood next to him, watching his fingers. Clark had his arm around Ellen. During a pause in Sean's efforts, Clark took the floor. "I think Ellen and I are close to finding the treasure," he said. "I've got the exact route Mosby took, and since we don't have to worry about being kidnapped any more, we can go back to our hikes."

"Also, the weather's getting warmer, and it will be more fun," added Ellen. "If we find something, we won't be digging through frozen ground."

"Don't forget you've got help from Horace and his dowsing rod," Gail added with a sly smile.

"Success is assured." Clark raised his glass.

"If you find the treasure, though," I said, "you'll have to sell it first before you have money to donate to the cause."

"Yes, that's probably true." Clark scratched his beard. "The NAACP won't want a bunch of old candlesticks and stuff."

Ellen sat twirling her wineglass thoughtfully. "I don't agree," she said. "We'll be able to donate it publicly to the NAACP, unlike you and your 150,000 stolen dollars. I'll bet the NAACP could raffle off Union bootie for a lot of money. Or contact an expert who'll find buyers for the stuff."

"You'll have to navigate the legal issues first," said Sean, twisting the piano stool to talk to Ellen and Clark. "The state of Virginia probably has laws connected to ownership of found objects and treasure salvage and such-like."

Clark pushed out his lower lip. "Maybe so." He sipped his wine. "We'll deal with that when we get to it."

"If you get to it," Gail muttered under her breath.

Mike hadn't joined in the festivities. He sat slumped over on the couch, staring mournfully into the wineglass. I took the seat next to him. "How are you doing?" I asked.

"I can't believe you didn't include me in planning the rescue or even this last visit to Rockwell's house. Why didn't you let me know what was happening?"

Here it came. The moment I was dreading. I began gently. "We were worried about you."

"Worried? Why? I am okay." He turned a puzzled face to me.

"Maybe not exactly about you." How far would I have to go to spell it out for him? I wasn't exactly unbiased.

He thought about this for a minute. I watched the shifting expressions n his face. He wasn't handsome, exactly, but his face showed the firmness of character. Finally, he said, "Do you speak about Sally Ann?"

I nodded.

He silently stared into his wineglass, mulling things over. He shook his head again. "You saw through her much more fast than me," he said.

"She worried me," I replied. "It seemed Rockwell knew stuff about us he shouldn't have known unless he had an informant."

Mike nodded. "I see."

"The only new person beside me who could have told him was Sally Ann."

He reached for the wine bottle to top off his glass. "Did all of you know?"

"Not at first," I said. "We decided it would be best not to risk her learning anything more from you." I rushed forward. "We didn't want to leave you out, but you were so taken with Sally Ann, and we might have been wrong about her."

He shrugged. "You had to do it, I guess."

"Yes, we had to do it. Too much at stake." I smiled at him. "Sally Ann turned out to be useful, though."

"How's that?" Mike asked.

"Since it was obvious you were one of us, yet carried on as if you knew nothing of the robbery and kidnapping, you fooled her into thinking Rockwell was on the wrong trail in suspecting us. It helped us get out alive when we threw the guilt onto Reg."

He nodded. "The whole thing turned out more complicated than we thought, but we did it, didn't we?" He held up his glass in a salute.

I raised my glass to his. "We certainly did."

"*Egészségedre!*" He looked into my eyes with a smile. "That is Hungarian toast. And this is one in Esperanto. *Je via sano!*"

I didn't try to repeat the Hungarian toast. Someday, perhaps.

Epilogue

June 10, 1964.

After seventy-five days of filibustering against the Civil Rights Bill, seventy-one senators voted to end the filibuster, four more than needed. On June nineteenth, the Senate voted seventy-three to twenty-seven to pass the bill.

And on June twentieth, I met Aunt Kay at Washington National Airport. She came striding off the plane wearing jeans and a sweatshirt. No pumps. Just blue sneakers. I almost didn't recognize her. Then she waved at me. I perceived her with new eyes, and this time she did seem like the kind of person who might own a VW bus.

"I've never seen you wearing jeans before," I blurted.

"We only got together for special occasions," she said, "or for lunch during work hours. I wear what's expected then, but this was a long flight, and I'm going home."

She hugged me and put an arm around me as we walked to the Baggage Claim. "How did it go?" she asked.

She already knew about the loss of her VW bus. I had to call her in Europe to get the car insurance settlement taken care of. So much had happened in the past six months, and I had played an essential part in all of it, even risking my life and worse, acting like a *femme fatale* luring men to their doom. It was about time I'd grown up. Aunt Kay no longer intimidated me, but I respected her and felt much closer to her. Oddly, she had to go away for me to get to know her. Perhaps tonight at dinner, all of us can fill her in on the rest of the story.

"I have a lot to tell you, Aunt Kay," I said.

***

June 21, 1964

The first day of the Mississippi Freedom Summer, James Chaney, Andrew Goodman, and Michael Schwerner drove to Neshoba County, Mississippi, to investigate the burning of a black church after a voting rights meeting. On their way home, they were arrested and jailed by the local deputy sheriff. The deputy sheriff and local Klansmen took the three men to a remote area, then tortured, murdered, and buried them.

July 2, 1964

The House approved the Senate Civil Rights Bill two hundred eighty-nine to one hundred twenty-six. Shortly before seven p.m. on the same day, President Johnson signed the Bill into law.

August 25, 1967

An American former neo-Nazi assassinated George Lincoln Rockwell in Arlington, Virginia.

Victory
Civil Rights Act of 1964
First 10 Titles

Title I—Voting rights. Requires voting rules and procedures be applied equally to all races.

Title II—Public Accommodation. Discrimination based on race, color, religion, or national origin is prohibited in hotels, motels, restaurants, theaters, and all other public accommodations engaged in interstate commerce; private clubs are exempted but the term "private" is not defined.

Title III—Desegregation of public facilities. Prohibits state and municipal governments from denying access to public facilities on grounds of race, color, religion, or national origin.

Title IV—Desegregation of public education. Desegregation of public schools to be enforced and the U.S. Attorney General authorized to file suits to enforce said act.

Title V—Commission on Civil Rights. The Commission established by the earlier Civil Rights Act of 1957 is expanded with additional powers, rules and procedures.

Title VI—Nondiscrimination in federally assisted programs. Prohibits discrimination by programs and activities that receive federal funds. If a recipient of federal funds is found in violation of Title VI, that recipient may lose its federal funding.

Title VII—Equal employment opportunity. Prohibits discrimination by covered employers on the basis of race, color, religion, sex or national origin.

Title VIII—Registration and voting statistics. Requires compilation of voter-registration and voting data in geographic areas specified by the Commission on Civil Rights.

Title IX—Intervention and removal of cases. Eases the movement of civil rights cases from state courts to federal courts.

Title X—Community Relations Service. Establishes the Community Relations Service, tasked with assisting in community disputes involving claims of discrimination.

Acknowledgements

I once ran a boarding house on Kilbourne Place in downtown Washington, D.C., and I mined the experience in writing this book. Although I took bits of personality from the real boarders in developing the characters, this book is a work of fiction. None of the fictional characters bears any resemblance to anyone I met at the real boarding house.

I drew the descriptions of George Lincoln Rockwell and the house from the well-researched and reviewed book, *American Fuehrer—George Lincoln Rockwell and the American Nazi Party* by Frederick J. Simonelli. Descriptions of Rockwell's men, house, and neighborhood are fictional.

The Bill of the Century: The Epic Battle for the Civil Rights Act by Clay Risen was also a helpful resource. Articles from the Internet supplied or confirmed additional information.

My first husband, Bob (Rel) Davis, was an active Esperantist in the Washington area, and our boarding house also became an "Esperanto Domo." We hosted Esperantists visiting Washington from all over the world.

The passage of the Civil Rights Bill of 1964 made a huge difference in the lives of African Americans and of all women in the United States. More legal battles had to be fought, but Title VII not only banned discrimination against African Americans, it also opened the door for women to gain access to credit cards and loans in their own names, join professional associations, like the National Press Club, that up until then were "men only," to enter restaurants and register at hotels without raised eyebrows and harassment, to be admitted to military academies as equals to men, and many other rights that had been denied to women.

In researching this novel, I felt great shame for the continuing racism in our country. Despite the succession of civil rights laws, its rampant racism continues. In this country, most African American mothers suffer intense fear for their children. Current events show their fear is justified.

But I also felt awed by those, both White and Black, present and past, who struggled and continue to struggle for equal rights, Many of them lost their lives. The fight has been long and hard and, again shamefully, it must continue as long as the evil stench of white supremacy exists. Black Lives Matter.

My thanks to Maureen Klovers, Millie Mack, Marilyn Magee, Laura Manning Johnson, John Morrison, Mark Willen, Janis Wilson, and Rog McIntire for reading versions of this novel. Their comments and suggestions were invaluable.

I also want to add additional thanks and much love to my husband, Roger McIntire, also an author and Professor Emeritus in Psychology, University of Maryland, for his constant support of my writing efforts.

Eileen Haavik McIntire

If you enjoyed this book, please place a review on Amazon.com

I always enjoy hearing from readers. You can reach me at eileenmcintire@aol.com

Visit my website at SecretPanels.net

The Shadow Series of Historical Mysteries by Eileen Haavik McIntire

Shadow of the Rock

Setting sail for American in 1781, Rachel Levy and her father Moses are captured by Barbary pirates and brought to Morocco for sale. The loathsome vizier forces Moses into slavery and Rachel into marriage. Rachel and Moses must use their wits to find a way to freedom.

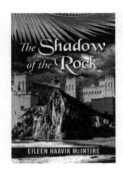

Two hundred years later, Sara Miller's sweet, loving grandmother Ruth is killed, and Sara discovers Ruth's buried past, long hidden by the terror of the Holocaust. Ruth's bequest sends Sara on a journey that will uncover Ruth's mystery and the link to their ancestor, Rachel Levy.

"A riveting tale of time and humanity, highly recommended." (Midwest Book Review). *"A bold adventure…Chapters move quickly in a mixture of danger, excitement, and pure enjoyment…"* (Foreword Reviews)

In Rembrandt's Shadow

It's 1616 in the Spanish Netherlands. Saul Levi Morteira rescues a family from the Inquisition and take them to tolerant, egalitarian Amsterdam. The family recoups its fortune and, in gratitude, commissions Rembrandt to paint a portrait of Morteira.

Four centuries later, Sara Miller and her friend Josh dig up the painting, hidden during the Holocaust. They seek the painting's rightful owner, but danger stalks them through the streets of Gibraltar, forcing them to flee to Paris. As they dodge thieves and a murderer, Sara and Josh struggle against impossible odds to fulfill a promise made sixty years earlier. Sequel to *Shadow of the Rock*.

The 90s Club Cozy Mystery Series
By Eileen Haavik McIntire

The 90s Club & the Hidden Staircase (No. 1)

The 90s Club at Whisperwood Retirement Village discovers a

simmering brew of thefts, murders, and exploitation bubbling beneath its luxurious lifestyle. Nancy Dickenson and fellow club members pile up clues like tricks in a bridge game to uncover the culprits—and almost lose their lives. The menace grows into a bloody climax and even Nancy's suspiciously wild kitty cat Malone takes part, turning the murderer's confidence into terror.

"With plenty of humor and its own original tale...a 'must' for readers of cozy mysteries." (*Midwest Book Review*)

The 90s Club & the Whispering Statue (No. 2)

Nancy Dickenson and the 90s Club at Whisperwood Retirement Village head south to Fort Lauderdale to rescue one friend and find another. Four attempts to murder Nancy's long-time confidant Peter Stamboul have failed, but in the placid lifestyle of his retirement condo, who would want to kill Peter and why? Adventurous young Jessica Cantwell took a job as crew on a boat, but when the captain is murdered, she disappears and becomes a "person of interest." Once again, murder and mayhem stalk Nancy and fellow 90s Club members Louise and George as they race to save Peter and Jessica's lives and, ultimately, their own.

"A fun read...nostalgia and...social commentary, wrapped up in an engaging mystery novel. (*Foreword Reviews*)

The 90s Club & the Secret of the Old Clock (No. 3)

Nancy seeks its secret as she and the 90s Club at Whisperwood Retirement Village discover swindlers are targeting and defrauding the residents. The scams are online, but the swindlers know too much to be strangers. Did they shoot and kill Nancy's new friend Betts? Nancy and the 90s Club pursue the killer and the con men, but the killer is no fool and attacks first. This time, the killer swears, Nancy will not escape.

"An impressively well-crafted and thoroughly entertaining mystery that plays fair with the reader..." (Midwest Book Review)

The 90s Club & the Mystery at Lilac Inn (No. 4)

Nancy and the able, alert, and active 90s Club at Whisperwood Retirement Village are given a free week at Lilac Inn Resort in exchange for solving the mysteries plaguing the inn. Someone is stealing the hotel's supplies and spreading rumors that the local legendary Green Monster and the Mothman are stalking the resort. Then valuable jewelry is stolen, and the inn's fortune teller is murdered. The 90s Club has one week to solve four mysteries before the current guests leave, and the inn goes bankrupt.

Psychological Suspense
The Two-Sided Set-Up

Melanie Fletcher flits from one bad relationship to the next, following an internal selection mechanism that steers her wrong every time. Then she meets the man of her dreams

and marries him. It only takes a few months for Melanie to realize he's an abuser and a criminal. Melanie escapes on a small trawler she owns, a secret she doesn't share with anyone, and runs for her life back to where it all began, her home, a small marina in tidewater Virginia. She needs to confront the demon who set her up for bad choices—her abusive, obstinate, drunk of a dad. Now he will set her up for the fight of her life.

"...a fast-paced and multilayered thriller with well-developed characters and colorful settings....An engaging tale for aficionados of psychological suspense." (Kirkus Reviews)

CPSIA information can be obtained
at www.ICGtesting.com
Printed in the USA
FSHW010851090421
80251FS